D1648908

JODI NIEHAUS

EXACTLY HOW IT'S SUPPOSED TO BE

A NOVEL

This is a work of fiction. Names, characters, and incidents are a product of the author's imagination or are used fictitiously. Any resemblance to actual persons, living or dead, is entirely coincidental.

First paperback edition February 2022

Design and layout by Brandon Niehaus

ISBN 979-8-9855811-1-9 (ebook)
ISBN 979-8-9855811-0-2 (paperback)

www.jodiniehaus.com

To my husband, Brandon, who encouraged me
every day to sit down and write the damn thing.

To Dax, Bridge, and Lennon, my inspiration
and motivation for everything.

And to my mom, Linda, who is the strongest
person I have ever known.

The universe has a way of meddling in your plans. Of spinning your world around when you just want it to stay still. Then, like magic, there are times when it suddenly makes perfect sense. When all of the little pieces fall together perfectly, proving all of the chaos was for something after all.

Chapter 1

I scan the room, but I don't see him yet. I do, however, spot a copper penny at my feet. *Never leave a heads-up penny on the ground.* I don't remember who told me that, but I think of it whenever I see one. I keep a small collection of the heads-up pennies I find in a neat little row on my nightstand where, for the most part, they just exist. I never think of them beyond the moment I find one and wonder if it might be a lucky one.

Before proceeding to the counter, I bend over to snatch the penny up and stuff it into my pocket. "Americano, black please," I say to Jesse, one of the baristas, who I don't know well enough to have any sort of real conversation with. He looks like he belongs in a nineties grunge band with unkempt shoulder-length hair and a black Pearl Jam t-shirt.

"Right on." Jesse turns around to pack espresso into the portafilter, revealing white paint stains on the back of his loose blue jeans. I wait at the bar for my drink and then head to my favorite table in the far corner. It sits next to an antique piano and beneath an oversized potted fern hanging from a chain attached to the ceiling. The top of my table is a decoupage of the faces of a dozen different house cats, each staring up at me with sinister eyes. I set my book on the face of the calico cat with the glowing green eyes and prepare to wait.

My back is against the wall so I can see everyone in the place: a chess match, a tea-drinking poet, and a table of four noisy regulars who think they run the show. This is all pretty standard for this establishment, a late-night independent coffee shop known for a cozy, laid-back ambiance and Irish coffees, heavy on the Jameson. Located on the outskirts of downtown Cincinnati near a bustling college campus, it has been frequented by college students and writers and hipsters since the 1970s. Sully's, it's called.

While I wait for him to arrive, I reach into my pocket and pull out the penny. 1992, the year I was born. That has to mean something, right? Maybe, maybe not. But there isn't any time to think about it because he's here, standing at the entrance looking for me.

My first impressions are that he is much shorter than I imagined, and his red hair is way brighter than it appeared in his pictures, almost fiery. He has a nice face, though. I like his blue eyes and the character that comes with his slightly crooked teeth, but I've never dated a redhead, so it's difficult for me to picture myself with him.

"So what do you do for fun?" is one of the first questions he asks me.

When you go on enough of these things, you hear the same questions over and over again, so I begin to recite my usual answer.

"Well, I spend most of my time in the kitchen, but I also really like to read. Kind of nerdy, I know. I like thrillers and memoirs mostly and an occasional romance here and there. Some of my favorites are—"

"I'm into science fiction," he interrupts. "Oh, and Stephen King, obviously."

"Obviously," I add, and I don't know if he senses the subtle sarcasm in my tone. I am also not sure if he realizes he cut me off mid-sentence, but I'm not surprised. A lot of men think this is appropriate to do on a date, and for the life of me, I can't tell if they think it's acceptable behavior or if they've simply developed a horrible habit they aren't even aware of at this point.

His name is Cory, and there is nothing outright wrong with him per se, other than the fact that he just interrupted me (which is an enormous red flag). He is thirty-three and works as an actuary, which tells me three very important things about him: he is intelligent (book smart at least), he has a steady income, and he has health insurance, all positive traits when browsing potential boyfriends. But after a good amount of the usual first-date banter, he shares his baggage with me. Cory has an ex-wife. However, the two of them divorced before having any kids, so it's really emotional baggage for him and not much beyond that.

The thing about dating in your thirties is everyone has baggage, and they feel the need to share their baggage on the first date because, frankly, there isn't any time to waste. In your teens and early twenties, a lot of people are still mostly blank canvases. Sure, the large majority of those in the dating pool have had breakups at this point, but compared to your thirties, the lack of life experience of someone in their twenties is just plain laughable. People in their thirties have been through some shit. Because of this, a first date in this decade of your life is the time to show all your cards and let your dates decide if your baggage is something they are willing to deal with.

So when I go on first dates, I always expect a big reveal if all else seems to be going well and sometimes even if it's not. A lot of people, I've learned, treat first dates like a therapy session. It's like they can't wait to put everything out on the table and then vent to you about it for the next two hours to give you a preview of what the rest of your life could be like if you ultimately choose them.

Cory's baggage is minimal at best, and I can tell he would sleep with me if I let him. But, he's pretty ordinary. He might find me endearing in the beginning, but I can already tell my millennial lifestyle, the fact that I work from home and voted for a Democrat, would chip away at him until he eventually ditched me down the line when the sex got too routine. Most likely, it would be for a predictable, plain woman who orders vanilla in a cup when she goes out for ice cream. I, on the other hand, get the chunkiest, most indulgent ice cream on the damn menu, and I'll never apologize for that. I don't even consider myself *that* unconventional, but I can already tell I'm too off-center for him, and he is much too conservative for me. This is one of the reasons I prefer to do coffee for first dates. I do not need an entire awkward dinner to be able to see if there is any chemistry with someone. Usually, I can tell if a date and I click in the first ten minutes, and the majority of the time, I sit through the next hour or two just to be polite.

I remember being fifteen and begging my parents to be allowed to have a boyfriend. I dreamt of kissing in cars and under the bleachers at football games, receiving a letterman jacket and a promise ring from some handsome boy I couldn't get off my mind. Everything about my relationship with my mythical, long-term boyfriend would be perfect. We would even share an apartment in college, sleeping in the same bed and playing house while our bills were paid by some imaginary entity, most likely a student loan agency. All of these hopes were in spite of my mother frequently lecturing me about not having sex before marriage. She actually still tells me this on occasion even though I just turned thirty. The difference between then and now is that dating is the very thing I wish I didn't have to do. I am ready to never have to go on another first date again, but first, I need to find someone who laughs at my jokes and calls me on my shit. That's what my dad always said is the key to his long-lasting marriage with my mom.

Lately, I frequent Sully's a couple of times a week meeting self-proclaimed eligible bachelors who also swiped right, and most of these evenings, I find myself playing a game where I identify all of the little fibs and exaggerations from their online dating profiles.

No, you are not six-foot, as much as you may want to be.
Having a paralegal certification does not warrant
you calling yourself a lawyer.
Scuba diving doesn't count as a hobby if you did it one time
on vacation five years ago.
Your "roommates" are actually your parents.

I'm not petty about this type of stuff. More than anything, it's amusing people tell these little white lies online without considering they will very obviously be uncovered on a date. I'm not looking for some perfect specimen to be my future husband. I don't need to be rich or someone's trophy wife, and I don't need six-pack abs on a boyfriend either. Most of all, I'm not interested in finding a man who feels like he has to lie about himself. All I *really* want is someone who is honest and self-aware and would be happy sitting on the couch eating takeout with me on a Friday night.

At the end of the evening, Cory asks me sincerely, "Would you like to do this again sometime?" His blue eyes look desperate but hopeful.

"That sounds nice," I reply, but I have no intention of seeing him again. In fact, at the first red light I hit on the drive home, I plan to delete his number from my phone. This little fib, the only one I allow myself to tell, makes the end of the evening go much smoother in my opinion.

When I arrive home, I whip myself up a quick stir-fry with some leftover rice and vegetables I have in my refrigerator. Then, I post up in front of the television with a glass of red wine and flip to a rerun of *The Office.* I want Pam and Jim love, the kind of love that looks effortless and fun and never too painful. But I think everybody does.

My silenced phone lights up next to me. It's my best friend, Sarah, FaceTiming me, so I mute the television and answer. We've been pretty much inseparable since high school where we met at tryouts for the freshman soccer team. It seemed like no time had passed before we ended up as roommates in college. As an only child, she's the closest thing to a sister I have ever had.

"Hello!" I answer, unsurprised to see her six-month-old baby boy's chunky face on the screen instead of hers. That's pretty standard lately.

"Hi, Baby Ace!" My baby talk is super high-pitched and incredibly embarrassing, but I have learned I have absolutely no control over it. I see any baby, and I suddenly turn into a vivacious cartoon character, lively and loud. "Look at the size of those jowls! You are the fattest little thing I ever saw! Can I eat you for breakfast?" Ace chuckles at my silly facial expressions as drool floods from his mouth like Niagara Falls. He has giant, bulging eyes and a bald, slightly lumpy head and sort of looks like a little alien, but he is still the cutest baby I've ever laid eyes on.

"Okay, Aunt Maddie," I hear Sarah say in the background, even though I'm still looking at Ace's enormous rosy cheeks. "How did tonight's date go?"

"It wasn't completely horrible, but Cory's definitely not a keeper." I sigh into the phone. I sound discouraged because I am discouraged. One can only find humor in the ghastliness of the online dating world for so long. Sarah's heard one too many of my first-date stories though, so I tend to spare her all of the dirty details these days.

"Listen, I don't think these dating sites you're using are going to work," she blurts out so quickly it's like she's been holding it in, ready to pop with this information. "I think you need to go out in public more, and you'll find someone nice and normal, not a weirdo looking for sex on the internet."

Now, Sarah's face is zoomed in close on my phone screen, and she literally looks disgusted when she says that last part.

"Oh, so going out to bars on a Friday night is going to produce a better quality of man than mathematical algorithms on my phone?" Sarah rolls her eyes, but I keep going. "All of those Silicon Valley tech studs aren't making millions off of these apps for nothing. And who knows? Maybe I'll even match with one of those tech studs." I really don't believe in the whole dating algorithm thing, but I'm just trying to get under her skin. It's what we do as sort-of-sisters.

Sarah is irked now. She lets out an exasperated sigh, and her nostrils are the most flared I've ever seen. "No, Maddie. I am talking Whole Foods, Trader Joe's, the gym, the dog park, the line at Starbucks. Those are the places where you can meet a nice man."

"First of all, Sarah, I don't have a dog. Second, you met Mike at a frat party, one where I recall you had like ten Jell-O shots and then had to make yourself throw up to stop the room from spinning." Mike is Sarah's husband who is super sweet, but there is no denying he was a big macho bro back in college. Sarah and Mike have been married for three years now, and Ace is their first child. Luckily, Mike grew out of his frat boy tendencies and is now a respected and well-liked high school history teacher and baseball coach.

"Correct, I was very wasted, but I was also twenty-one. Mike and I are now happily married, and the past is the past. Don't think I don't see you trying to change the subject either. You are *thirty* Maddie. Not to mention, the world is so different now." She emphasizes the *thirty* as if this is a very important point she's making, like she is letting me in on a secret. Unfortunately, I am well aware of my age and also the fact that most of the worthwhile men have been snatched up already.

"Maddie, you are an influencer for God's sake. You even have a little blue checkmark next to your name. What you need is the kind of man who goes to the grocery store and works out and lives his life out in the real world, not some dude who plays video games and swipes left or right on random girls' profiles while he takes a poop."

"Oh my god, Sarah! Where do you get your information? I'm pretty sure I'm your only single friend, and you haven't had a first date in ten years. So, who on earth do you know who finds dates while they poop?"

"I just know it, okay? That's what men do. They are gross, and the ones who don't have wives or girlfriends are even more repulsive. When I started dating Mike, he was sleeping on a mattress on the floor. He didn't even have sheets on the bed. He slept in a sleeping bag, Maddie! A fucking sleeping bag!" She's practically yelling at me, but she stops to take a breath and begins again, now calm and soft, like I'm fragile. "I get that you have a badass job as a food blogger and you get to work from home, but please try to leave once in a while and stop trying to find love online. Get off your phone, and get out of your house. If you do, I promise you'll find someone before your eggs are too old to produce babies."

"You are batshit crazy, Sarah. You know that?"

"I know I am. That's what happens when most of your conversations are with a baby." Then, she hangs up without even saying goodbye.

I get it though. I really do. Sarah's concern is not unwarranted. I do spend a lot of time in my house. It's the very nature of my job, and there are a lot of days I don't even leave. After I got my business degree, I spent the first couple of years after college at a boring, entry-level cubicle job. My salary was barely enough to pay my rent, and I was always stressed out. At night and on the weekends, I started spending time in the kitchen to decompress. It wasn't long until food turned into my full-time hobby. I took pictures of my dishes and posted them on social media, a world that was nowhere near as vast then as it is today. It took a lot of time and countless hours of slaving over a hot stove and spending way too much time on my computer, but my persistence paid off in the end. I have a job I love where I don't have to deal with boring Excel sheets or petty office drama. But, I'm lonely.

I fall asleep that night thinking about Sarah's advice. Tomorrow, I will stay off my phone, get out of my house, and live my life.

The next morning, I wake up to a cool breeze on a picture-perfect sunny day. It's Saturday, my favorite day of the week. I tie my long, unruly hair back so it's out of my face and off my neck. Then, I throw on a simple yellow sundress and some oversized sunglasses before I am out the door. In my front yard, I notice my first peony of the season has bloomed, and I take it as a sign of good things to come.

At the Row Street Farmers' Market, I visit my favorite vendors first for my fresh weekly produce. But with Sarah's insistent voice in the back of my mind, I linger a little longer, perusing more booths than I normally would, observing who else comes to these things and realizing I am always looking at the food and never looking at the people.

There are mostly women, lots of women, most of whom are over fifty, equipped with sun visors and canvas bags hanging from their wrists. The only men I see are either with the aforementioned visor-wearing women or pushing double-strollers next to perfectly toned, beautiful, blond wives. This is why I'm single. The good ones, the best ones, were all taken in their twenties by the girls who were on homecoming court in high school. Here I am, the ex-knitting club member who had a mouth full of braces and very bad bangs, and as everyone probably guessed, I'm all alone.

What are all of the single men doing right now? I wonder. Sadly, I don't have an answer to that question, but I force myself to stay out anyway. I take a walk in the park, roam around Whole Foods, and then sit in Starbucks while I sip on a flat white. Only one other table is occupied, a little old couple eating scones at one of the café tables. I watch them for a while, admiring the way they don't need to fill the silence with small talk, perfectly comfortable in each other's presence. I'm not going to find that kind of companionship here. I don't know where I'm going to find it, but it's definitely not here.

It's late afternoon when I finally return home to tend to my croissant dough, a true labor of love. The rest of my day will be spent buttering and folding and buttering some more, and at the end of it, I will have a delicious physical representation of all of the hard work I put in. I wish dating were like that:

you put in the work, and then you're guaranteed a reward. I always thought my soulmate would find me when the time was right, in some serendipitous moment where every detail happened to align perfectly, like it was meant to be. But it turns out when you spend approximately ninety percent of your time at your own house, love doesn't just come knocking at your door. Life isn't like a romance novel after all.

While my dough rests, I open one of the dating apps on my phone and sift through an endless list of men who all start to look the same. A montage of poorly taken selfies in bad lighting. I've basically been doing my own version of speed dating lately, trying to increase my odds of finding love by forcing myself to go on as many dates as possible, but I'm starting to think I was meant to be alone. Not everyone gets the fairytale, the family and the career. Little did I know, I chose my fate long ago, before I even knew it was a choice.

When I get up to do another round of dough proofing, I hear a *ping* from the next room, and when I return, I see an alert. I have both a match and a message, so I click on his profile.

Josh, a project manager with dirty blond hair and bright white teeth. His profile states he likes jogging, is an avid skier, and recently moved here from Louisville for a job. We talk back and forth for a short while, and then he asks me if I'd like to meet up. I skim through his profile again before replying. An avid skier from Kentucky? I highly doubt it, but what have I got to lose? Maybe he travels a lot.

Sure, I reply. *Sully's Coffee House at 8?*

See you there. He adds a smiley face emoji, which I have to admit is a turn-off, but I am in no place to be picky.

At 7:45, I arrive at Sully's and take my usual seat at the cat table. Whenever I'm on a blind date, I prefer to be the first one there. I order a drink and start to read my book (I bring one with me everywhere, a habit I developed in middle school), but I only make it through a couple of pages when I recognize Josh from his pictures standing at the entrance. I do a shy wave from my table in the corner to let him know it's me. He walks towards me with a toothy grin that resembles the Cheshire Cat, and the sight of it makes me shiver a little in my seat. His hair is slicked back and almost looks wet. Before he even takes a seat, he pulls my paperback from my hands.

"Whatcha reading?" Josh asks, examining the front cover while losing my page. "Never heard of him," he continues, handing me back my book and sitting down across from me. "I'm a John Grisham fan myself. You really should check out—" and that is exactly when I stop listening. There are very few people in this world I trust book recommendations from, and I can already tell this guy is not one of them.

"This cat table is kind of creepy, don't you think?" he asks, when I finally tune back into his incessant talking. I don't think he's even heard me speak yet.

I defend my favorite table. "I like it. It's quirky."

"Really? You like this?" His nose scrunches. "I'd hate to see what your house looks like if this is your style." He chuckles at his own joke, and for the next twenty minutes, Josh babbles on as I tap my foot on the table leg, waiting for him to ask something about me. I begin to feel like I'm going to crawl out of my skin if I don't end it soon. When he tells me his last relationship ended because he cheated, but apparently, it wasn't really his fault because *she wasn't emotionally invested anymore,* I take that as my cue to tell him I have to be up early, and we should call it a night.

Josh stands up to leave, and I excuse myself to the restroom so he won't try to walk me to my car. Once I'm hopeful the coast is clear, I return to my table to get my things. But beneath my book, I notice a folded piece of lined paper. The edges are torn, like it was ripped out of a notebook either carelessly or because the writer was in a hurry. I unfold it to reveal a handwritten note, scribbled in blue pen:

You are too perfect for all of them.

I take a step back as goosebumps erupt all over me. Quickly glancing around the room, I look to see who might have put it there, but everyone appears busy, in their own little worlds, talking or writing or reading. Not a single patron is even looking in my general direction, so I walk up to the counter and get the attention of one of the two baristas working tonight.

"Excuse me, did you happen to see who left a note on my table?"

The guy who I ask is relatively new. I've only seen him working here a few times in the past month or so. I think his name is Max or Jack. I've heard people say it but haven't paid much attention.

He nods and leans in close, like he's trying to be secretive. "I did. It was the guy who just left. He was sitting in the corner on his computer with the thick black glasses." He points in the direction of an empty table near the entrance.

I know the guy he is talking about. There's a man who looks like an academic type, probably in his early forties, who is here all of the time. He's either on his laptop or furiously writing in one of those cheap composition notebooks. It doesn't make sense to me though because I come here often, and I've never seen him even glance my way before.

"What did it say?" Max or Jack asks. "Sorry if that's nosy. I saw him over by your table, and I was curious what he was doing."

It strikes me that I've never noticed how attractive Max or Jack is before. He has sun-kissed olive skin, a chiseled jawline, and just the right amount of scruff on his cheeks to make him look rugged but also sexy, like a mix between a lumberjack and a Calvin Klein model. He gives off that tall, dark, and brooding vibe all women swoon over without looking a day over twenty-five. As a card-carrying member of the Thirty and Up Club, I can't do anything other than admire his good looks. I've always considered myself average-looking. Average face. Average body. Nothing special. Though I will give myself credit for making great strides in the looks department since my teenage years. It's a wonder what a little bit of exercise and cutting out soda can do.

I hesitate for a second to show him the note because I'm a little embarrassed by the whole situation, especially since I have now realized how incredibly handsome he is. But it's still in my hand, and I have no real reason to say no, so I give it to him. I lean against a bar stool, trying to play it cool as he opens it, like this sort of thing happens to me all the time, but I'm nervous and self-conscious as I watch his eyes move over the message.

He folds the note back up and returns it to me.

"He's right," Max or Jack says with a sweet smile.

Chapter 2

The following day, Sarah calls at seven in the morning, waking me from a deep, Nyquil-induced slumber to invite me over for dinner that night.

My eyes are still closed, too groggy to face the daylight. "How are you possibly thinking about impromptu dinner plans this early?"

"You've obviously never had a six-month-old baby before. I've been up since 4:30 watching Cocomelon and reading mommy message boards to figure out how to get this kid to sleep through the night. Just say you'll come." Then, she promptly hangs up the phone. She always does that, hangs up so she can have the last word.

I send her a text a few seconds later: *You never waited for my answer.*

Three little dancing dots show me she instantly begins typing her response.

Sarah: *Ace started crying, and I figured it's a yes.*

Me: *Why do you figure that?*

Sarah: *C'mon, Maddie. What else are you doing?*

Nothing. Absolutely nothing.

Me: *See you at seven.*

In all honesty, I look forward to any time someone invites me over for dinner because, while I love cooking, it's nice to get a break once in a while. Not to mention, I spend most of my time in the house I bought two years ago. Purchasing my home meant moving across town from both my parents and Sarah, but I fell in love with the storybook gables, the cobblestone chimney, and the massive maple tree in the front yard. Besides, I craved a fresh start somewhere new. Caught up in all of the little details, I didn't consider the bigger picture, how much time I'd be spending alone.

After trying and failing to fall back asleep, I finally roll out of bed and text Sarah again offering to bring dessert. I drag myself to the kitchen to throw together a tiramisu. It's simple and elegant. Every time I make it, everyone raves over it. It's one of those things people think you spent way more time on than you actually did. It also tastes even better when it's been sitting in the refrigerator for an entire day, and I am up early so I might as well.

During the remainder of the morning and into the afternoon, I work on a few recipes and even manage to fit in a quick nap. When I got home from Sully's last night, I stayed up late overthinking everything, mortified at the reality of strangers in the coffee shop forming opinions on my pathetic dating life. So, on a whim and after half of a bottle of sparkling wine, I deleted every account on every dating app I have.

Sarah was right. Online dating doesn't work, at least not for me, and the last thing I want is yet another humiliating encounter with a gorgeous man.

I arrive at Sarah and Mike's house a little early, tiramisu in hand. They live in a modest but adorable craftsman-style home in the newer suburbs just north of Cincinnati. The type of street where kids are always outside riding bikes or playing basketball in the cul de sac. It's the kind of neighborhood you want to raise a family in, with sidewalks, golden retrievers, and minivans as far as the eye can see.

Mike opens the door when I arrive. "The Mad Hatter, come on in!" He makes a grand gesture with his arms like he is welcoming royalty into his home. Mike has a million different nicknames for me and pretty much calls me anything but Maddie. I instantly notice he is wearing a plaid button-down shirt, which is a little odd. Enough to make me wonder. Usually when I come over, he's in jeans and a Carhartt t-shirt because he's been out mowing the lawn or working on some house project in the garage.

"Thanks for the grandiose entrance, Mike. Now where is your fat baby so I can snuggle the crap out of him?" I step into the entry and glance into the living room to the right. The Reds versus Dodgers game is playing on the enormous television mounted above the brick fireplace. Ace is lying on a rug in the middle of the room. He's on his belly with his head up, looking straight at me with those cute little alien eyes. He smiles when he sees me, revealing two bottom teeth and a mouth full of pink gums.

"C'mon, Stephenson!" Mike yells loudly and seemingly out of nowhere, which startles Ace, and he starts to cry. When he picks Ace up to comfort him, Mike sniffs the air and makes a face like he's in the presence of a dead body.

"Just in time, Madster! I think Little Man took a dump. In the mood for a diaper change?"

I shake my head. "Not a chance. How about you take care of the poop while I put the tiramisu in the fridge?"

Mike's eyes light up. "Oooo, I'll change a million poopy diapers for your tiramisu. I think you put crack in it."

"Shhh, don't reveal my secret ingredient," I whisper.

"Don't worry. I won't tell Sarah. She's a party pooper," Mike murmurs, his voice low.

"I heard that!" Sarah calls from the next room.

"Just kidding, babe!" Mike shouts, and then turns back to me, a mischievous grin plastered across his face. "I'll be back in a minute. I've got a flight to catch." Mike pivots Ace now so he is belly down, cradled in both of Mike's palms. He proceeds to fly Ace around the room like he is a human airplane, sound effects and all. Ace is smiling and giggling, loving every second of it. They disappear up the stairs to his nursery, and I saunter into the kitchen where I find Sarah peeking into the stove.

"That husband of yours was made to be a dad," I tell her.

She spins around, setting her worn oven mitts on the island counter. "Don't I know it. Sometimes I think he only married me so he could have babies."

"Yeah, right. He's obsessed with you. Not all of us can be so lucky." Sarah rolls her eyes but doesn't argue because she knows I'm right. Mike is so in love with Sarah, *and* he is an amazing dad.

He would have ten kids if he could, but Sarah, who is a labor and delivery nurse, would prefer to wait a year or two before she gets pregnant again. She had a traumatic birth experience with Ace that ended in an emergency c-section and a blood transfusion, so even though she wants a big family too, I think she's still recovering from that experience.

"So what are we having for dinner?" I ask, noting the heavy scent of garlic in the air.

"Lasagna, salad, breadsticks, and… a special guest," she says, and as if that was some sort of cue, there is a knock on the front door.

"What did you do?!" I ask Sarah accusingly.

She makes pouty, apologetic eyes that let me know I am not going to be happy. "I'm sorry I didn't tell you. I had this great idea, and so I went with it, okay?"

"Tell me you're not setting me up with someone tonight, Sarah."

"Okay, I'm not setting you up with someone tonight." Her voice goes up an octave, and she flashes me an impish grin.

"C'mon. You could have at least warned me. I'm in yoga pants, and my hair is a frizzy mess. I was planning on getting wine drunk with you while watching *Shark Tank* and venting about life. I'm not at all prepared to be on a date tonight." I crumple over, resting my elbows on the granite countertop and cradling my face in my palms. There's nothing I can do about it now.

"Please Maddie, you always look amazing, even when you don't try. Those yoga pants are hot by the way. Plus—" Before she can continue, I hear Mike answer the front door followed by the sound of footsteps headed in our direction.

I quickly stand up tall, pulling my shoulders back and straightening my posture.

"Maddie," Mike says, walking into the kitchen first, and I know something is up because he just called me Maddie for the first time in the decade I've known him. "I'd like you to meet my cousin, Jack." And just like that, I am shaking hands with the sexy barista and wishing I were anywhere but here.

"Very nice to meet you," Jack says with a coy smile. Unsure of why he is acting like we haven't met before, I take his lead anyway and pretend this is the first time I've seen him.

"Nice to meet you too," I say, imagining how perfect this could be if I had the forewarning to make sure I looked in the slightest bit presentable for a blind date, especially with one who is so damn good-looking. Sarah screwed me on this one, so I have Mike pour me a fat glass of wine to help me loosen up. This guy is out of my league anyway.

"Jack recently moved to town from… what city were you living in again?" Sarah turns to him to ask.

"Albuquerque," Jack replies with a slight head nod.

Sarah looks to both of us with a glimmer in her eye. "Ah, that's right. Well, Jack just moved here, and I thought you two could be friends." You can see how proud of herself she is for this secret setup. *She has no idea.*

"So you're Mike's cousin? I'm practically a part of the family, so how have I never met you before?" I attempt to sound casual, but inside my stomach is doing backflips, still trying to overcome the shock of this strange coincidence.

"Family drama, pretty much," Jack says. "My dad and Mike's dad are brothers. My parents divorced when I was young, and my mom moved my sister and me to Arizona with her." He sounds bored with his own history, like he's reciting rehearsed lines. "We weren't really around my dad's side of the family much growing up. Mainly some holidays here and there. Anyways, I recently moved here for a job and called Mike to hang out."

"We haven't seen each other in probably ten years," Mike adds.

Sarah interjects because she can't help herself. "And I thought you two have a lot in common, so you should meet!" I flash Sarah an aggravated glare and don't even try to hide it from Mike or Jack. Sarah continues, looking directly at Jack now, "For example, Maddie is the biggest bookworm I know. I haven't seen her without a book for as long as I've known her." Then, she shifts her glance to me. "And Jack is Xavier University's newest literature professor."

"Adjunct professor," Jack clarifies. "It's not a full-time gig or anything but enough to get my foot in the door."

"Wow, that's impressive. I never would have... you look so... are you like a Doogie Howser type?" I ask, awkwardly trying to figure out the politest way to tell him he looks really young.

"I know. I know. I've always had a babyface. I still get carded when I go to bars."

"Me too!" Mike practically yells. We all burst into laughter because Mike has a pretty intense receding hairline and has looked like a thirty-five-year-old for as long as Sarah and I have known him.

"I'm actually thirty-two," Jack adds. "I just finished my doctorate in the spring."

The baby monitor on the counter lights up, and the sound of Ace crying from upstairs engulfs the kitchen. "Babe, can you please come help me with Ace?" Sarah asks Mike.

"Uh, sure?" Mike says like a question, clearly confused about what help Sarah might possibly need with what is likely a routine diaper change. However, I can see right through Sarah and her little scheme. Jack and I are left standing at the island with nothing to do but talk to one another, a setup indeed.

"Can I pour you some wine?" I ask Jack, an attempt to fill the uncomfortable silence.

"Thanks, but I'm more of a craft beer guy myself. Wine gives me headaches." Jack walks to the refrigerator and pulls out a can of Rhinegeist. When he turns around, I can't help but admire the way his jeans fit his body perfectly, like they were made for him. He cracks his beer open as he looks back to me.

"What are the odds?" He studies me for a moment. "I had no idea last night that I would be your next victim." The same sly smile from when Jack first laid eyes on me tonight graces his face yet again.

"Sorry for the disappointment. For the record, I had no idea Sarah was planning any of this. If I did, I would have tried a little harder." I gesture to my messy hair and outfit.

"I think you look gorgeous. You don't have to try very hard."

I feel my cheeks turn hot pink and remind myself he is out of my league. I'm average, and he is, well, perfect. All I have to do is look at him to know that much. But I remember what my dad always told me: *Take the damn compliment. Men don't want an insecure woman.* So rather than argue the point, I simply say, "Thank you," and quickly change the subject.

"So, what's a lit professor doing working at a coffee shop? I thought for sure you were a student at UC when I saw you at Sully's, not a professor."

"Ah, I knew that was coming. Well, it's the start of the summer term. I didn't actually get hired to start teaching until the fall semester, but I wanted to come early so I could find a place to live and get settled, you know?" I nod and take a sip of my wine. "I stopped at Sully's for coffee one day and saw a sign posted that they were hiring for one night a week."

"Saturdays?"

"Yep, Saturdays. I've met a lot of cool people there, obviously." He motions towards me. "And if anything, it forces me to leave my apartment. I tend to be a homebody."

A handsome single guy who likes to hang out at home and read for fun? I blink a few times to be sure he isn't a figment of my imagination because as it turns out, Jack really is exactly what I've been looking for.

"I feel you on that," I tell him. "I work from home now, and I love it. I've done the cubicle thing, and it wasn't for me. It's amazing how dramatic people in an office environment can be over every little thing: missing Post-its, stolen parking spots, broken copy machines. I just couldn't do it anymore."

"So what do you do now?" Jack sounds like he's genuinely interested, which I have to admit, is an endearing quality. When most people ask you about your life these days, it's out of obligation, maybe even politeness, but definitely not interest.

"I started with a food blog, but now I mostly do recipe development. I don't love being on social media all of the time, so I actually pay someone to do that part of it now."

"Wow, you must be pretty damn successful to be able to do that." His dark eyes are locked on mine, and I can see he's impressed.

"I'm proud to say that I am, but only because I worked my ass off for all of my success. Nothing has ever been handed to me. I make the food and send Margot the pictures, but she posts everything, comes up with witty captions, and responds to comments, that sort of thing. She keeps me relevant while saving me probably five hours of every single day."

"Ah, that's how you have so much time to date so many men." Jack wears that now familiar smirk.

"Hey now!" I act like I am offended but very quickly concede. "I know there's been a lot of them lately. I've been trying the online dating thing, and I've… well, I've been failing very badly at it." I stumble over my words as I watch my fingers trace the rim of my wine glass, avoiding eye contact with Jack because I know I'm blushing yet again. Jack has seen and probably heard me on some of these encounters with strangers from the internet. Not to mention, if he has truly listened in, he may know more about me than I even realize.

"Is it that important to you, having a boyfriend?" And there is something about the way he asks this. With this one question and the tone in which he says it, the entire dynamic of the conversation has shifted. Like he has gone from being impressed with me to feeling sorry for me in a single moment.

My shoulders stiffen as my arms cross over my chest, the need to defend myself for going on a few dates suddenly overtaking me. "It turns out there aren't many good guys left in the dating pool, and I don't want to be one of those cat ladies. Have you seen how in love Sarah and Mike are? I want that for my life."

"They are pretty perfect, but why do you think you need a relationship to be happy?"

It feels like I'm being interrogated, and I have to remind myself I barely know this guy. He doesn't deserve to know anything. "I didn't say I need it to be happy. But doesn't everyone want someone?"

"I don't," Jack says, matter-of-fact. "I'm too selfish right now to be in a committed relationship. There are things I want to do before I settle down… *if* I settle down. Maybe I never will. I don't feel like I need to." He's so casual about it, like he's blissfully unaware lots of people want someone to love more than anything else. I'd venture to say most people do. I've met plenty of guys like Jack though. The ones who think they're too good to settle down, like a relationship will hold them back in some way. I don't want to waste my time on someone who is so self-centered he can't even imagine fitting another person into his present or his future.

Thankfully, Sarah and Mike return from the world's longest diaper change bringing our conversation to an end. "I hope we aren't interrupting anything! Who's ready to eat?" Sarah winks at me.

For the next two and a half hours, the four of us sit around the dining room table and have dinner, drinks, and dessert. Despite the fact that I have completely written this off as a date, we all have an absolute blast together. Unfortunately for me, Jack is charming and funny and fits right into our loud and sarcastic banter like he has been hanging out with us forever.

A few times, I even catch him looking at me mid-bite from across the table, and when he sees me spot his stare, he quickly shies away. Maybe I'm not as out of his league as I initially thought. If he hadn't made that jerky comment earlier, I would probably be swooning over him just like Sarah wanted.

Jack is undeniably attractive, and I don't think anyone could argue that point if they wanted to. However, I can't let myself get involved with him no matter how charismatic he may be. I'm thirty, and there's no time to waste anymore. I know his type well. He's the kind of guy who wants you to come over and watch a movie, have casual sex, and still pretend you are only friends at the end of the night. He wants you to promise him you won't catch feelings or fall in love. Then, the first time the topic of being exclusive comes up, he will drop you like a bad habit, all because he has commitment issues and doesn't want to have to get over his Peter Pan Syndrome. I am not twenty-five anymore, and I am definitely not falling for that. So, I'm careful to keep my guard up and to resist his charm.

After dinner, the men clear the table and take care of the dishes while Sarah and I curl up on the couch with our mugs of decaf coffee. She whispers to me so Mike and Jack can't overhear from the next room. "Did I do good, or did I do good?"

"Way out of my league," I whisper back.

"No way. He may be really hot, but I promise you, he's super nerdy like you. You guys are perfect for each other." She puts her feet up on the brown leather ottoman and leans back into the couch cushions, soaking in the glory of her perceived success.

"He told me he doesn't want a girlfriend," I inform her.

"He's full of it!" Sarah practically shouts the words, forgetting Jack is in the next room.

"Shhhh!" I don't want Jack to hear any part of this conversation.

"Sorry," she continues, in a hushed tone. "No single guy *wants* a girlfriend. Love just happens when it happens."

"No one said anything about love. You are getting way ahead of yourself, Sarah."

"I don't think I am."

Mike and Jack appear in the doorway at the same time Ace starts crying from his nursery again. "That's my cue." Sarah stands and heads for the stairs. "Milkmaid reporting for duty."

I stand too, leaving my cozy imprint in the couch. "It's getting late. I think I'll head out. Thanks so much for having me over. I had a really great time."

"I think I'll do the same," Jack says. "Dinner was wonderful, Sarah. And Mike, I'll text you about those Reds tickets later this week."

I give Mike and Sarah a quick hug before heading for the front door. Jack walks out with me. His very practical Honda Civic, which appears to be brand new, is parked behind my Subaru. We make our way to our respective cars without uttering a word, but when I open my door, Jack turns to me. "I think your tiramisu was one of the best things I've ever eaten." He looks flawless in the moonlight.

"Thank you. It's one of my favorite desserts. A classic."

He steps towards me, fiddling with his keys in his hand. "Hey, it's still pretty early, and you and I don't have to deal with midnight diaper changes. Would you by any chance be interested in an after-party?"

An *after-party?* He sounds so cheesy, and I can't tell if he's serious. "What do you have in mind?"

"Well, I would suggest a bar, but you don't seem like that kind of girl. And I'm not that kind of guy. I did pick up some DVDs I had on hold at the library this afternoon if you're interested."

"DVDs? From the library?" I try to conceal my laughter. "Okay, any doubts I had about you being over thirty are now completely out the window. Are you sure you're not in your forties? Fifties, maybe?"

He stands tall, confident in himself, and he doesn't even flinch at my joke. "I'm not in the least bit ashamed. I'm an old soul. Always have been. And I'm a frequent visitor to my local library. So much so, I've even considered getting a bumper sticker so everyone knows."

I can't help but laugh now, and he does too. I want to go to his place. Well, my body wants to go at least, but I already know exactly what will happen if I were to say yes. I would inevitably start looking through Jack's book collection (as a literature professor, I imagine it's an impressive one, too). We would get into a deep conversation about our favorite books of all time, never even turning on a movie, and I would assure myself he is different than I initially suspected. We'd have too much to drink, and before I know it, I would be unbuttoning his shirt as he slides his fingers into the waistband of my yoga pants while I worry about whether or not I'm good enough for him. We would have sex right there on his couch, and I would drive myself home at four in the morning sexually satisfied beyond measure, wondering if his opinion on love is negotiable.

But, alas, my brain reminds me of what he said earlier. Jack is too selfish for a relationship. He knows this about himself. He told me as a warning. *Don't do this to yourself, Maddie. It won't end well.*

"So are you in or out?" he asks. His voice is so deep, and his full lips look so soft. I want those lips on mine, and it takes all of the self-restraint I have to say what I say next.

"Sorry, I'm going to have to pass tonight. Maybe another time. Goodnight." Jack gives me a little wave, and I get in my car and close the door. As soon as I sit down, I lean forward, press my forehead to the steering wheel, and let out a heavy sigh. I wish I were the kind of girl who could sleep with a man and not develop feelings for him.

Chapter 3

Three days after the setup at Sarah and Mike's, it's early afternoon when I am finally relaxing on the couch for a brief break from work. I spent the morning recipe testing followed by washing a million dishes, and now I'm casually researching food trends on my laptop. But I let my mind wander to Jack for a moment. For the most part, I have put him out of my mind, though in this indiscriminate time in the middle of the day when I would normally be scrolling through dating apps, I can't help but daydream about what might have happened had I attended his proposed after-party. However, the past is the past, and I learned a long time ago I have to let what already happened go.

My phone rings on the coffee table beside me, pulling me back to the present. It's an unknown number, but for some reason, I have the inclination to answer, something I very rarely do.

"Hello?" I say, like it's a question.

"Hey, Maddie?" The voice is familiar, but I can't pinpoint the caller right away.

Still unsure of whom I am speaking with, I reply rather formally, "This is she."

"Hey, uh, it's Jack. Jack Keller. I hope this isn't weird, but Sarah gave me your number." I didn't even know his last name until now. He sounds less confident than I remember, like he's not sure if calling me is crossing some sort of line.

"Oh, hi." To say I am surprised by Jack's call is an understatement. I wait for an explanation while my brain runs through every possible reason he might have to contact me. He wants my tiramisu recipe. That must be it.

"This might seem kind of random, but the head of the English Department at Xavier gave me two tickets to *Hamilton* at the Aronoff Center for tonight. I was wondering if you'd like to join me?" An awkward pause follows his question.

"Oh, wow," I finally say, realizing I'm supposed to respond. I am both surprised and confused by his request. *Why me?* "I know so many people who are obsessed with that show, but honestly, musicals aren't really my thing, and I'd hate to waste a ticket."

"No, that's perfect. That's what Sarah told me. I'm not into musicals either, and I think it would be way more fun to go with someone who won't take it so seriously. Plus, I still don't have many friends around here, and I thought maybe we could be. What do you say?"

"Umm, I do have some deadlines I have to meet." I am apprehensive for the same reasons I didn't go to his house three days ago. Jack is exactly the kind of guy I have been trying to avoid. He is gorgeous, afraid of commitment, and I can already see him ripping my heart into a thousand shredded pieces.

He senses my hesitation. "Maddie, I think I may have given you the wrong first impression of me. Let's start over tonight. Can I pick you up at six?"

"Sure," I say, and my jaw drops when the single word leaves my mouth. I am stunned by my response because I hadn't even agreed to go in my head yet, and then all of a sudden, my mouth just blurted out an answer.

"Great! Text me your address."

As soon as we hang up, I immediately regret agreeing to go, and I spend the next three hours combing through my closet trying to find the perfect outfit to wear on a date with a man who is not interested in any sort of relationship with me. Though I suspect he may want to sleep with me, a desire I would have succumbed to ten years ago when I thought I could change people, but not anymore.

After rifling through my closet, I settle on a long, navy floral dress I find deep in the depths of my wardrobe. I only remember wearing it once to a wedding a few years ago. The bottom is flowy, and the top dips all the way down to my sternum, complimenting my long and mildly curvy figure. I wonder why I haven't worn this again because I have to admit, I look good. Really good. My dark hair drapes down my back in loose waves, and my makeup is soft and subtle, like the pastel lilies on my dress. I put on a single piece of jewelry, an understated rose gold necklace adorned with a small pendant, an origami crane.

Jack arrives in a dark gray blazer layered over a white dress shirt with no tie. His hair is just the right amount of disheveled to look the professor part, and the stubble on his cheeks is only slightly visible, easily mistaken for a shadow in the dim light of the early evening. He is the kind of handsome I have only seen in the movies, the kind of man reserved for only the most classic and stunning of heroines, the Natalie Portmans and the Kate Winslets. I smooth my hands over my dress, and I watch him take a full breath when he sees me.

"You look beautiful," he tells me, as simple and lovely as a compliment can be.

On the drive, we listen to Band of Horses, and Jack tells me about the time he saw them play at a music festival in Colorado. He went by himself so he wouldn't have to worry about anyone else. That way he could come and go and do as he pleased without the responsibility that often comes with other people. He talks about the girl he met there with the henna tattoos who offered him acid, but he turned her down. She kissed him on the mouth before disappearing into the crowd, and he never saw her again. Sometimes he thinks about what she might be doing right now, where she is and what her life turned out to be. He is a good storyteller. I could listen to him talk all night. *Let's skip the show,* I think to myself, but I don't say it out loud.

Our seats are better than either of us imagined, and as we wait for the show to begin, I watch the thousands of chairs surrounding us fill up. There isn't an empty space in the entire theater. Jack lets me have the armrest, and when the lights go down, it's simply magical. I resist the urge to whisper to him as much as I actually want to. My mind isn't focused on the musical. It's on everything happening around me. The outlandish costumes, the red velvet seats, the scent of rosewood and patchouli drifting from the lady a few seats over. Jack and I giggle when the middle-aged man next to us mouths every word to every song as he pats his leg with his palm to the beat. At one point, I cross my right leg over my left, and when my ankle brushes Jack's leg, I get goosebumps. *Don't fall for him. It won't end well,* I repeat in my head to help me believe it.

I don't think Jack pays much attention to what's happening on stage either because at intermission, we don't talk about it at all, instead commenting on the people we see, how intense they all are, and what kind of posts we think they are making on their Instagram stories right now. We drink cheap house wine in the foyer, leaning against a tile wall, our elbows touching, flocks of passionate theatergoers passing us by.

Then, I see him. He appears suddenly and completely unexpected, like the onset of an earthquake. I freeze and do a turnabout to face the wall. Jack sees in my face that something happened, but he doesn't know what.

"Are you okay?" he asks, concern folded into his furrowed brow.

"Yes, I'm fine. It's nothing." I am fast and short with my words. He knows I'm lying.

His hand gently takes hold of my wrist. "Maddie—"

"It's just an ex. One I really don't want to see."

Jack shifts his gaze from me to the crowd, looking out into the sea of people. "Who?" His head turns slowly, scanning the possibilities.

"The guy in the blue checkered shirt with the beard to your right. His wife is wearing a long red dress. Running into exes, it's the price you pay for living in the same city your whole life." I try to sound casual, like I'm not *that* bothered, but I'm not doing a good job of it. My voice is shaky, and I am flustered.

Jack identifies him in the mass of people. Then, he leans in close to me and brushes my hair away from my ear with his fingers and whispers, "You got the good end of that deal, Maddie." I like that he reassures me, that he thinks so highly of me even though he doesn't know the least of it. He moves his warm hand to my waist and turns me back around slowly. "Don't hide. Let him see what he's missing."

Facing me now, Jack's hand remains on my waist, his body so close to mine that nervous butterflies crowd my stomach wanting him to get even closer, to touch me more, to move his hands to other places. *It's chemical. Physical. That's all it is,* I tell myself. My breathing starts to get heavier against my will, an involuntary heat rising inside of me, just before Jack smiles and says, "They look like brother and sister."

The tension in my body melts into laughter. "I always thought that too!"

But when my laughing finally fades, Ben and his wife are still standing there. Only a few steps away, I can make out the subtle facial expressions they give one another, and it's almost unbearable to watch. "She was the one right after me. The girl he dated right after we broke up, I mean. He married her."

Jack shakes his head, taking my hand and leading me back to our seats to watch the rest of the show, but I can only think about the intermission, replaying it all in my head. *Ben, his wife, Jack, me.* I don't know if Ben saw me in the foyer, but I hope he did. I hope he saw me with Jack and wondered how I've been.

After the show, we are struck by the smothering heat of summer as we exit the air-conditioned venue. Jack and I get ice cream cones to cool off and sit on a wooden bench in Washington Park right outside the theater. The stars hang in the air, bathing in the glow of the silver moon. We watch all of the people coming and going from restaurants and bars, passing through the park as a means to an end. It seems like we're the only ones sitting still. The only ones content where we are and who we're with.

I wonder if Jack simply can't think of anything else to say or if he really wants to know, but he asks me about Ben while we sit on that bench. "What happened with that guy anyway? Your ex. He obviously meant a lot to you."

And maybe it's because I already feel some weird and unexplainable connection to Jack or maybe it's because I've had a few glasses of wine and want to stop myself from thinking about having sex with him tonight, but I do tell Jack about Ben. "He was the only one I ever loved, and I didn't know it until it happened. I thought I loved other guys before him, but then he came along when I was twenty-two, and he swept me off my feet with his guitar and the way he didn't take the world too seriously. I learned what being in love was from him, and it was perfect, our relationship that is, until it wasn't. It's the same old story for everyone who's fallen in and out of love, I suppose."

"So what happened? Where'd it all go wrong?" Jack is intrigued. He really does want to know.

I stare at the blur of neon restaurant lights ahead. "Everything and nothing I guess you could say. It was a classic tale of being too young to be that serious. Of wanting to change parts of someone who doesn't want to change. Of falling too hard too fast without enough experience to really know how to handle any of it. I wanted John Cusack outside my window with a boombox in the pouring rain."

"In the pouring rain?" Jack gives me a curious look.

"John Cusack is *always* stuck in the rain," I inform him.

"Of course he is." Jack rolls his eyes and laughs. "Everyone wants a romance like the movies, don't they?"

My gaze turns to Jack now. His ice cream is gone, and his hands are resting on his legs. All of his attention is on me. "I don't know. I never thought of it like that. Maybe that's where everyone learns about love. Unfortunately for me, Ben wasn't John Cusack, and I couldn't make him John Cusack. That isn't why it hurt so much to see him tonight, though."

"So what makes it so hard?"

"Do you know how it feels right after a breakup, when you're letting someone go, and deciding to stop loving that person hurts so fucking bad that you take it out on each other in the worst possible ways? You can only see in red." I tuck my hair behind my ears and attempt to explain something I really don't even know how to put into words. "I wish I could go back in time and make it suck less for both our sakes. The fighting, the revenge, the horrible things we both said, I would take it all back if I could. But however bad it was then, in the midst of it, I still refuse to believe we were never meant to love each other."

I pause for a moment to think about it all, and then I tell Jack something I haven't told anyone, not even Sarah. "I still think of Ben sometimes. Even now that the acceptable amount of time to think about an ex has long since passed. Sometimes he shows up in my dreams, completely uninvited. It's not that I want him back, because I don't. I just don't feel like there was ever closure, if that makes any sense. I've always wanted one last conversation to say, *Hey, no hard feelings. I hope you found the kind of happiness I always wanted for you. I hope when you think of me, it's not all bad.* Sorry, I'm rambling. I think I needed to say all that out loud." I twirl my fingers in my hair the way I do when I'm nervous, deciding I must be more intoxicated than I realize to have said all this to him.

Jack rests his hand on my thigh. "Don't apologize. I like listening to you talk. Do you want to hear something crazy?" We're sitting so close on the bench, our hips are pressed together. We may be in a public park where anyone can see, but our whole conversation feels so intimate.

"Of course, I do. I just sat here and spilled my guts to you. Tell me anything." I wipe my mouth with my napkin, then hold it crumbled in my hand.

"I don't know how any of that feels, everything you just talked about. I've never had a breakup because I've never been in a real relationship. I guess I don't know what love is, the romantic kind anyway." My eyes widen with his confession. A thirty-two-year-old man who has never, not once, been in love? This may in fact be the heaviest baggage I have ever heard on a first date, and that is saying a lot. He looks at me, and my expression must demand further explanation because he continues even though I haven't said a word.

"I told you my parents got divorced when I was young. Well, it was a bad divorce. There was a lot of fighting. So much so, I would lock myself in my room and put my headphones on, blasting my iPod at the highest possible volume to drown out the yelling."

Jack's eyes follow a pigeon eating remnants of spilled ice cream and popcorn on the bench across from us. "And my mom basically used my sister and me as pawns when she moved us to Arizona. She wanted to make my dad as miserable as she could. Over the years, not only did I see my dad way less than any kid should see their dad, but I had to endure the countless boyfriends my mom brought home. There were dozens of them over the years, some who were assholes, some who were okay, and even one or two I hoped she'd marry to end the cycle. But guess what?"

"What?" I hope for a happy ending to the somber story of his upbringing. It's enough to make me feel guilty for my own, one filled with parents who loved each other and still do.

"My mom is still alone and unhappy." Jack's mouth melts into a slight frown. "All she wanted her whole life was love. It was all she cared about, and she has nothing now. No career, no husband, and two kids who resent her for what she put them through. If I learned one thing from my mom growing up, it's that whatever love is, I'm not interested."

He looks up to the star-scattered sky. I look up too. "So here we are, two single thirty-somethings eating ice cream cones on a park bench. More than anything, I want to find love, and you want nothing to do with it," I say.

"And here we are *together,* the irony of it all," Jack adds.

I shake my head. "I don't think it's ironic. I think it's the universe trying to tell us something, send us some sort of message."

"Maybe. But there's something I want you to know." He pauses for a moment, inhaling the midnight air, alive and warm. "All that stuff with my parents was a giant mess, and when I told you at Sarah's that I'm not looking for a relationship, that's why. So I don't want you to take any of what I said personally, and I think you might have. You are beautiful and smart and funny, but I'm just not meant to be in love. I was hoping we could be friends though."

"I would very much like to be friends with you, Jack Keller."

I have had more fun with Jack tonight than I've had on every date from the past six months combined. There is indisputable chemistry between us, and if being friends is all we can be, I am willing to accept that if it means I can have more nights like this one. More nights when I'm not all alone.

"Just so you know, I don't have sex with my friends," I tell him.

Jack wears that trademark, troublesome grin on his face. "Got it," he says and moves his palm from the top of my thigh. "That's a damn shame."

I look down at my phone to check the time.

"11:11, make a wish."

Chapter 4

"What are you cooking this week, Madeline?" Mom asks from across my kitchen table.

I place my napkin on my lap the way she taught me to always do when I was a little girl. "Whelp, one thing I know I'll be doing is figuring out what to do with the abundance of zucchinis in my garden. I'm bursting at the seams with them. Probably zucchini pasta with a fresh tomato sauce."

"That sounds like the perfect, light summer meal," Mom says, then takes a bite of the chicken parmesan on her plate.

Dad sets down his fork, a confused expression spread across his face. "How in the heck are you gonna make pasta out of zucchini?" Mom and I giggle, not even bothering to answer his question.

This is our typical Wednesday evening, sitting around one of our kitchen tables eating a home-cooked meal and talking about our week ahead. We've had dinner together every week since I moved out of their house over a decade ago when I started college.

Food has always been a part of our story. When I was young, I made dinner with Mom every night, acting as her sous chef. On slow, lazy Sundays, we would bake pies and cakes from scratch. My parents still live on the other side of town in the home I grew up in. Upstairs, my periwinkle bedroom is still intact, complete with posters on the walls and glow-in-the-dark constellations stuck to the ceiling. They both retired recently. My mom, Anne, taught preschool for twenty-seven years in the back of a little church near their home. She loves kids, she always has, and her personality is one toddlers are drawn to. I've seen her in her classroom, and the way she reads and sings songs with them is pure magic. She is completely patient and understanding with the enormous emotions that flood their tiny little bodies.

My dad, Dave, worked in banking for thirty years, which doesn't fit his personality at all. In another life, I think he was an engineer of some sort. Or a park ranger. He never sits still and loves to be outside. He also loves to fix things. Anything from a rickety lawnmower to a leaky faucet, his toolbox is always nearby. Sometimes I joke that I think he breaks things just to be able to put them back together. He's the type to come home from work and spend hours tinkering with some little project he has going, having to be called in by Mom for dinner. It's hard for me to even picture Dad sitting at a desk all those years because at home, he never sits. It's not in his nature.

"When can I come over next week to start the demo?" Dad asks over dinner, eyes gleaming like a kid on Christmas morning. Demo is Dad's favorite part, and he's anxious to get started. He and I spent weeks making the plans for my downstairs bathroom. My goal is to maintain as much of the old home charm as I can, which includes keeping the antique mirror and avocado-colored tile, but we decided to take down a wall to make it larger and then add a clawfoot tub and shower. I offered to hire a contractor for all of that stuff, but Dad insists on doing it himself. "It keeps me young," he always tells me, but at sixty-five, I can't help but notice his body slowing down, the way he holds his back and groans at the end of the day. One of the hardest things about growing up is watching your parents lose their vibrancy, their immortality.

"Let him do what he can, and you can hire someone for the rest," Mom tells me. "He likes to feel like he's helping."

I think about my schedule before responding. "Thursday would probably be best because I have a few recipes due to some clients earlier in the week."

"Why don't we move dinner to Thursday next week then?" Mom suggests. "I'll bring dinner over to your place when you and Dad need a break."

"That sounds great, Mom."

Dad nods his head in agreement, and we move on to other topics. My cousin Delilah's upcoming wedding, the postponement of their annual church festival, and of course, Ohio State Football, Dad's favorite topic. After a while, I get up for a moment to refill Dad's empty glass. When I sit back down, he takes a long sip of his fresh iced tea and sets his cup on the table next to a lone lemon wedge squeezed dry. He looks at me, his eyes a little glossy, and asks, "So Maddie, what's a good day to come over next week and start the demo in the downstairs bathroom?"

I start to laugh, but he doesn't, and neither does Mom. Dad looks confused by my reaction, so I stop, realizing he has absolutely no idea he asked me the same question mere minutes prior. My glance shifts to Mom, who is peering down at her plate avoiding eye contact with me. Panic rises in my gut, but I keep it in, holding myself together. *It could be a fluke,* I tell myself.

"Thursday is good, Dad," I say with a delicate smile, but inside of me, anxiety is already wreaking havoc. I inhale a long, deep breath, and it takes all of my willpower not to run to the bathroom and throw up.

"Very good," Dad says, his trademark response for everything. That's how he always ends a conversation before moving on to another: *Very good.*

Once we finish dinner, Dad takes some measurements in the bathroom while I interrogate Mom in the kitchen as she rinses the dishes. I stand next to her, loading them into the dishwasher when she passes them to me.

"What was that all about?" I ask in a hushed tone, worried Dad might overhear us.

"It's nothing. It's all going to be okay."

But I don't believe her. Something about the way she says it makes it hard to. "We don't keep secrets, Mom. Tell me what's going on."

She shakes her head, her eyes focused on the congealed mozzarella she's scrubbing from a white plate. "To be honest, I don't know."

"What do you mean you don't know? Is this like a regular thing?

How long has it been happening?" I want to know every detail, hoping I'll find solace in her words, that it won't be as bad as I'm making it out to be.

"It's happened before, but it's more frequent lately," she confesses, almost wincing at the words. "He asks the same question two times, even three times, one right after the other. And..." She pauses and pushes out a slow, sullen breath before continuing. "He keeps losing his socks. He talks about it all day long. *Where are my socks? They keep disappearing. Where are those damn missing socks?* I have no idea what he's talking about. All of his socks are right there in his drawer, but he insists they keep going missing."

"It sounds like—" But I stop myself mid-sentence, fearful my words might will something into existence.

"He has an appointment with his doctor in two weeks," Mom says, gently.

"So he knows something's wrong?"

"Yes, he knows. We've discussed it."

Tears form in my eyes, but I stop them before they fall. *We don't know anything yet. It could all be okay,* I try to reassure myself. However, I can't help but worry about the future of our little family, what might happen if Dad is sick. It's always been just the three of us.

My parents spent three years after they got married trying and failing to get pregnant, and finally, by some lucky chance, I came to be. For the next decade after I was born, they wanted to give me a sibling. Dad wished for a whole basketball team, and Mom hoped for three. "Two girls and a boy," she told me. I don't know all of the details because I was young, but I know they went to fertility doctors and did everything they could. Lightning just wouldn't strike again. Or maybe it wasn't supposed to.

There were so many nights Mom cried herself to sleep as I peeked through a crack in their bedroom door. Dad lay next to her in bed, rubbing her back for as long as the tears lasted, humming made-up melodies to calm her nerves.

"What's wrong with Mom?" I would ask him the next morning.

"She wants to give you a sister," he would say.

The three of us never hid things from each other. There can't be secrets in a family so small, so they always told me the truth whenever I had questions. Each night, I looked out my window and made a wish on the brightest star. "Please give Mom a baby. Please give her a baby," I would repeat over and over again to whoever might be listening in the sky. It didn't make me sad that she felt like she needed more kids because every chance she got, she would tell me, "You are the sun, the moon, and all the stars, Maddie June. You are enough for me."

"And the trees and the leaves and the Blue Jays and the Cardinals?" I would ask.

"All of those and more, my sweet girl."

I never got a sibling, but I think it made the bond between my parents and me that much stronger. Now, the thought of one of them not being okay is enough to break me. They're all I have.

Once my parents leave, I'm left alone in my empty house. I quickly find that being by myself makes the panic more difficult to suppress. I start to feel like I am suffocating. My breaths are short and shallow, and I can't seem to get enough of them. Every effort to distract myself is a failure, and I end up lying on my back on the living room floor staring up at the speckled ceiling, overwhelmed with worry and a sense of helplessness. My chest is uncomfortably tight, and my fingers are clenched into fists. If I stay here, I am going to be awake all night conjuring up the worst-case scenario in my head, and that is exactly what I shouldn't do.

My first instinct is to call Sarah. It's what I have always done when I feel like this, when I need someone to show me the other side to a story, to talk me through something I can't rationalize myself. But Sarah is a mom now, and it's unfair for me to expect her to stay up late and watch *The Great British Baking Show* while drinking just enough alcohol that I don't have to think when I fall asleep. So, I call Jack instead.

"Sorry if this is weird or too much. Something happened. I need to get out of my house." Jack doesn't ask a single question. He simply tells me to meet him at Sully's thirty minutes later.

When I arrive, I don't see Jack anywhere, so I have a seat at the cat table and send him a text: *Here.* The vibe at Sully's isn't the same tonight. Normally, when I am waiting for a date, I am hopeful, at least a little. Tonight though, the dim lighting is much too dark, and all of the tchotchkes that give the place its character make it feel like the walls are closing in around me. Claustrophobic and exhausted, I would like to be hopeful, but I'm not.

Jack replies just in time because sitting here, my whole body is fidgety and restless.

I'm on the patio, he writes.

I knew there was a deck out back because of a sign that hangs near the restroom door, but I have never so much as glanced out there, assuming it was occupied by hipsters smoking cigarettes, a scent I could never grow to tolerate. To my surprise, when I walk to the back past a hidden nook with a shabby couch and a few small tables, the space is captivating. It resembles an enchanted treehouse, completely surrounded by trees and covered by branches filled with leaves. A wood-burning fireplace acts as the focal point, and a million twinkle lights surround the perimeter, even lacing up into the branches overhead. No one is smoking, one of the many trends that must have disappeared when I wasn't paying attention, like skinny jeans and side parts.

Jack is sitting at a table in the corner in a blue and white raglan shirt. He types on a laptop, eyes locked on the screen and lips pursed in such pure concentration, I almost don't want to interrupt. He doesn't notice me until I pull out the chair across from him. He immediately shuts his computer and sets it to the side.

"Sorry, do you have work to do?"

"Oh no, that's nothing," he says, waving his hand as if to shoo away a fly.

The table is wobbly. My chair is wobbly. Everything in this place is unsteady, and I recognize that's a part of the charm. It's what differentiates Sully's from the Starbucks and Caribou Coffees of the world, along with the shots of Jameson and cat tables. But tonight, the shakiness of everything around me only contributes to the uneasiness burrowed deep in my gut.

"First things first, what would you like to drink?"

Jack talks as if he has prepared an agenda for our evening.

My head still feels foggy, and my mind keeps finding its way back to Dad and his lost socks. "Anything."

Jack nods, understanding I can't think right now. "I'll be right back."

He stands up and walks inside. I can see him through a clouded window as he steps behind the bar and makes my drink himself, chatting with Holly, one of the baristas on the clock. I know her from coming here so often. She has blue hair and a septum ring, and she seems to always be at Sully's, whether she's working or not.

Jack returns to our table a few minutes later holding a pint glass in each hand. He places one of them in front of me. "It's an Iced Metro Coffee."

I shrug, the tightening in my chest beginning to soften. "Never heard of it."

"Well, it is the most popular menu item here at Sully's. You'll like it. Everyone does." Jack sits back down in his chair across the table from me.

"What's so special about it?" I ask, conspicuously examining the glass.

"Well, there's a secret about the Iced Metro Coffee, you see," Jack whispers now, like he is going to reveal something to me no one within earshot can hear.

"Really?" I lean forward, intrigued.

"Yes. But first you must promise you won't tell anyone what I'm about to tell you." He is as serious as a heart attack as he holds his pinky finger out over the table. I interlock my little finger with his.

"Pinky swear," I promise.

Then he stands, bending his body over the table so his face is only inches from mine. "The Iced Metro Coffee is not real," he murmurs, and I can smell the espresso on his breath. "It's not a real thing." Jack sits back down, peering around the patio to make sure no one else is listening. I look back at him, my eyes narrowed and confused.

"What do you mean it's not a real thing?" I ask.

"It's made up. A figment of the imagination. Everyone loves it. The regulars rave about our Iced Metro Coffee." He waves his hands around as he talks. "If you go on *Yelp,* you'll see dozens of reviews mentioning it. *Best drink I've ever had,* people say. What nobody knows is that every single bartender who works here makes it differently. There is no recipe. It's not real."

I glare into his eyes, trying to read him. *Is he being serious right now?* "So you're telling me everyone here just puts whatever the hell they want into a pint glass and calls it an Iced Metro Coffee?"

Jack weaves his fingers together behind his head and leans back in his chair. "That is precisely what I'm telling you."

My arms fold over my chest. "I don't believe you."

"Maddie, I even confirmed it with Jon." Jon is the owner of Sully's who every patron knows well, a white-haired old guy in his seventies who opened the coffee shop sometime in the 1970s. He sits at the bar every night drinking fully caffeinated black coffee until he is ready for bed. Sometimes Jon walks around and talks to people, sharing stories about the years he spent traveling Asia studying Buddhism, but mostly he stays to himself, sitting at the bar and jotting things down in a tiny notepad.

"When I first started working here," Jack continues, "a couple of the baristas taught me how to make it differently, so I went to Jon so I would know how to make it the right way. Do you know what he said to me?"

"What?" I ask, still trying to figure out if Jack is exaggerating about all of this.

"He said the Iced Metro Coffee is just a concept. An idea. Then he told me it can be whatever I want it to be."

I giggle. "That sounds like Jon, alright."

"Oh, yes. It's all *just a concept,*" Jack repeats, laughing as he says it. "He did say it has to taste good though."

I lift my glass and finally take a long-awaited sip, letting the taste settle on my tongue before swallowing. "Jack, that is very, very good. It might be one of the best drinks I've ever had. What's in it?"

"I'll never tell." He gives me a disarming smirk, and his smile oozes the kind of comfort I need right now. It's hard to believe we barely know each other because we talk like we've been friends for years. "Now, on to the next thing." Jack moves to the next item on his imaginary to-do list.

"What's on our agenda, Dr. Keller?"

"You called me because something happened. So, you have two choices."

"Lay 'em on me."

"Well, you can tell me what happened, and I will listen to you all night if you'd like me to, or…" He pauses and takes a drink, then sets his glass back down on the wobbly table. "We can avoid whatever happened entirely and play *Scrabble* instead."

Without the slightest bit of hesitation, I choose. "*Scrabble*." I know I don't want to talk about what happened tonight, especially because there isn't anything to talk about really. I have no answers. Everything is speculation at this point. Panic-inducing speculation at that. The reason I called Jack is so he could help me get my mind off of it. I don't want to dive headfirst into the possibilities, the reality of it all.

"I thought you might say that, so I swiped this from inside." Jack reaches over to the seat next to him where he already has an ancient *Scrabble* game waiting. He sets it on the table between us. The box is torn to shreds, but surprisingly, the game itself appears to be in very good condition. He sets up the game board, we each pull our seven letters out of the red velvet bag, and before he even takes a peek at what he has, he looks at me with his flecked brown eyes and says, "Ladies first." Then, he peers down at his row of letters and begins to study them intently.

I get lucky with my first round of letters and lay down the word *bridge*. "I'll keep score," I say, removing the scrap paper and lead pencil nub from the box. I write both of our names at the top of the page and underline them, then write *12* beneath mine. "Your turn."

I can't remember the last time I played a board game, or any kind of game, and I can sense the youthful competitiveness building inside of me. It's a feeling I don't have often these days, not since being on the soccer field in high school where Sarah and I both played the front line. Jack's eyes travel from his letters to the board and back again. Back and forth, back and forth. He breaks for a moment to look up and sees me staring at him. "Don't forget to get your new letters," he says.

I promptly shift my glance, embarrassed he caught me watching him, and I reach my hand into the bag. The wooden pieces move between my fingers, nostalgia in my touch. I used to play *Scrabble* with my parents around the kitchen table along with *Yahtzee* and *Battleship* and a million other games that helped to shape my childhood. They taught me a lesson or two about how to win and lose gracefully. Or at least try to.

Jack lays down *clover* using the *e* in *bridge*. "Sixteen."

"What was your favorite board game when you were younger?" I ask while documenting his points.

"*Risk*, hands down. My friends and I played it at every sleepover for like six months straight."

"What is it with guys and *Risk*? I swear that's every guy's favorite board game."

Jack looks at me like I'm crazy not to know. "Strategy, war, world domination, what's not to love? Let me guess yours." He ponders for a moment. "*Candy Land*?"

"C'mon. *Candy Land* is for five-year-olds."

"Hmm…" He thinks on it longer this time. "*Monopoly*?"

"Are you being serious right now? Nobody likes *Monopoly*."

Deep lines form on his cheeks when he laughs. "You're right. That game sucks. So give it up. What is it?"

"*The Game of Life*," I say, and Jack begins nodding his head.

"How did I forget about that game? My sister made me play it with her all of the time."

"I loved it so much." The mere mention of that game brings me back to the family room in my parents' house. On the weekends, the three of us would sip on orange soda with a bowl of pretzels and M&Ms to share between us while we played *The Game of Life* around the coffee table. There was a time when I would beg them to play it with me every single day. I never cared that having kids would put me at a disadvantage. I always wanted four so I could fill my vehicle completely, preferably two boys and two girls. It was probably a reflection of what I dreamed my adult life would be like before I even hit double digits myself. I wanted the game to be real, to skip childhood and go straight to the fun stuff like buying a house and getting married. I was so eager to race into the future when I was young. Now, I would love nothing more than to sit at that coffee table, knuckle-deep in M&Ms, just one more time.

"Let me guess, you had to name all of your kids?" Jack wears a playful grin from ear to ear.

"Of course. That's the whole reason I wanted to play. It was always some mouthful of elegance like Sabrina Victoria or Sebastian Constantine."

"Sebastian Constantine?" He bursts into laughter, and I reach across the table, nudging his shoulder with my hand.

"Whatever. I like it." I smirk at him because I know the name is a bit much. "My turn," I say, looking back down to my letters and changing the subject from my apparently stereotypical ways. I lay down the word *hoax* above *bridge*. In the process, I form three more words: *ob, ar,* and *xi.*

"Let's see." I begin to count the points in my haul. "Thirty-four," I determine. "You can check my math if you want."

He leans over the board, inspecting my last move. "I don't need to. X-i? That's not a word. How do you even pronounce that? What is it?"

"Dost thou want to challenge me?" I reply in my best Shakespearean accent.

"Maybe I do." Jack narrows his eyes and stares at me, trying to determine if I'm pulling one over on him. "I have a doctorate in English Literature, and I do not know of a word *xi* in the English language."

"Then challenge me. I dare you." I rest my elbow on the table and lean into it, waiting to see what he'll do. But he can see I'm too confident, and I am because I do happen to know I am right. That was the only way I could beat my dad, by learning two-letter words, especially the ones with the most valuable letters on the board.

Jack's gaze as he attempts to read me is so deep, I worry he might even be able to tell what I'm thinking, which would not be good because I'm thinking of how utterly perfect he is.

"You're either some sort of *Scrabble* guru, or you're trying to swindle me. Or both," he says.

My poker face melts into chuckling now. I'm smiling so much my cheeks are starting to hurt. "Swindle you? I wasn't aware there were any stakes involved in this game."

"Good thing that wasn't established yet. Either way, this is war." He can't contain his laughter anymore either, and he finally lets it out. His smile is so familiar already. A cozy couch, a warm fire.

"Hey," I say, resting my fingertips on his, shifting the tone of our banter for just a moment. "Thank you."

"Anytime, Maddie. We're friends." He lets his eyes rest on mine for another long second before looking back to his row of letters.

Chapter 5

"Maddie, please come over here NOW," are the only words Sarah says to me when she calls the next morning at six. She hangs up, and I drift back into a shallow sleep, looking back at my call log a few minutes later to verify it wasn't just a dream. Since she is calling *me* instead of 9-1-1, it's safe to assume it's not a real emergency and probably just her being melodramatic about Ace's runny nose or eating some expired meat. She tends to be high-strung when it comes to that kind of stuff. Motherhood also seems to bring an entirely new level of anxiety I have yet to experience.

I let my eyes close again, fully awake now. My mind lingers to last night, to Jack's strong jaw, to his perpetually messy hair, and to the tight fabric outline his shirt formed over his arm muscles. But a queasy feeling overtakes me when I remember why I was with Jack last night. My stomach sinks into the rest of my body like a lead balloon. *You don't know anything.* I have to continue reminding myself of that to keep from falling apart, but I know that uneasiness in my gut will be there, nagging at every unoccupied moment until I have answers. *Stay busy.*

I roll out of bed and brush my teeth. Remnants of mascara are smeared under my eyes, and my whole face looks puffy, like I'm hungover. I guess that's what happens when you hit thirty and stay out late. Last night, Jack and I sat on the deck at Sully's until after midnight. We played another round of *Scrabble* and talked about books, a topic that was actually way more pleasant to discuss with him than I expected. Considering he has a doctorate in English Literature, I assumed Jack would be pretentious, that he would judge my amateur taste in reading material, but he was the opposite. Not only did we bond over our fondness for Hemingway but also our love for modern, page-turning thrillers with gimmicky storylines: someone locked in a basement, a controlling husband on the edge, a repressed housewife turned murderer.

"Life is too short to waste time reading books you don't enjoy," Jack said, and it's true. It got me thinking life is too short for a lot of things.

On the way to Sarah's, I stop for a couple of coffees and chocolate sprinkled donuts, the same remedy Sarah and I used to survive our college hangovers ten years ago. To think how much our lives have changed in a decade, how different we are now. In the blink of an eye, we went from all-nighters and fraternity parties to late-night board game sessions and baby blowouts.

Sarah messages me again while I am stirring cream into her coffee at the donut shop counter: *Are you on your way!?*

Be there in five, I reply, and I speed up my leisurely weekend pace back to my car.

When I pull into her driveway, Sarah is hanging out the front door to her house waving for me to come inside, like I have to come quickly or I'll miss something. She must have been standing at the window waiting for me since she sent that text, a toddler with an eye out for the ice cream truck.

I clutch the donut bag under my arm so I can grab the coffees with both my hands. Then I shimmy out of my car, careful not to drop anything. Arms full, I shut the door with a bump of my hip. "What is going on?" I ask.

Sarah is standing barefoot in the doorway in her red plaid pajamas. I hold out one of the coffees to her. "Cream only, the way you like it."

She takes it from me without saying a word, her expression troubled. I follow her into the kitchen where she promptly sets the cup down on the counter. "That's just it, Maddie! I made coffee when I woke up like I always do. It's my favorite part of the morning. Usually, Mike and I have a cup together before he heads into work. Today, I took one sip, and—" she sticks her tongue out and makes a face expressing pure revulsion.

"Okay? I don't get it. Maybe you need to clean your coffee pot." I'm not following her train of thought here, and I think maybe I am still half-asleep, so I take a big gulp from my paper cup. It burns so good going down, and I regret not adding a shot of espresso because this already feels like it is going to be a very long day.

"It had me thinking that maybe..." she hesitates, clearing her throat before continuing, "I might be pregnant."

Sarah watches me closely to gauge my reaction as my eyes widen and my jaw involuntarily drops. "Oh boy!" is all I manage to get out before Sarah starts to get panicky.

She begins to ramble in her flustered state. "I know. I know. This is crazy. Ace is only six months old. That would mean, if I'm pregnant, I will have two kids under two, which is INSANE! They could both be nursing at the same time. How would I even manage that? My boobs would fall off." She clutches her breasts with her hands. "Let alone the expense. I'll have to take more time off work. I don't even know if I'll have enough paid time off for another maternity leave by then, and then what do I do? Just go unpaid? Or do I send my brand new baby to daycare at two weeks old? Are babies even allowed to go to daycare at two weeks old?" Her eyebrows arch, asking a question of me I can't answer. "Mike is a teacher. We can't live on his income alone. This is crazy. Everything about it is just crazy."

"Okay, calm down." I place my hand over hers on the countertop. "When was your last period?" I ask, attempting to talk her through this.

"Two years ago, Maddie! You don't have periods while you're pregnant or nursing." With that, she throws her hands up in the air and starts pacing back and forth in the kitchen. Obviously there are some things I don't know here, so I can see my job is purely to be the voice of reason, to calm her, to help her see whether she is pregnant or not, it will be manageable.

"Let's go get a test," I suggest. "You know, so we can know for sure before we make a big deal of it. You might be freaking out over nothing. Besides, I don't think you can get pregnant if you don't have periods."

"That's why I called you. I already went to the drug store this morning to get one. I need you here while I do this." She pulls a pink box from a plastic bag on the counter.

"You went to the drug store in *that?*" I look her plaid pajamas up and down.

"It was a drive-through," she replies nonchalantly.

"You can get pregnancy tests from a drive-through window?!"

"Are you kidding me? You can get anything from a drive-through now."

I shake my head in disbelief. Then, I pull a donut out of the bag, take a giant chomp out of it, and proceed to say with a stuffed mouth, "Let's do it."

I follow Sarah to the bathroom where I stand in the doorway and watch her pee on a stick. This is the kind of thing that doesn't phase you after fifteen years of friendship. We've seen each other at our worst, squatting on the sides of houses to pee (or puke) at college parties. Heck, I even watched her deliver Ace. I don't think any situation could be embarrassing for us at this point. That's the beautiful side of friendship, when there's nothing left to hide or be ashamed of. A best friend knows every part of you.

Sarah sets the test on the counter, pulls her pajama pants back up, and then puts the toilet lid down so she can sit on it. Meanwhile, I lean on the doorframe and examine my still-puffy face in the toothpaste-splattered mirror straight ahead, pressing into my cheeks with my pointer finger.

"Well, this might be the first time I've eaten a donut in the bathroom," I joke, trying to ease Sarah's nerves.

"You have to be the one to look. I can't. Oh my god. I'm going to vomit." There is no distracting her. She has a one-track mind right now.

"Well, we're in the right place if you do have to hurl."

"Very funny," she says, never looking up. Her eyes are fixed on the timer she set on her phone.

"Can I look yet?" I peek over to the counter.

"No! You have to wait five minutes. It's been less than one." She talks like she's some sort of pregnancy test professional, throwing her arm out to stop me from getting too close.

"But Sarah, I don't think you have to wait five minutes." I reach over her arm and pick up the test. I hold it to face her so she can see the results for herself. "You are very, very pregnant, my friend."

She jumps up from the toilet now and snatches the test from my hands to inspect it for herself. "Holy shit! No fucking way! No fucking way!" She cradles the test in both of her hands and glares at the two pink lines staring back at her. "Maddie, this may be TMI, but Mike and I have literally only done it once in the past month. I'm just not feeling very sexy, and I'm really tired all the time, so we haven't been doing it."

She says *doing it* like she's in the sixth grade, afraid to say the word *sex,* and I can't help but giggle. "We were in the same health class together freshman year, don't you remember? Ms. Lambert said it only takes one time."

"No fucking kidding. It was the margaritas! We had margaritas one night with Mexican takeout, and we were pretty tipsy, and he didn't pull out in time."

I hold up my hand and shut my eyes so she spares me any more detail. "Okay, now that's TMI."

"What do I do!?" Her tone is desperate, as if she has never done this before, like she's a scared teenager instead of a wife and mother (not to mention a labor and delivery nurse) who very much has the ability and means to take care of two children.

"Well, the first thing you do is you tell Mike. He's going to be so excited Sarah! This isn't something to freak out about. This is good news, really good news," I reassure her.

Then, reality hits her like a blinding bolt of lightning, fast and all at once. The split second of shock and fear has passed, and she can allow herself to be excited. This isn't a tragedy. It's just the opposite.

"Oh my god." She closes her eyes and inhales, filling her lungs with a calming breath. "I'm pregnant," she whispers. Cupping her hands over her face, she starts to cry soft, happy tears. We hug right there in the bathroom before we begin jumping up and down, basking in the excitement life can bring in unexpected moments.

"You are the best mom, Sarah. This is one lucky babe. And I'm just going to say this now, I really hope it's a girl. She can be your little mini-me."

Sarah smiles. "Our little mini-me."

Ace begins babbling in his crib, wanting to nurse after his morning nap. I take Sarah's hand in mine and squeeze tight, the way we say *I'm here* without uttering a word. We let go, and she tends to Ace while I head back to the kitchen to microwave my coffee. I can drink hot coffee, and I can drink cold coffee, but I cannot do room-temperature coffee.

"I didn't know it was going to rain," I call to Sarah as I peer out the bay window and watch a single crow, black as night, peck at worms in Sarah's backyard. The tiniest ray of sunlight begins to peek through the dense gray clouds. "I might need to borrow an umbrella. That sky looks ominous, and I have some errands to run."

"No problem. I have a few in the garage," Sarah says, returning to the kitchen with Ace in her arms. He kicks his legs with vigor when he sees me. I take a seat at the small kitchen table, and Sarah sits opposite me, Ace on her lap. He reaches for everything within arm's length to put in his mouth.

"So, are you going to tell Mike *tonight?*" I ask, both of my palms wrapped around my warm coffee cup.

Sarah bounces Ace on her knee. "Of course. You know I can't keep a secret from him for long. But *how* should I tell him? Should I make it special? He was with me when I took the pregnancy test with Ace, so we found out together."

"How about with a million balloons?" I suggest.

Sarah starts to laugh at the initial silliness of my idea. "Balloons? This isn't a kid's birthday party."

"It doesn't matter. Imagine walking into your house to find a million floating balloons. So many you can't even see inside. Balloons everywhere. You know something big is happening. And it's something good. You never see balloons at a funeral. Only at a party."

"You know what?" Her pupils move to the tops of her eyes. "You're fucking right. Balloons are even happier than flowers. There are hundreds of flowers at funerals but not a balloon in sight."

"Get the balloons," I say, and I stand to leave. Sarah follows me to the door with Ace on her hip. As I step out, I turn around to tell her, "And you better tame that potty mouth before Ace's first word is *fuck.*"

"I know. I've always been a fucking sailor." We burst into laughter.

Once I'm in my car, I roll down the window to shout, "You better text me after you tell him!" She gives me a thumbs-up, and I drive away.

Nearly twelve hours later, I am sitting on my couch with a bowl of homemade pasta and pesto reading on my tablet when I hear the *ding* of a text message on my phone. I pop up to check it, anxious to see Mike's reaction to the news. Instead, I find a text from Jack.

Jack: *Have any plans for this weekend?*

I admittedly get more excited than I should. *We're just friends. That's all we are,* I remind myself.

Me: *Why? Should I cancel them?*

I try to avoid outright telling Jack I'm a loner and have no plans other than to drink wine by myself and read, the standard weekend protocol for me.

Jack: *Well, I happened to see signs for an entire festival devoted to goetta downtown. Never had it, don't know what it is. I Googled it, and it looks like some kind of weird meat patty, but if it's special enough for an entire festival, I need to get me some of that.*

I smile at my phone and reread his message at least three times before I begin to type a response.

Me: *There are four types of people in this world, Jack Keller. The purists, the ones who dip their goetta in maple syrup, the ones who dip their goetta in ketchup, and the ones who don't know what they're missing.*

Jack: *Which one are you?*

Me: *Maple syrup, all the way.*

Jack: *Interesting. I'm even more intrigued now. Are we talking real maple syrup or that Log Cabin shit? Also, is that a yes?*

I prop myself up on the couch, sitting on my feet now. My stomach is doing somersaults, and I can't make it stop. *Quit getting so excited. It's not a date.*

Me: *Mrs. Butterworth's, and yes, of course I'll go to Goetta Fest with you. I haven't been in so long.*

Jack: *Awesome, I'll pick you up tomorrow night. Goodnight, Maddie.*

I set my phone face down next to me without texting him goodnight. I am irritated he makes me breathless every time we talk. I am annoyed he makes me laugh without even trying to, that when I get a message from him my neck gets hot and my head gets foggy. And I hate that he is so goddamn handsome. The truth is I haven't even been able to think of going on a first date with anyone else these past few days because I know no one will compare to the chemistry Jack and I have when we're together. Despite my best efforts to evade his charm, I'm already in too deep, and I need to swim to shore before I drown.

My phone dings again, and it is exactly what I have been waiting for, a four-minute video of Mike opening the front door of his house to a sea of pastel pink and blue. Sarah is holding the phone on the other end of the ocean of balloons, Ace wriggling in her arms at the bottom left of the video screen. Mike, who is awestruck, makes his way through the whimsical maze of ribbons hanging from each balloon, and when he finally reaches Sarah, his eyes are wet. He knows. He doesn't even have to ask. Mike takes Ace into his arms, and Sarah holds the phone out in front of them to reveal a kiss more beautiful than on their wedding day. By the end of the video, I'm crying too. All I can think about is how much I want a love like that. A love Jack isn't willing to give me.

Chapter 6

"What are these for?" I ask Jack as he stands just outside my front door the next evening holding a bouquet of wildflowers. They remind me of a summer sunset, vibrant shades of orange and purple and fuchsia.

The corners of his eyes crinkle as he smiles softly. "I saw them and thought of you."

Jack carefully wipes his feet on the doormat before stepping inside and following me to my kitchen. I place the flowers in a ceramic vase on the countertop. It's Jack's first time in my home, and I watch him admire the space, taking in each of the details I toiled over during the renovation. I follow his eyes as they move from the quartz countertops to the tile backsplash to the pendant light fixtures, and I feel a sense of pride that I was able to create this reality for myself, the one he is seeing now.

"Thank you. They're perfect." I arrange the flowers in the vase. "I didn't know friends bought friends beautiful bouquets of flowers for no reason."

"It's not for no reason," he says very casually, clearly leaving out the rest so I have to keep prying.

"Really?" I ask, taking the bait.

"It's a thank-you." He pauses for a moment, shifting his weight onto one foot and leaning against the counter. "For giving me a second chance after that bad first impression. I know it hasn't been long, but I like being your friend a lot, Maddie." There is a sincerity and a sweetness to what he says. He means it.

"I like being your friend too," I say, but then I shy away, shifting my gaze to the window when I see how intently he is looking at me. He makes me the kind of nervous that gives you sweaty palms and a hitch in your breath. The kind of nervous I haven't felt in so long.

"Shall we?" He gestures for the door.

I look back at him now. "We shall. Goetta awaits." I grab my wallet and follow him to his car.

We drive downtown, and Jack pays ten dollars for a parking spot in an underground garage. For that price, we still have to walk a half-mile south to the festival, which consists of dozens of covered booths, an enormous stage, and a handful of carnival rides along the river. I almost wore a sundress with sandals, but when faced with the prospect of a long walk in the humidity of an Ohio summer night, I am happy to have dressed more casual, opting for a simple white tank top, denim shorts, and white sneakers. Jack did the same, and in sneakers and a t-shirt, I am in awe of how good he looks no matter what he wears.

The crowd of drunken Midwesterners chugging German beer and feasting on sausage is almost overwhelming. I haven't been to a festival like this in years. The air smells of fryer oil with the occasional waft of cigarette smoke. In addition to goetta being turned into almost every cuisine imaginable (goetta mac n' cheese, goetta egg rolls, goetta gyros, etc.), there are also the typical festival booths, which include impossible-to-win games and deep-fried everything from Oreos and Twinkies to pickles and goetta, of course.

I tell Jack he has to try the Midwestern delicacy and namesake of the festival first, in its purest state, so he can form an opinion before he tries all of these crazy carnival concoctions. Surprisingly, it is much more difficult to find a plain piece of goetta than we realize. But in the tiniest booth in the furthest corner of the festival, we discover good old-fashioned goetta patties, fresh off the griddle and perfectly crispy, just like Mom used to make for slow weekend brunches at home.

Goetta and fresh-squeezed lemonade in hand, we have a seat on an empty bench overlooking the river a few yards away from the hustle and bustle of the event.

"What do you think?!" I ask him before he even finishes his first bite.

"It's..." He pauses to finish chewing, and I can see him ponder this new, unique flavor. "It's delicious. I'm kind of surprised actually. It's way better than the chili you guys rave over, that's for sure." Jack continues to devour his goetta as I take in the magnitude of his last statement.

"Wait. You don't like our chili? How are you even allowed to be here?"

Cincinnatians are incredibly loyal to our chili and even more defensive than we are about goetta. It's basically a thin meat sauce we serve over spaghetti noodles topped with shredded cheddar cheese, onions, and sometimes beans. We also put it on hot dogs, and it's safe to say most people here will eat this meal on a weekly basis.

Jack's grin shows me he is satisfied he's gotten under my skin. "Maddie, chili does not belong on spaghetti. I also heard there's chocolate in it?"

"What's wrong with that? It's a fact of life that chocolate makes everything better, and I've made so many amazing recipes with chocolate as the secret ingredient: Mexican mole, dry-rubbed ribs, and yes, chili."

"Well, I can only make pasta with jarred sauce, and that's about it, so I'll take your word for it. But that doesn't change the fact that your chili sucks." He nudges my shoulder playfully and laughs at himself. Then, he sets his hand back down next to mine on the bench. Our fingers overlap for an instant, sending a tingle up my arm. It's hard for me to even pretend to be annoyed with him.

Once we finish our food, we meander through the swarms of people, breathing in the scent of funnel cakes, fryer grease, and sweat. The humidity has my entire body uncomfortably damp, like I wish I could rub a deodorant stick over every inch of me. I pull my hair up into a loose, messy bun to get it off my neck as we walk to nowhere in particular, the way you do at festivals, wandering and walking and watching until it's time to sit and eat again. There's no point in even trying to talk more than a brief sentence or two when we are in the swallows of it all. The cover band and the drunk middle-aged women demand attention and ungodly decibels. Jack takes hold of my hand as we move so we don't lose each other in the throngs of people. The blood in my body starts to race a little faster, adrenaline pulsing through me. This is the effect he has on me, and I don't think he even knows it.

We stop at the main stage at the center of the festival where there is a motley crew of characters, musicians and dancers dressed in neon colors, entertaining the intoxicated spectators with everything from Journey to Bruno Mars. Jack and I sit down in folding chairs near the far side of the stage drinking cherry slushies spiked with vodka and observing people making fools of themselves. It's so much fun, we have another drink and continue to watch the debauchery unfold. I unconsciously find every excuse to touch him as we sit. My knee innocently brushes his. My hand skims his forearm. He makes me laugh so hard, I clutch his shoulder and squeeze. I never realize what I'm doing until afterward, when each graze of our bodies sends flutters straight to my stomach. Every touch giving me a little more life, driving me a little more crazy.

The first few chords of *Blister in the Sun* begin, and suddenly, Jack takes both my hands in his as he pulls me up from my chair and leads me to the chaos of the makeshift dance floor, a patch of lawn in front of the stage. Everyone is twirling and spinning and gyrating, not a single inhibition in sight.

"This is my song," he tells me, holding my hand while belting out the lyrics and dancing beneath the stars. I dance too, without even thinking twice about how silly I might look or how much rhythm I lack. Because with Jack's hands on my waist moving me to the music, I can't focus on anything but him. As he whirls me around, a kaleidoscope of flashing lights spin with me, dizzying me, hypnotizing me, and it all feels so surreal, like a dream. The energy radiating from his touch. His warm breath on my neck. His fingertips pressing into my back. I would never do this kind of thing on my own, dance in a crowd of strangers, but Jack puts me at ease, making me forget I'm supposed to be nervous. He makes me feel free.

When we finally make our way out of the pulsing crowd, bathed in sweat, Jack and I stroll side by side away from the mayhem of the stage until we can finally hear one another speak again.

"We're starting to hang out a lot, Jack. I already have a best friend, you know," I joke, as I wipe my face and neck with a napkin I snatch from a nearby booth.

"Well, when your best friend has a baby and goes to bed at seven, it's time to add another best friend to the mix." Jack smiles, then takes a swig from a plastic water bottle he bought for a buck and passes it to me. He motions for me to follow him, leading me to a stretch of grass far from the commotion where we plop down to rest. Our backs to the city skyline, we face the darkness and calmness of the river.

My eyes are on Jack as his face tilts upwards to the sky. "When I was in undergrad, I considered majoring in astronomy and astrophysics," he tells me, and I think about how I like to learn these little things about him, the little details other people don't know.

"A far cry from an English professor, what would you have done?"

His eyes stay fixed on the stars, his arms wrapped around his bent knees. "I don't really know, actually. It was an idea I had in high school. I've always been mesmerized by the stars. I used to set up a tent in my backyard as a kid, and I'd lie in the grass and study the patterns they made in the sky for hours. I'd get so lost in them, I would fall asleep right there on the lawn, never even making it to the tent."

I look up now too, the brightest star in the sky capturing my gaze. "You know, when I was little, I used to look out my window and tell the Man in the Moon what I was thankful for every night. Sometimes I still do. My family was never very religious. I didn't grow up praying to a god or anything like that. But my parents taught me to be thankful. *Don't wish upon a star for things you don't have,* they would tell me. *Instead, say what you're thankful for.*"

"I like that," Jack says, and he rests his palm on my lower back. "There's so much magic in the sky. Not many people pay enough attention to it."

I soak in his touch, the feeling of safety and protection it brings. "I think you're right about that."

We sit quietly for a while watching the reflection of the moon on the river. I silently count the fireflies around me as a gentle breeze sweeps across my skin. I could sit next to Jack like this for hours. There's no need to fill the gaps in the air with words. I start to think he could too, until he breaks our blissful silence.

"I've been having a lot of fun with you, Maddie, *but—*" and my whole body stiffens. I can sense the atmosphere shift with that one measly word, but. His hand moves from my back, finding a new place to rest on his lap. "I understand if you need to, you know, not see me as much, to, uh, give yourself a chance to find a boyfriend or husband or whatever it is you're looking for." My stomach drops with his words. I don't know what I was expecting him to say, but it definitely wasn't that. So I don't say anything for a while.

The truth is, until Jack, I honestly didn't know there were people who don't have some sort of romantic relationship as an end goal for their lives. I thought that was a part of the journey along with everything else. You live, and you love, and you die. Love is an essential component of the whole experience. But Jack has proven me wrong yet again. His innocent touches have nearly electrocuted my insides, but I realize now they likely mean nothing to him. A touch like any other touch.

Jack acts like a friend, a best friend, and in the short time I've known him, I truly would trust him with my deepest secrets. The unfortunate thing for me, though, is the more I know about him, the more I like, and the further I fall into this bottomless pit I know I won't be able to escape from. I live for the conversations we have that go deeper than the surface, that catch a glimpse of something more, something beyond what we already know. And when we're in the midst of these exchanges, I don't want them to end. I am willing to stay up late, lose a full night's sleep to keep them going. It's like I'm a lust-filled teenager willing to sacrifice my freedom to stay out with a boy past my curfew, to make the night not have to end just yet.

And frankly, all of that scares the shit out of me, because what am I supposed to do now? Continue a friendship with him? All the while watching everyone around me fall in love and create these beautiful little lives and families?

You can't change a person. I learned that at twenty-three when Ben smoked weed and played video games until three in the morning while I wanted to go to bed at a reasonable hour and begin building our post-college lives together. All I wanted was for him to take me out to dinner instead of spending another night at home watching him drink beer and get high with his friends.

Sarah frequently told me I could do better than Ben, but I was adamant she didn't understand our relationship. She didn't see what we were like alone together. He was so sweet, and I could tell he loved me in the way he kissed me. I wanted so badly to change him, to make him the kind of guy who would want to settle down with me. I didn't realize it until this moment, but I have been holding on to that same hope for Jack these past couple of weeks. I have been unintentionally wishing Jack will eventually turn into the kind of guy who wants to be in love. And if I let this relationship keep going the way it is, I'm bound to resent him for not reciprocating the feelings I have for him. I'm bound to resent myself for letting it get to that point. I have to end this before I can't go back.

"I think that's a good idea," I say finally, as all of these thoughts, these doubts, fly around in my head making me unsure of everything.

"What's a good idea?" I can tell he's not exactly sure where my head is, and this revelation is new to me too. It's something I only decided mere moments ago when I recognized I was holding on to false hope.

I scoot myself a few inches away from him, creating the distance I need. "You're right. You and I have been spending a lot of time together, and I'm sorry, but I don't want to wake up ten years from now and wish I'd gotten married, wish I had tried harder to find someone to love me." There is callousness in my voice, and I wish it didn't have to be like this.

Jack looks solemn, every bit of festival-induced jubilation drained from his perfect face. "I understand. And I don't want to get in the way of any dreams you have for your life. So if we can't be friends—" He stretches his hand out to touch my leg but quickly pulls it back, realizing he shouldn't.

"No." I interrupt him because even the thought of saying goodbye to this person who was a stranger only weeks ago is unbearable to me right now. I can't say goodbye completely. At least not yet. "All I mean to say is we can't keep accelerating at this pace. Let's be honest, I'm not going to meet my future husband while I'm hanging out with you." My tone is a little lighter now.

"Really? I'm shocked." He laughs, some of the color coming back to his cheeks now. And we leave the conversation there to settle, nothing decided, but our intentions are clear.

We talk in the grass about other things, work and life and dreams, until our buzzes wear off, and he drives me home. Instead of simply dropping me off in the driveway, he turns off the car and follows me to my door like a gentleman. Tension builds as he stands in front of me on my porch. There is usually a lightness between us, but the air is heavy around me.

"I had fun tonight, Maddie."

I nod, and there is a moment, a very brief one, when I think he might lean down to kiss me. I'm torn inside, like I want him to and I don't all at the same time.

"Goodnight," Jack finally says. I don't bother to watch him walk to his car or drive away. Instead, I slip into my house, go directly to my bathroom, and splash cold water on my face.

Chapter 7

In the days leading up to Dad's appointment with his doctor, it's as though time is inching towards an imminent doom. Every free moment I have is overtaken by the churning of my insides, that anxiety you feel when you are sure something bad is about to happen. There is a constant pit in my stomach, one I can only seem to bury with work. So, I spend all of my time in the kitchen, hiding in the pots and pans and measuring cups, all the while knowing whatever is six feet under will claw its way out soon enough. And then it finally does.

The morning of the appointment, I wake up with a tightness in my chest and lie in bed reading long past the time I usually get up and start my workday. Even though I want to ignore the colossal elephant, my mind and my body will not let me pretend it is like any other day. I keep my phone attached to my side, waiting for Mom to call with a full report from the doctor.

"We have a referral to a neurologist," Mom says when she finally calls me late in the morning. I am unsatisfied from the start. I crave definitive answers, a yes or no, a right or wrong, a 6+7= 13. Unfortunately, she has none of that to give me.

"There isn't a simple test the doctors can do to know for certain," Mom explains. "Dr. Sherwood asked a lot of questions about Dad's memory and the concerns we've had at home. He ordered some routine blood work, but other than that, there isn't much he can do right now. The neurologist will do more cognitive tests and possibly even some imaging of his brain, but…" I hear hesitation in Mom's voice as she says the word I hate more than any other, *but*. There's always a condition, a caveat, to keep things from being too good or too stable or too easy.

"But what?!" I ask impatiently. I don't even realize how frantic I am until the words burst from my mouth. *Just say it. Don't make me beg for information I don't even want to hear.*

"I don't know if you knew this, but your great-grandpa, Grandpa Hank's dad, likely had early-onset Alzheimer's. There weren't as many tests back then to be completely certain, but he started to lose his faculties when he was in his fifties, and when he passed away a few years later, he didn't know anyone or anything, so…" She pauses again. All of this stalling is only contributing more to my panicked state.

"So? What are you trying to tell me exactly?" My heart is beating out of my chest.

Then she blurts it out, sounding frustrated with my inability to give her the time she needs. "It's hereditary. Early-onset Alzheimer's is hereditary."

And just like that, there is nothing else to say. It might as well be an official diagnosis in my mind. Mom tries to temper the blow, explaining Dad has an appointment with the "...best neurologist in the city. No, not just the city, the best neurologist in the whole tri-state region" and everything "will be okay." But I only catch snippets of her words because all I can do is try to keep breathing as my whole universe shatters to pieces.

Thinking back to the days leading up to the appointment, I don't know what solace I thought would come from having an answer, from knowing why Dad's mental state was quickly declining. It was only a few days ago when I watched him search my house high and low for the measuring tape he swore he left on the bathroom counter, practically throwing a temper tantrum over the mishap only to find it in his pocket after twenty minutes on a rampage. This was not my calm and even-tempered dad, the one who rarely lost his cool over anything.

By the time Mom and I hang up, that pit in my stomach has transformed into a volcano, one that has just erupted. I finally have an answer, or at least I think I do. But it's the answer I feared most. I trudge through the remainder of the day, my mind somewhere else entirely. That night, I'm afraid to go to sleep because there is no reprieve from a dark room alone with your thoughts. So I stay up late watching television on the couch. Soon enough, that becomes my new routine: work and watch TV and busy myself so I don't have to think about Dad.

The next time I see him, Wednesday for dinner, Dad doesn't talk about the appointment, and I don't want to be the one to bring it up. The only time his state of mind is mentioned in the following weeks is when Mom asks for symptoms to write down in a diary she is keeping for his doctors. She was instructed before seeing the specialist to keep a record of all concerning behavior in regards to his memory and mental state. She asked me to keep a record of any incidents that happen while he is at my house working on the bathroom renovation.

The truth is (and this might be the hardest part of it, too), a lot of the time Dad is perfectly fine, his normal and happy self. He's the same Dad who can't help but constantly teach me new skills like how to fix a clogged pipe or how to patch a tire. The Dad who insists on calling me Madeline instead of Maddie, who still tells me every time he leaves my house to lock my door behind him, even wiggling the knob a minute later to make sure I do.

But then, just as I think to myself, *Maybe he's fine. Maybe Mom and I are overreacting and nothing is wrong. He is getting older after all. This might all be a part of it, a normal part of aging,* I am inevitably interrupted by a forgotten name in a story, the same question asked three times, a lost drill bit, and my heart crumbles to pieces all over again. I am devastated not only for him and for me but for Mom who experiences this pain repeatedly each day. She can't busy herself to pretend it's not happening like I do. There's no escaping it in your own house. She never complains or cries to me, though. All she ever says is, "It's going to be okay," and I hope she's right.

As the days pass by, painfully slow, I am like a zombie, simply going through the motions of everyday life, hiding from my feelings as much as I possibly can. My appetite is nonexistent, which makes being around food all day difficult. I stay in bed longer, but I am sleeping less, so my eyes are perpetually half-open, begging me for a good night's rest. I don't call Jack, even though at times, it's all I want to do.

Then, late on a Friday evening, Jack texts me out of the blue, writing: *Hey, how have you been?* It has been over a month since I have seen or spoken to him. In the midst of this mental hell I've been living in, I have pushed the prospect of a romantic relationship aside. After our night at the festival, I kept my promise to give us some space, to not let Jack become my whole world. Instead, I've been spending more time with Sarah, the only socialization I am interested in right now, watching her once flat stomach slowly but surely distend.

"I read your belly gets bigger much faster with the second baby," she told me, and she was right. It turned out she also discovered her pregnancy when she was much further along this time. At her first doctor's appointment after getting the positive pregnancy test, she was shocked to find out she was already sixteen weeks along, due in five months.

"How on earth did you not know?" I asked her.

"I have no idea! I was still nursing, so I wasn't having periods. And I was still losing the baby weight from when I was pregnant with Ace."

I don't tell Sarah about my dad yet. It's not that I am keeping a secret from her, though perhaps I am. It's just that when I am alone, all I can think about is Dad and the future of my small family. When I am with Sarah and Mike and Ace, it's the only time I can laugh and pretend life is the same as it was before I found out Dad is sick.

So, as I lie there, staring at Jack's text on my phone, I consider deleting it, not replying at all. Then whatever we had, friendship or flirting, could fade away. Just disintegrate into the universe like it never happened. I don't have the time or energy for it anyway. But it's not that simple. Life never is. I still think about him, more than you should probably think about someone you have only known for such a short time. He didn't technically do anything wrong. If anything, Jack has been completely and utterly honest with me from the start, and I did tell him I still want to be friends.

I know I can't ignore him, so I text him back.

Me: *I've been okay. Some family stuff, that's about it. How about you?*

I don't think I could be more vague if I tried, but sympathy isn't what I need or want right now.

Jack: *Work stress for me. Syllabus planning and such. I wanted to check-in and make sure you're doing well.*

His text makes me sad for some reason, like I am a trivial afterthought, a goldfish that needs to be fed while you are on vacation. It doesn't help that I'm so vulnerable right now, from Dad, from keeping everything hidden so I can try to ignore it, and from not having anyone to share the brunt of the hard stuff with. I am a chipped glass, ready to shatter with the weight of a feather. So, when I respond a few minutes later asking Jack to come over, I know I am breaking my own rules, but I don't even care. I just don't want to be alone right now.

Jack tells me he could use a break from staring at his laptop and arrives at my house half an hour later. He is wearing an open cardigan over a t-shirt and rectangular glasses with thick black frames. For the first time, I imagine what he would look like standing behind a podium at the front of a university classroom.

We sit on my couch for hours, never even checking the time. Some random indie movie plays in the background, but we don't pretend to watch, instead talking about what we've missed in each other's lives over the past month. He tells me about the curriculum he's been planning for his fall courses, a couple of English 101 classes and one upper-level American Literature course.

"You have to be tenured before you get the cool seminars," he explains. I think it's sweet he asks for my feedback on the books he's chosen.

"How long have you known you wanted to be a professor?" I ask him.

He tells me he's not sure. He started undergrad *Undecided,* and when it came time to choose a major, he chose English because the only hobbies he has ever stuck with are reading and going to the gym.

"I'm too squeamish to be a doctor and much too passive to be a lawyer. What else is there?" he asks, and honestly, I don't even know.

Every career in the business field is all the same, schmoozing the people above you with a goal of eventually running the place (except the people who run the place always turn out to be the sons or daughters of whoever started the business in the first place, so what's the point of it all?). That's why I got out. I'm not up for schmoozing of any kind. I want to do my own thing.

"But I do want to write a novel someday," Jack adds.

"It doesn't need to be a bestseller or anything. Just an itch I need to scratch. I think I've got one good one in me. Maybe two if I'm lucky." I would love to read any story he writes.

I tell Jack about my latest contracts, the biggest of which is a series of fall pie recipes, revamping classics to make them new and modern for a high-end flour and baking company. I also talk about my adventure babysitting Ace a couple of weeks back for his first full night away from Mike and Sarah. They wanted to celebrate their wedding anniversary with a fancy dinner and a romantic night alone in a hotel suite void of poopy diapers and baby bottles. Ace was inconsolable for what felt like hours when he realized his mom wasn't going to be putting him to bed, but when Mike and Sarah returned home the next morning, I said Ace was "absolutely perfect," and he "didn't fuss a bit." When I started babysitting for a few neighbors as a teenager, Mom told me you should always rave about the children to their parents. "No one wants to come home to hear their kids were terrors," she said. "They'll blame that on you."

I still don't tell Jack about Dad. It's possible I don't have the words yet, but I convince myself there is no point in bringing down a perfectly lighthearted evening, and for the first time in a long time, I don't feel a weight bearing down on me.

It seems like no time has passed before I need to retrieve a second bottle of wine from the kitchen. The first we finished so easily in the midst of conversation, I barely noticed I had been drinking, but I can tell he is buzzed and so am I. His eyes are glossy, and his lips are tinted red from the cabernet.

I return with full glasses, and when I sit back down next to him on the couch, Jack says, "I missed you, Maddie," out of nowhere.

The sincerity in his voice makes me realize how much I have missed him too. I swore off the possibility of us a long time ago, but now that he is here, sitting next to me, I can't stop thinking about how he smells like cinnamon. I can sense the warmth radiating from his body without even touching him, and I wish I hadn't gone so long without seeing him.

"I missed you too," I say, and though I know the alcohol is the only way either of us worked up the nerve to say these words to one another, it doesn't matter because this is the moment we are in, and I want to live in it.

Then, something happens. Something completely unexpected, but I would have waited for forever for it. I don't know who leans in first because I'm too busy trying to calm my thumping heart. It might have been me, but it might have been both of us, too tired of acting like there isn't something more than what we've acknowledged. Neither of us wanting to tuck away our attraction any longer. Jack's lips part just slightly, and then they meet mine, kissing me slow and tender to start. But then, almost urgently, his hands grasp my face as mine grip his thighs. His tongue slips into my mouth and sweeps across mine, and even though we've been drinking wine, he tastes like chocolate and espresso. We kiss so long and so hard I think we both forget to breathe, neither of us wanting to let go. The most perfect, firework-inducing kiss of my life.

I bring my hands to meet his on my face, interlocking our fingers. Starved for him, I slowly guide both our hands down to my waist, but he quickly pulls away, practically panting the words, "I'm sorry."

I lightly shake my head and pull his face back to mine, his soft lips back on my lips for another full minute before I move my mouth to his ear and whisper, “Don’t be.”

Jack drifts to my neck, kissing the sides and the front before finding my mouth again, and my whole body shivers. I don’t know what’s come over me, maybe it’s the booze or maybe it’s that I’ve wanted this for so long, but I don’t think I could stop myself if I tried. What we’re doing feels so natural and so right, running my fingers through his tousled hair, touching him the way I have only been able to reluctantly dream about until now. I never want it to end.

He pulls me on top of him, my legs now straddling him on the couch, our faces never parting. I pull up on his shirt, and he raises his arms in the air to help me take it off, revealing an effortless tan and a tattoo on his chest.

“A wind-up bird,” I say, and he nods. My fingertips run over it, admiring the colors, the technique, like a watercolor painting. It’s one of those tattoos that means something I can tell, but I don’t ask him. Tattoos like that are for sad things usually. We haven’t gotten to that stuff tonight, the reality of life.

“I want you, Maddie. I’ve wanted you for a long time,” he says, breathless, cupping my breasts over my shirt. I am on my knees, my head tilted downwards to look at him. His words are everything I have wanted to hear since the beginning, since that night when he told me we couldn’t be anything.

He pulls my shirt over my head, and then his hands fall back to my waist. They raise me up so he can kiss my chest while hooking his thumbs into the waistband of my jeans.

My hands are on his shoulders, gripping his muscles as he starts to sweat, his hips rocking beneath me.

But then he stops, releasing a heavy breath. "I have to tell you something."

"Okay," I manage to mutter, a little shocked he is thinking about talking right now because that's the last thing on my mind.

"I wrote it."

"Wrote what?" I lower my body back down so my eyes are in line with his. He looks nervous.

"The note. The one in the coffee shop that I blamed on Chad." *Chad,* the guy with the glasses in the corner. The one with the laptop and the notebook. I didn't know his name until now. He doesn't look like a Chad.

"Why? Why did you write it?" I think back to that night, to the handwritten words sloppily strewn on the paper, clearly written in a hurry. *You are too perfect for all of them,* it read.

"Because you seemed like you needed to know. You are perfect, Maddie. In every way."

He pulls me in to kiss me again, but before our lips meet, I stand up, taking his hand into mine. I lead him back to my bedroom. He sits on the edge of my bed, and I nudge his shoulder so he will lie down on his back. I lie next to him, face down on my stomach.

He turns his head to look at me. "I'm sorry I didn't tell you sooner."

But I don't care that he lied about it. We didn't know each other then. I care about right now. This moment. "Stay with me tonight," I say.

"Are you sure?" I know what he's thinking. He is thinking back to when I told him I won't sleep with him, when I said I won't have sex with someone who is just a friend. Tonight, I'm breaking my rules.

"I'm sure." I crawl to the top of my bed now and lay my head on a pillow. He follows me up, his body parallel to mine. We are both on our sides facing one another. Jack squeezes my hip with his hand, and he pulls me in so close I can feel the way he wants me. We kiss as he glides his hands over my body, exploring every curve as I get lost in his touch. I wait for him to go further, to slide my pants off and take this somewhere new. But he never does.

"Let's not go too fast," he says, and I nod my head, disappointed but grateful he doesn't want me to be a one-night stand. At least that's what I'm hoping. I don't want that either. So as much as I want him to take all of me tonight, we stop. Jack and I fall asleep in my bed, his arms draped over me, our bodies molded as one. The intimacy I've been craving. For the first time in months, I'm not jolted awake in the middle of the night with cold sweats and a racing mind.

Chapter 8

The next morning, I don't have to wake up wondering if what happened between Jack and me was all a lustrous dream because he's still lying next to me, my body cradled in the crook of his arm. My back is pressed against his chest, and when I twist to look at him, to see his familiar face for the first time in the morning sunlight, his cheeks are a soft shade of pink.

"Let's get breakfast. I want pancakes," he says.

We sit in a vinyl booth at Sunnyside, an old-fashioned diner down the street from my house. While we're eating, Sarah calls me four times a few minutes apart, but I keep sending her straight to voicemail. I don't want to tell her where I am or what I'm doing right in front of Jack. I would rather spill all the details when I can talk without him listening in. When I can tell her Jack and I kissed, and it was everything.

During breakfast, the interactions between Jack and I aren't awkward the way it usually is the morning after waking up next to someone you drunkenly hooked up with the night before.

We act like a couple, casually drinking coffee and eating crispy bacon and syrup-soaked carbs like we do this all the time, unconcerned about how we look or who might be watching.

Our long and lazy breakfast stretches into the late morning. Jack pays the bill, and he drops me back off at home afterward. It catches me by surprise when he kisses me goodbye, short but sweet, like he is letting me know it wasn't the wine last night that made everything happen the way it did. He wants me to know it wasn't a mistake.

"I'll text you tonight," he says, the way a boyfriend nonchalantly speaks to his girlfriend. All of this is so unexpected. It's surreal.

I rush into the house so I can return Sarah's call, dialing as I slip off my shoes and gently kick them into the closet. I'm anxious to tell her everything that has transpired over the last twelve hours. When she answers, though, I can tell something is wrong in the way she says, "Hello," the sound of an empty gulp following the single word. She's been crying, her voice hoarse and nasally.

"I'm sorry I didn't answer earlier. I didn't know you were upset," I say.

She ignores my apology. It's clearly the last thing on her mind. "I'm at University Hospital. Can you come here now?" she asks, urgency in her tone.

My purse is over my shoulder, and I'm clutching my car keys in my hand before Sarah even finishes her sentence. "On my way. Do you need me to bring anything?"

"No," she pauses. "I mean, I don't think so. I don't know. Just come."

It's a fifteen-minute drive from my house to the hospital, and I have to pee, but rather than stop, I put it out of my mind by running through every possible scenario for why Sarah could be there in my head. *Ace rolled off of the couch. Or he had an allergic reaction to peanut butter or strawberries or something. Kids are allergic to everything these days. No, it couldn't be. He would be at Children's Hospital, not University.* So my mind moves to Sarah now, and the only thing I can think of is—that must be it. There is nothing else it could be.

Sarah lost the baby.

With the tragic realization that Sarah will not be pregnant anymore when I see her next, my hands start to shake. I slam them against the steering wheel, overwhelmed by preemptive grief as I circle around the cave-like parking garage, an underground maze without an open spot in sight. *Why is it so damn full?*

It has been over two years since I have been to a hospital. The thing about hospitals is every time you go to one, you think about the last time you were there. Same as funerals. As I impatiently navigate the parking lot, my mind goes to my routine pap smear three years ago when I had abnormal cells appear on my results. It had never happened before, and apparently these were "precancerous" cells. I remember the phone call from the nurse to tell me this. The whole conversation was very impersonal, and she sounded like she was reading from a script. It might have been my ignorance or the wording she used, but I translated her words to mean, *You have cancer,* so I went into full panic mode. I spent hours reading horror stories on the internet and then calling my mother in pure hysterics, crying to her about how I am going to die or end up infertile so she will never have grandkids.

My outpatient surgery to remove and test the precancerous cells wasn't scheduled until three weeks after the nurse's phone call, so I had nightmares about the cancer growing inside of me. *This is an emergency,* I thought to myself. *The cells need to come out right now. This is three weeks of the cancer spreading.* Afterward, I remember waking up thirsty, so thirsty I thought I was choking. I could barely talk as I coughed out the words, "Water. I need water," to my empty recovery corner, not a nurse in sight. Finally, an old mean one came over and told me in deep grunts that I couldn't have water yet before walking away. I was scared and cold and thirsty. And the worst part was there were no answers right away. I still had to wait for the results.

It was a few days before my doctor called me to let me know the biopsy came back negative, and the cells were only "mild," whatever that means. In a fraction of a second, my life returned to normal. This event I had dramatized in my head, one I blew up into this huge, life-changing affair, quickly dissolved into a memory. Not even a memory. Something less significant. A mere hiccup.

"That's what this could be," I say out loud to myself as I pull into a narrow space in the corner of the garage that might not even be an actual parking spot. "It's just a hiccup."

I make my way to the main entrance of the hospital where I spin in circles trying to orient myself with the chaos of the lobby. *Where the heck am I supposed to go?*

There are a million floors and wings in this place. It's both confusing and cruel to see people wide-eyed and clearly out of tears, probably having the worst day of their lives, in the same room as perky greeters and valet parkers. A coffee kiosk sells sprinkled donuts and frappuccinos to everyone who is there for something insignificant, something that will soon be even less than a memory.

I call Sarah. "I'm here, in the lobby. Where are you?"

"The ninth floor. Go to the front desk, and turn left. The red elevators, not the blue ones."

Sarah is waiting for me when the elevator doors open. There isn't the sweet scent of coffee and pastries like the lobby up here. Instead it smells sterile, like rubbing alcohol and latex gloves. She doesn't smile when she sees me, but she looks more put together than I was expecting in jeans and a fitted blouse, one that shows off her pregnant belly, now well into the second trimester. Her face is stoic, revealing nothing, but I am shocked she is not in a hospital gown. If she's not the patient and neither is Ace, then who?

It didn't even cross my mind that something could be wrong with Mike. Mike, who competes in obstacle course races. Mike, who runs sprints with the teenagers at his baseball team practices. Mike, who is about to be the father of two perfect children.

"What happened? What's wrong?" I ask Sarah, my body beginning to shake against my will, fear pulsating through my veins. I can feel the weight of my words in the air, and she hangs on to them. She doesn't blurt out an answer because she can't. It's stuck in her throat, something she doesn't want to say out loud. She's afraid to.

Sarah turns around and walks down the long white hallway to the other end of the floor. I follow her to a row of chairs that has been separated from the nurse stations and patient rooms by an opaque wall, showing only shadows of what's behind it. With no other waiting areas or so much as a coffee maker in sight, this little room appears to be the closest thing you can get to an escape up here. She sits down in one of the olive-colored, vinyl chairs, the kind your legs stick to if you are wearing shorts, and I sit next to her, reciting little prayers in my head until she begins to speak.

"He started having these headaches," she says, staring down at the floor and then out the window. Anywhere but in my eyes.

"It was *Mike* who had the headaches?" I ask to be sure.

"Yes, and they were nothing." She says the word *nothing* with force, with conviction, shaking her head side to side while her hand rests on her stomach, slowly moving her palm back and forth over her baby bump. "They were mostly in the mornings, and he would take some over-the-counter headache medicine, and then that was it. There was nothing to them."

"Okay," I say, waiting for the other shoe to drop, waiting to hear what's left of this story. *Why are we in the hospital then?* But I don't ask her that question because she resembles a ghost, pale and lifeless. I let her take the time she needs.

Sarah takes a few deep breaths before she continues. "Last night, we were getting ready for bed. It was like eight o'clock or something. I was reading a book, already lying down, and Mike was in the bathroom brushing his teeth." She talks like a robot, trying to keep her emotions at bay as she continues to peer out the window at the full parking lot, thousands of cars in long, neat rows.

"He started to say something to me, something about baseball practice. I can barely remember now. But then his words became unintelligible. Like a mix between a stutter and some foreign language. I couldn't understand anything he was saying, but I thought it was a joke. I thought he was making some sort of joke that I didn't get yet, and so I laughed a little. Then he collapsed, completely unconscious on the bathroom floor. His head was bleeding. He hit something when he fell."

I pull her into me now, wrapping my arms around her stiff limbs. I don't care if she doesn't want to look me in the eye or if she's trying to be brave. She needs a warm body to collapse into. She needs to know it's okay to not be okay. With her face buried in my chest, she starts to cry, her body shaking ever so slightly. But she pulls away gently and slowly, wiping her eyes with the backs of her hands, attempting to compose herself before she tells me the rest. There's more.

"I called 911," she continues. "An ambulance came, but I couldn't go with him because of Ace. He was still sleeping in his crib. It was a whole thing. Not only an ambulance but two police cars and a fire truck. The whole neighborhood must have been looking out their windows, but no one came outside. Once the first responders loaded him in, I ran barefoot to the next-door neighbor's house, Molly, the one with the twins, and I asked her to watch Ace. I've been here ever since."

"Oh my god, Sarah. I am so sorry I didn't answer your call earlier. I didn't know." My body is heavy with guilt. How do you ever make this up to your best friend?

"It's okay," she says, looking at me now for the first time. The whites of her eyes are bloodshot, and her pupils are dark and massive. "I could have texted you or kept calling. I think I wanted to be alone with him. We didn't know anything yet, and I wanted it to just be us."

We didn't know anything yet. She didn't know anything then. But she does now.

"What is it, Sarah? Is Mike okay?"

"A few hours ago, they did an MRI once he was conscious again and stable. He was awake and acting normal, just tired and confused by it all, so I thought maybe it was a fluke. Like he didn't drink enough water or something. But on the MRI, they found a tumor in his left temporal lobe."

Every part of me reacts physically to her words. My hands go straight to my face, covering my mouth as my jaw drops. My legs are limp, like I couldn't stand or walk if I wanted to. I begin to rock involuntarily in my chair as my shoulders crumple over. My brain gets foggy and my vision gets glossy, and all I want to do is to go back to yesterday when Mike was fine, when Sarah was fine.

"So what happens now?" I ask, barely whispering, not even certain the words exit my body.

"There's a lot of different things that can happen depending on the doctor." She starts to talk like a nurse now. Scientific. Objective. Potentially optimistic. "But I was told generally they start with a biopsy. They go in, they remove what they can, and they see if it's cancer."

"When does this happen? Today?" I am completely clueless. She's the nurse, albeit she helps deliver babies every day, but Sarah is still the person I go to with every medical question I have.

"They gave me a list of oncologists, and I have to pick one. First, I need to figure out who takes our insurance, and then I choose from a giant list of names to decide who will slice my husband's head open and operate on his brain. How fucked up is that?" Her voice quivers a little. She's telling this story to someone for the first time of what will be many. She's realizing it's not a bad dream.

"It's really fucked up," I agree.

I don't tell her it's going to be okay the way Mom does when she talks about Dad. There's no reason to get her hopes up or promise her something I can't deliver. None of us have any idea how all of this might turn out. It may very well not be okay. So instead, I take her hand in mine, and I ask her, "What can I do?"

"I don't know yet. I just know I'm going to need you," she says.

"You've got me, Sarah. Whatever you need, I'm here."

Chapter 9

Understandably overwhelmed, Sarah asks me to help her with sorting through the list of potential doctors for Mike. Before leaving the hospital to watch Ace at their house and begin my research, I make a trip down to the hospital cafeteria to get Sarah some food. When I return, she is standing at the window like a statue, completely motionless. I place my palm on her back, just barely touching her, but wanting her to know I'm here. She is caught in a stare, peering out at cars in search of parking spots beneath a perfect, cloudless sky. It's the kind of day you'd want to have a picnic in the park, but here we are.

"Please don't tell anyone yet," Sarah says, her mouth hardly moving to form the words. "I'm just not ready for flowers and cards to start flooding the house. The only ones who know right now are you and Mike's parents. Nobody else. At least not until we know more."

"Of course," I say. "I won't tell a soul."

Mike has three brothers, one older and two younger, two of whom have wives and kids of their own, and they don't know about him yet. He comes from a close-knit family of competitive boys, The Wolf Pack, as they call themselves. They all live within an hour radius of their childhood home twenty miles north of Cincinnati, but when Sarah mentioned calling one of them, Mike insisted on not worrying anyone.

"They'll all give me shit," he apparently told her when she tried to convince him.

The dynamic of siblings is one Sarah doesn't fully understand. She is an only child like me, and her parents live a plane ride away in Ft. Myers. We both have mothers who wanted siblings for us, but neither ever got so lucky. Sarah's parents moved down to their condo in Florida full-time a few years back when they both retired from their jobs as teachers. She said she doesn't want to tell them yet because she knows they will catch the first flight back to Cincinnati, and she's not prepared for it. Less than twenty-four hours into this new reality, she is overwhelmed enough and still trying to cope with the shock of it all.

There will be time for the inevitable casseroles to start arriving nightly and for extended relatives and long-lost acquaintances to send a million Facebook condolence messages, but for now, what we need is a plan to get Mike and Sarah through this hiccup. That's all it is.

I spend the next twelve hours on my laptop researching every oncologist within a reasonable driving distance of Cincinnati. Jack texts me as I am scrutinizing resumes from

Mike and Sarah's couch, Ace asleep in his crib upstairs. I don't want to lie to Jack. He asks if he can see me tonight, but I don't even respond. My focus is on finishing a condensed list of doctors to pass along to Sarah, complete with detailed notes about each one. Around one in the morning, when Sarah finally returns home to get some rest, I give her the list.

"Thank you so much," she says, as she collapses onto the couch, her eyes half-shut already.

"Why don't you go to your bed? You'll be way more comfortable there."

"I don't want to sleep there without him." A single tear rolls down her cheek as her eyes shut completely. I drape a throw blanket over her, kiss her forehead, and drive back home.

Over the next couple of days, Jack texts me a few more times, saying things like, *Hey, I was thinking of you,* or *Did I do something to upset you?* I never reply to any of his messages. It feels wrong that Jack and I had such an amazing night together the very same night my best friend's life fell to pieces. Not to mention, I know his cousin has a brain tumor, and I can't tell him.

I wish I could talk to Jack about all of it because he feels like my only saving grace as I attempt to survive a sea of tragedy. My mind keeps thinking back to all of the authors I've read who have written about the agony life can bring. How to persist and overcome misfortune when entire periods of one's life are marked by death and failure and trauma. These authors write about how to come out stronger on the other side of it, but truthfully, no one ever remembers that part of the book, the part where some lesson was learned or some good came from all of the setbacks. They remember the trauma, the loss, the death, and the pain. It's the sad story that sticks with you, the one you can't imagine ever having to experience yourself. I have never been able to relate to those stories before, the stretches of life when it seems like only bad things happen in a relentless universe. That is until right this very moment, when all of the people I love in this life are suffering, and there isn't anything I can do to stop it.

Sarah chooses a doctor quickly because we all know there isn't any time to waste. She has an appointment for Mike within the week. In Dr. Matthew Huber's pictures online, he looks like he can't be any older than thirty-five, though his graduation years suggest he is probably closer to forty-five. He is Ivy League-educated, specializes in brain cancers, and is very involved in ongoing research and clinical trials. One of the reasons she chooses him is because he is so proactive, calling her personally and insisting they meet soon and act fast after she called his office and left a message for him with the receptionist.

"Whatever you need," I keep telling her. "I can babysit. I can research. I'm all yours, Sarah."

Mike is still in the hospital being monitored, resting when he can, but Sarah says he is in good spirits. "He's optimistic. He says that no God he believes in would take a husband from his pregnant wife." She smiles when she tells me this, and it is the only time I see hope in her eyes.

A craniotomy is scheduled for one week later. Mike is able to spend a few days at home before the procedure. Dr. Huber plans to remove as much of the tumor as possible and then biopsy it. He discussed what will happen afterward with both Mike and Sarah if the tumor is cancerous, likely radiation, chemotherapy, and possibly clinical trials.

"He said that's just to prepare us for the worst," Sarah says, "but it could be benign. He says he sees a lot of benign tumors, so first we have to see what we're dealing with."

The morning of his operation, I arrive to the hospital at six and sit with Sarah in the waiting room. Mike's parents are there, frequently fielding calls from his brothers, who now know everything, and sending them updates as we receive them. Sarah's parents have arrived in town too. They've become Ace's primary babysitters while Sarah spends all of her time caring for Mike, monitoring him in their home almost twenty-four hours a day prior to his surgery.

There are a lot of people who know about Mike now since he is a well-liked teacher and coach at a prominent high school near their home. The school year just started, and Mike is officially on medical leave for the time being. Word travels fast. Sarah's house is already filled with huge displays of love: cards from students, flowers from coworkers, and even a six-foot-tall mural from one of the art classes. I find it amazing how fast the news has spread and how many people care so much.

Despite Mike's condition being out in the open, I have yet to tell my own parents. It's one of the first real secrets I have ever kept from them, which I feel badly about, but I am hesitant to put anything else on the two of them right now. I want them to focus on Dad's health, and that means not weighing their minds with more bad news.

I assume Jack knows too, though I haven't heard from him in days, not that I was expecting to. I never called or messaged him back, and eventually, he just stopped contacting me. It's strange to think I haven't seen him since breakfast on the day everything changed. It's also weird to even imagine going back to that morning, a state of mind I am not sure I will ever know again. What's happening right now is enough to change the course of lives forever.

The surgery itself takes six hours. However, by the time we finally hear from the doctor, we have already been at the hospital for closer to nine. Sarah asks me to come with her and his parents to hear the update.

"It was a successful surgery," Dr. Huber tells us as soon as he walks into the small, bare conference room where we meet with him to discuss the operation. There are a few lone chairs and a small table, everything stark white.

Dr. Huber sits down in one of the chairs before he says the rest, looking Sarah in the eye when he speaks. "Mike did great. He's in recovery now. I was able to remove most of the tumor. About 95% of it. We'll get the biopsy results back in a few days. In the meantime, Mike will stay here for observation, and he'll be able to go home in a couple of days. Once we get the results, we can discuss what happens next. My office secretaries will call to schedule it." He isn't robotic when he speaks the way a lot of doctors can be, but I still can't figure out if any of this is good news.

Mike's parents look relieved, happy even, but Sarah looks so exhausted, pale white skin and gray around her eyes like a ghost, a mere shell of the woman she was weeks ago. Her belly is so big now, only a few months from her due date. She looks the same size she did at nine months pregnant with Ace. In all honesty, I can't even believe a precious little life can be growing inside of her when on the outside she looks like she is just barely alive.

While we wait for the results of the biopsy, the seconds of each passing day tick by slower than I have ever felt time pass. The first time I actually get to see Mike after his surgery, he is in a recliner chair in their living room, a bandage wrapped around his head and a bowl of ice cream on his lap. He's watching the MLB Network, the Reds versus the Cardinals.

"Hey there, Madster," he says when I walk into their house without knocking like I always do. "Sarah's back in the nursery, but, hey…" He pauses, seeming tired. His voice is slower and softer than usual. "Thanks for your help with Ace and everything else. You've been great."

I have thought a lot about what I would say to Mike when I saw him after his surgery, but nothing feels right. Standing over the chair, looking down at him, I hold back the tears that want to fall. "Shit, Mike. I'm so sorry this is happening."

"You know, it sucks. I'm not gonna lie. But my mom always told me God only gives you what you can handle, so I must be a badass mother fucker."

"You are, Mike. The baddest mother fucker I know." Instead of going back to find Sarah, I sit next to him. "So how about those Reds?" I ask.

Three days later, Sarah tells me in a text that the tumor was malignant. I suspect she doesn't call or tell me in person because everyone can appear strong in a text message.

A glioblastoma, she says. *Appointment tomorrow to discuss treatment.*

I don't call her because she obviously doesn't want to talk, and a quick Google search informs me that this is the worst-case scenario. I skim through dozens of articles online looking for something to give me some hope, but all I see are the same words and phrases I don't want to see: *terminal, palliative care, the most aggressive form of cancer,* and then the worst part, *12-18 month average survival.*

I feel sick. I run to the toilet and throw up. My body is hot and shaky, and what I need is for someone to hold me, to let me crumble. But the only people I have ever turned to for that are my parents, who don't know yet, the thought of telling them making me even sicker, and Sarah who is in the damn brunt of it. So, I lie on the bathroom floor, shivering, my cheek against the cold wall, and I count the chartreuse tiles until I pass out right there on the bath mat.

It's three in the morning when I wake up to the sound of my phone ringing. Completely out of it, I don't even look to see who is calling before I answer.

"Hello?" I'm still half-asleep, though I am awake enough to know middle-of-the-night phone calls usually signal bad news. More bad news is the last thing I need.

"Maddie, I just heard. My family's got this whole phone chain going, and I'm at the end of it. Are you okay?" Jack's tone is low and hoarse.

I squeeze my eyelids shut and sit up. "He's *your* cousin, and you're asking if I'm okay? Are you okay?"

"No, Maddie, I'm not. It's fucking awful, and I'm worried

about you because you're closer to him and to Sarah than I've ever been. Are *you* okay?"

"No," I reply without explanation, without even pretending to be strong.

"Do you want me to come over?"

"Please," I say, my voice trembling.

"I'll be there in twenty."

Jack rings my doorbell fifteen minutes later. He is in gray sweatpants and a faded white t-shirt with a rip near the neckline, and he doesn't waste a second before he pulls me out onto the porch and wraps his arms around me. In the pale light of the lamp post, he holds me, giving me permission to fall apart. I breathe in the cool, fresh air I didn't know I needed. Jack doesn't say anything for a while, and neither do I because his embrace, the fact that he is here right now at a quarter past three in the morning, says more than words ever could.

My face still pressed against his chest, my fists clenching the back of his t-shirt, I finally break the silence. "I don't know how to do this Jack. I don't think I can do this."

"What don't you think you can do?" he asks gently. I stare down at his Converse sneakers and think for a while about how to answer his question before I say it out loud.

"Life. It's too goddamn hard. I don't want to do this anymore." But I realize he still doesn't know everything. He still doesn't know about my dad. Nobody does.

I look up into his eyes, the ones that somehow seem to understand me. "I know I'm being vague, but it feels like my whole world is crashing down around me, and I'm too tired and overwhelmed to try to save it, you know? I don't even know where I would start."

Jack takes my hand and leads me to the porch swing where we both sit side by side. My feet hang a few inches above the ground, but his are firmly pressed on the concrete. They rock us back and forth.

"I get it," he says. "I remember when we left Ohio, when my mom tore us away from everything we knew to start this new life my sister and I didn't want. At that point, I didn't even try to fight it. I knew nothing I did would change the final result, so I sucked it up. But you know what? I wish I fought harder to stay with my dad, to say that I wanted to stay. Even if the outcome was the same, I wish I'd known I tried."

"My dad…" I begin to say, desperate for Jack to know the whole story, for someone to understand why I'm such a mess. "His doctor suspects he has early-onset Alzheimer's. It all happened recently, right before everything with Mike, and it's just too much all at once."

Jack's eyebrows shoot up as he lets out a deep sigh, before looking at me with apologetic eyes. It's then I start to cry. "I wish I could take it all away for you. I really do," he says, rubbing my shoulders as he talks. "You know, Robert Frost said, *The best way out is always through,* and I really believe there's something to that. You have to face your suffering and fight it and feel it. It may not change the outcome, but it will change you."

"Will you come lay with me?" I ask, like a kid who is afraid of the night, the monsters under the bed and the absence of light.

"I will," he says, taking my hand into his and leading me first to the kitchen to get us both a glass of water and then back to my bedroom. I light a lavender candle to calm my nerves. Jack pulls back the covers of my bed and gestures for me to get in. He covers me up before climbing in next to me. We both lie there, fully clothed beneath the blankets, and I bury my face in his soft t-shirt, tangle my toes with his, and ask him the weirdest question I think I have ever asked anyone.

"Can you read me something? Something mindless, without a story, without any rhyme or reason to it." Jack doesn't ask for any further explanation of this admittedly odd request. He thinks on it for a moment, then digs his phone out of his pocket, and a minute later, he starts to recite some sort of list.

"Adidas Fleece Hoodie Men's Size Medium, Deco Chef Two Pound Stainless Steel Bread Maker, Honeywell Home Programmable Thermostat in White, Chanel Quilted Leather Medallion Tote Handbag."

He goes on like this for a long time. My mind briefly conjures up an image of each item in my head before moving on to the next. It's like one of those brain teaser games, only this one could go on forever.

"What is this that you're reading?" I finally ask him.

"It's just some random eBay seller's list of items for sale. Do you want something else?"

"No, I like it," I say, so he keeps reading.

"Hasbro Marvel Legends Series Six Inch Collective Action Figure Unbeatable, Dyson V8 Animal Plus Cordless Vacuum…" he drones on.

Chapter 10

Once I've had the time to talk with Sarah and let the initial shock of the biopsy results soak in, I decide it's finally time to tell my parents about Mike. I have been avoiding the topic on the phone with my mother for over a week now, and keeping it a secret has been eating away at me. I resolve to call Mom to tell her. I don't want to do it in person because I hate the level of vulnerability I feel when I cry in front of other people, even my own parents. It's always been like that. If I'm going to cry, I would rather do it alone in a hot shower where I can pretend it's not happening at all.

"Oh, Maddie," Mom says to me, pure sorrow in her voice. "He's so young." *So is Dad,* I think to myself.

Mom asks a lot of questions, all of which I answer. *Sarah's doing the best she can. The baby is due in a few months. Yes, she has all of the babysitting help she needs. No, don't bother sending flowers, but a home-cooked meal might be nice.* And finally, our conversation concludes with Mom saying, "Tell her I'll be praying." And for my mom, that is not just an empty promise.

We may have been the kind of Catholics who only showed up to church for the biggies, like Easter, Christmas, and the occasional baptism of a cousin, but the sky could be caving in and Mom would still say her evening prayers.

That night, I drive to Sarah's house to drop off dinner to her, and when she opens the front door, she looks like she hasn't slept in days. Her eyes are droopy and swollen, and her limbs look heavy on her body.

"Chicken pot pie and those tree trunk cookies you like." I pass off the insulated bag of food. Years ago, I made these super flat and chewy salted chocolate chip cookies with deep wrinkles in them for my blog. Sarah teased me that they looked like tree trunks, but then she devoured an entire plate, raving that they might be the best cookies she has ever eaten. To this day, she begs me for the *tree trunk cookies* whenever she needs to drown her sorrows in sugar.

"You're the best," she says, blowing her disheveled hair out of her line of vision, the slightest smile on her face. "Please come in and eat with me. Mike is asleep. He had his first chemo treatment today, and I really don't want to eat by myself."

"Of course," I say, accepting her offer and following her into the kitchen.

Sitting across the table from her, just the two of us, nibbling on our dessert at the same time we're eating our dinner, it's like we are back in college eating pizza and drinking cheap beer. Except now, we are much older, a little wiser, and faced with the awful reality of her husband's cancer.

"Have you and Mike talked about…" I pause, realizing there are so many things she's dealing with, pressing matters beyond the shock of it all, "everything?"

"We've talked about treatment. He's doing the chemo and radiation Dr. Huber suggests, but Mike doesn't want to uproot our lives and go to clinical trials across the country. He wants to be home."

"Are you okay with that?"

She shrugs. "I'm trying to be. But it kind of feels like he's giving up. If it were me, if I was the sick one, I would do anything. I would move to Antarctica for treatment if it meant I'd have a better chance. So, it's a point of contention between us. I've been researching, and I've found clinical trials in other places, but he asked me to stop looking. *I trust Dr. Huber,* he told me."

"Maybe if you explain your point of view—" I say, but she interrupts.

"I've tried. It's no use." Sarah shakes her head back and forth as she speaks. "He's not open to it. And so I'm doing my best to honor his wishes. I don't want to fight with him."

"I get it. But you have to remember to take care of yourself too," I remind her.

"I know. I'm really trying. I worry about this baby every day." She rubs her stomach as she talks. "I worry all of the stress and tears and lack of sleep are going to mess the baby up. But every night I cry into my pillow, and I think about how unfucking fair all of this is. Why us? What did we do to deserve this? Mike is so young. I'm so young. We were supposed to grow old together, to raise our kids, to be grandparents. I want to scream and punch things, and the only reason I'm holding it together is for Ace and this one."

Then I ask her a question I'm afraid to know the answer to.

One that scares me so much, I hesitate even asking, but it affects everything, and so I do. "Is the doctor hopeful, Sarah? I mean, is there a way Mike can fully recover from this?"

Her eyes slowly close and open again as she exhales. "It's terminal, Maddie. He can fight for more time, but that's all we have."

I knew this was a possibility, but that doesn't stop the tears that burst from my eyes as I reach across the table and place my hand on hers. I don't say anything for a while. I just let myself cry, and Sarah does too. "I'm here for whatever you need, Sarah. You know that, right?"

"What I need is a miracle and a big ass glass of wine." She wipes her cheeks with her fingers and laughs at herself. "But I've got three more months left for the wine part."

"I promise once you deliver that baby, I will buy you the fanciest, most expensive wine your heart desires."

"Not necessary," she says. "Anything at Costco will do."

We spend the rest of the evening on the couch watching *Real Housewives* of some east coast city I can't even remember. I finally tell her about Dad and about Jack and about everything else I have been hiding as we sip on our seltzer waters and stuff our faces with more food. I've never been one to keep secrets, and lately, it's all I have been doing.

"Please don't keep things from me, Maddie. I want to know what's going on with you. And I don't want to talk about Mike's cancer all of the time. Share all the good things and all the bad things with me just like we've always done."

"From now on, I will. I promise."

Sarah gives me a look, the one she gives me that says, *I'm serious Maddie. I'm not messing around.* So, I say it out loud for the first time.

"I like Jack. I mean, I really like him." I cover my face with my palms because I can feel myself blushing.

She has an I-told-you-so-smile plastered across her face. "I knew you would."

When I get home, I pour myself a glass of wine and sit on my back porch. The late summer air is cool the way it is after rain, and the nostalgic scent of lawn clippings and charcoal grills whirls around me. I raise my glass and say a silent *Cheers* to Sarah, and then I open my book. It's one I started weeks ago, but I stopped reading it the day before Jack and I kissed, the day before Mike went to the hospital. I couldn't pick it back up until now, and I am not sure why now suddenly feels okay for some reason, why it's any better than yesterday, but I trace my fingers over the letters on the cover, *What Comes After.*

After a while, I go back inside, relocating to the kitchen with my book. I read standing up, hunched over the counter, so lost in the story I forget why I came inside in the first place. A few chapters in, I hear a knock on my front door releasing me from the book's trance. I look at the clock, and it's quarter to ten, not crazy late, but definitely not early. It's enough to startle a single woman home alone, so I tiptoe across the room to my phone to check my front porch camera, careful not to make any noise.

As I open the app to see who is out there, the unexpected visitor knocks again, and I jump. Then, on my phone screen, I see Jack, hands in his jean pockets, rocking back and forth on his sneakers from toe to heel. I exhale a shaky breath as my pounding heart slows down. He has on a worn leather jacket that makes him look like one of those bad boys your mom warned you about in high school but also sort of like the "cool" dad of your middle school friend who drove her to school on his motorcycle.

I peek in the hall mirror before answering. A messy bun, off-the-shoulder knit sweater, and leggings, a pretty standard look for me. I wipe away the smudged mascara beneath my eyes with my thumb, then open the door.

"To what do I owe this pleasure?" I ask, leaning against the doorframe, ankles crossed.

"Oh, I was just in the neighborhood." Jack acts incredibly casual for someone showing up uninvited at this time of night.

"Really? You live on the other side of town." He ignores my comment as his eyes shift down to the book tucked under my arm.

"What are you reading?" he asks.

I pass the book to him so he can see. "Some new author. It's her debut novel. Maybe sort of a mystery? Not sure yet, but I liked the title."

"I like the title too," he says and inspects the front and back cover before returning it to me. There is an awkward pause that lingers in the air, and I am still trying to figure out why he's here.

"So, do you want to come in?"

"Actually," he says, both hands are back in his pockets now, and I can tell he's anxious for my answer before he even asks the question. "I was wondering if you would want to go for a drive?"

"Now?" I look down at my watch. "It's kind of late."

"Please?" He makes this sweet little puppy dog face with pouty lips and a scrunched-up nose, and I already know I won't be able to turn him down.

"What the hell." I set the book on the front hall table and grab a light jacket from the closet.

When Jack turns on his car, the talk radio he must have been listening to on the way to my house startles me when it begins blaring from the speakers. He hurries to turn the volume down.

"Must have been some heated discussion you were listening to. What was it about? Politics? Religion?" I ask, giggling at how nerdy he can be.

"No, nothing like that. It was about relationships." He has a smirk on his face, like he has a secret he's keeping, or he's embarrassed, or both.

"I didn't know you were a Dr. Drew fan," I joke.

"There's a lot you still don't know about me." Jack's eyes are on the road, but mine are on him.

"Tell me some things I don't know." Even though I sound flirty and incredibly generic, I really do want to know the little things, all of his little habits and quirks.

"Well, let's see." Jack tucks his top lip under the bottom one while he thinks. "I am the undefeated geography bee champion of South Pointe Junior High. I think that may have sadly been my peak in life. Hmm... what else? The first concert I ever went to was N'SYNC with my sister, and I actually kind of enjoyed it. And, I love going to the dentist."

"The *Celebrity* tour?"

"I think so?" His forehead wrinkles.

"I went to that too! But seriously, you love going to the dentist?"

He nods, and my mouth twists. "I *hate* going to the dentist. I'd rather get twenty flu shots than get my gums poked at with that metal hook thing. You must be a masochist because the dentist is the absolute worst."

"Really? I feel refreshed afterward, like I've just taken a long, hot shower."

"Masochist."

He briefly takes his eyes off the road to look in my direction. "Your turn. I want to know things most people don't know about you."

"Fine. I guess that's only fair." I contemplate for a second, considering my own idiosyncrasies as I watch the outline of trees pass by the window. It's so dark outside, everything is only black and gray. Eventually, I start rambling whatever comes to mind.

"Umm… I hate the first and only tattoo I ever got. It's all crooked and wonky, like a prison tattoo."

"The one on your ankle?"

"That's the one. But I've never admitted it to anyone because my parents were so adamant I would regret it. I swore I never would."

"That's a good one," he says, and I keep going.

"Since we're bragging about childhood accomplishments, I was the spelling bee champion of St. Gabriel Elementary School every year except for in the second grade."

"Woah, I'm in the presence of a legend. They probably still talk about you at good ole St. Gabe's. But if you don't mind me asking, what happened in the second grade?"

"Nate McCoy happened." There is contempt in my tone.

"What do you mean?"

"Well, we were down to the final two, Nate McCoy and I standing with our backs against the lockers. He was tall, dark, and handsome. That's every girl's type, by the way." I give him a head nod, and he laughs. "So Nate got eliminated on the word *February,* which meant if I could spell *Saturday,* I would win, but I threw it." I can't believe I'm telling him this. I also can't believe I am still so angry about this trivial life moment from over twenty years ago. Perhaps it isn't as trivial as I would like to believe, though.

"What? Why on earth would you throw it?" Jack looks mindblown, jerking his head back and then peering at me wide-eyed.

"I thought he wouldn't like me if I beat him. So I snuck an *O* in there. S-A-T-O-R-D-A-Y, *Saturday.*"

"An *O*? C'mon Maddie, that's not even believable. I bet your teacher could see right through it."

"Probably, but I was seven and in love. The thing is, when I let him beat me, he didn't turn to me and tell me he loved me like I imagined he might. He laughed in my face as he spelled *Saturday* correctly and took on the title of best speller in the second grade."

"Fucking brutal."

"I know. But from that moment on, I vowed never to dumb myself down for anyone, especially a boy, ever again. It wasn't worth it. So I kicked his ass every year after that until we went to high school."

"There you go. I like a headstrong woman. But, that story is exactly why I hesitate when it comes to falling in love. I've seen it change so many people and not for the better most of the time. My mother is the perfect example."

"What do you mean? How did she change?" I pry deeper into his dysfunctional family history as my fingers fidget with all of the buttons on the door.

"How *didn't* she change? She dated a dude who rode motorcycles, and she was suddenly one of those biker chicks in all leather and metal studs. She dated another guy who was super outdoorsy, always camping and hunting, and the next thing I know, she's no longer a vegetarian and cooking freshly slaughtered bison in our tiny kitchen, blood literally everywhere. She lost herself in every man she ever loved. Well, every man she *thought* she loved."

"Sometimes change isn't bad. Look at Mike," I tell him. "He was a beer-guzzling frat boy no one could take seriously before loving Sarah turned him into one of the greatest people I've ever known. He made her better, too. So much better. And my parents, I couldn't even imagine one without the other. I've never seen them have a serious, *oh-shit-I-think-my-parents-are-getting-a-divorce* fight. They just bring out the best in each other." I can't help but try to defend love, to force Jack to recognize that it's not always one person losing their identity, sacrificing oneself for the sake of not being alone.

"You're lucky to have grown up with them then. That's not the case for most people."

I never thought about it that way before, but I guess I am lucky. My parents' relationship, their unceasing affection for one another, their complete mutual respect, it's something I've taken for granted. "Most people today get caught up in the story, the image, and what they can post on social media, and they don't pay enough attention to the people they're choosing. At least in my opinion," I say.

"I think you might be right." Jack pulls into a parking spot in an almost empty lot.

I've been looking at him, so deep in our conversation, I haven't even paid attention to where he was taking me. My eyes shift from his profile to the sign in front of us: *Cincinnati Observatory.*

"The Observatory, huh? I can't say I've ever been here."

He turns off the car, races around to the passenger side, and opens my door before I even have the chance. It's the kind of thing you don't really see men do anymore. The Observatory is at the top of a giant hill in a secluded park, so there is no hustle and bustle anywhere close. It's a towering building of red brick with stone columns and a huge metal dome on top.

"Is it even open?" I ask, looking at the time on my phone which now reads twenty after ten.

"I'm not sure. Let's see." He takes my hand in his as we start to walk. It surprises me, but I don't pull away.

I notice a few cars on the other side of the parking lot, so I am hopeful we'll be able to go inside. When we enter the lobby, a lanky-looking boy with braces, probably not even old enough to drink, says to us with a noticeably nasally voice, "Welcome to *Late Night, Date Night* at the Cincinnati Observatory."

"Late Night, Date Night?" I say to Jack with a surprised tone. He raises and lowers his eyebrows with a suggestive look on his face. I laugh and ask, "Did you know about this?"

"I didn't. But it seems kind of perfect. The universe must have sent us here."

The teenage boy guides us on a brief tour along with three other couples who have shown up for what is apparently an actual event. I wonder whether they planned this or if the universe sent them here too.

The first couple appears middle-aged, a little older than my parents, probably in their late sixties. They look like the types of people you find at the zoo on a Sunday morning with expensive cameras, the ones who take pictures of all of the plants and animals like they work for *National Geographic* or something.

There is also a super young couple, maybe seventeen. They are definitely still in high school. She looks like one of those gorgeous nerds who doesn't know how pretty she is, and he is clearly a football player, wearing his letterman jacket and matching red sneakers. I instantly fall in love with the sight of them. They hold hands with their fingers interlocked, and they both look so nervous they could puke. I imagine him giving her a promise ring in her driveway at the end of the night before he drops her off. She'll write about it in her journal in her light pink bedroom that her mother painted that color before she was even born.

The last couple I am not in the least bit interested in. They look like bored, judgy Yelpers in their late twenties, so I don't pay them any mind. They're busy taking mental notes of everything that annoys them as evidence for their two-star review.

At the end of the tour, the nasally-voiced boy takes us to the roof where we are given access to huge telescopes I imagine cost six figures apiece. Before we are left to walk the perimeter and gaze up at the sky, our tour guide provides us with some brief instruction. "Tonight you will see the Full Sturgeon Moon.

This one," he gestures to a particular microscope to his left, "is one of the oldest working telescopes in the world, a Merz and Mehler refractor from 1845. If you'd like to look through it, I'd be happy to help you. In your brochure, you have a guide to help you identify constellations and any other astronomical objects you may see. Enjoy!"

The air smells of pine and musk. Jack and I circle around the perimeter of the space, finally settling on an open telescope. I bend slightly to peer into the eyepiece but step back when I realize I have no idea what I am doing.

"Can I help?" Jack asks.

"Sure. Do you know how to use one of these?"

"Sort of," he says, making a few adjustments to the telescope, then telling me, "Here, try again."

Now, looking back into the eyepiece, everything is clear. The sky is so vast, I could lose myself in its depths. The brilliancy of the stars, electric yellows and whites floating in a sea of midnight blue. It's all made even more majestic in the glow of the moon. A calmness comes over my body, a calmness I haven't felt in so long. This might be the closest to the Man in the Moon, to God, I've ever been.

"I don't even have the words," I say to Jack, still peering through the telescope. When I finally pull myself away to look at him again, I ask, "How did you know I needed this tonight?"

"I didn't. It was the universe that brought us here, remember?"

I nudge his shoulder. "Seriously though, what made you want to bring me here?"

"Well, I was listening to NPR, and this relationship guru said the key to romance is in doing spontaneous things. I had the idea to take you to the moon."

With a confidence I've never really known in myself before, not with men at least, I step so close to him, I can sense the heat radiating off his skin, a stark contrast to the cool air entering and exiting my lungs at a rate much faster than my usual breathing. I gaze up at him, and he peers back at me, mere centimeters of space separating our bodies.

"Why is it that you always smell like cinnamon rolls?" he asks.

"I'm not sure, but I think I like that about myself." I start to giggle like a lovestruck teenager.

He lowers his face and presses his lips to mine, sending a tingle up my spine. He is soft and sensual and sweet, the kind of kiss that keeps middle school girls up at night, what they dream kissing will be like one day.

"You always taste like vanilla." He breathes into my mouth, one hand on my face holding me steady and close.

"You always taste like espresso," I whisper back.

We separate before we know we can't stop, and he guides me to a bench where we sit next to each other, his arm around me, claiming me as his. I watch the middle-aged man kiss his wife's cheek, her pale skin shimmering in the moonlight. I see the nerdy girl, self-conscious in her own skin, sit taller when the football player speaks to her. He is probably telling her how beautiful she is, and she is probably hearing it for the first time from a boy she really likes.

"You know, vanilla and espresso are so compatible, they're practically peanut butter and jelly," Jack says.

"They're practically tacos and Tuesdays," I add.

"Ooo, that's a good one. I don't suppose there's a late-night taco joint nearby? That actually sounds really good, and I've been eating frozen dinners all week."

"I don't know of a taco place, but I'm pretty sure there's a sushi spot just down the hill in Mount Lookout that's on bar time," I say, recalling Sarah, Mike, and I gorging ourselves one night after too many drinks at the tavern across the street.

"You're speaking my love language, Maddie," Jack says with a grin.

"I thought you didn't have a love language?"

"I'm learning that I might."

He kisses me the casual kind of kiss two people in love have without even thinking twice. The kind of kiss I have been wanting from someone like him for so long.

"Let's go," he says, and we spend the rest of the evening smashing half-price sushi rolls and casually kissing like it's no big deal.

Chapter 11

At the onset of autumn, I spend a lot of time watching the premature burgundy leaves fall from the oak tree in my backyard while I reflect on the recent months. A lot of things have changed quickly. Some I saw coming, and some I didn't.

My work always picks up in fall, naturally, because every working mom in America wants a new, fresh list of easy and healthy slow cooker meals for weeknight dinners. The younger, more adventurous moms want recipes for their air fryers and Instant Pots. And then of course, there are the Thanksgiving side dishes and the homemade pies followed by Christmas cookies and cocktails. It's all very predictable. My social media feeds and blog get ten times the hits from September to December compared to the rest of the year, so I am constantly working, either in the kitchen fine-tuning recipes or on my computer growing my following and keeping up with contracts. Though it helps to have Margot working for me, it's still a twelve-hour-a-day job during this time. But I welcome the chaos of it all because even in the thick of it, I am grateful to be thinking about butter to shortening ratios in the perfect flaky pie crust, even if it doesn't change the fate of Dad or Mike.

After Labor Day, Jack started his first fall semester as an adjunct professor at Xavier University, and he was as busy as I was, working tirelessly to make a great first impression on his English Department colleagues. He worried even more about what the students thought of him. After all, they are the first ones to have him as their instructor, and they will be the ones whose words will begin building his reputation at the college, especially as a new, young professor fresh out of graduate school.

Despite our busy schedules, we still saw each other as frequently as we could since the night he took me to the moon. Jack became a regular taste tester of my recipes, and I became a frequent visitor of his library, an entire wall of books in the condo he rents close to campus. He constructed the bookshelves by stacking planks of wood and cinder blocks, which surprisingly look way more impressive than you would imagine when books are stacked from the floor to the ceiling spanning the entire length of a room. His collection is separated into fiction and nonfiction, and then each book is shelved based on the author's last name. I loved that even though he may have had laundry strewn about and dirty dishes in the sink, every single book was always in its correct place.

We spent all of our free time together, talking and laughing and making out like teenagers. There were so many late summer nights that turned into coffee and French toast the next morning. Despite all of the time we spent with each other, Jack and I still hadn't made our relationship official, and we still hadn't slept together. The first time you have sex with someone is a climax moment, one I was trying to wait for, and I think he was too. Like a slow-burn romance novel, the longer you wait for it, the better it will be. The problem with waiting for anything, though, is that if you put it off for too long, sometimes you miss your chance.

It was late when Jack called asking if I would like to come to his place Friday night to celebrate finishing his first official week of classes. I was already in bed, but I answered anyway, anxious to hear his voice. We hadn't seen each other in a week due to hectic work schedules. I offered to bring over Thai takeout and homemade apple pie with a crumble topping and caramel drizzle, the dessert Jack told me he used to request for his birthday every year. His mom would always buy the Marie Callender version from the freezer section of the grocery store because "she couldn't even handle slice and bake cookies," according to Jack.

At the end of the week, I arrived at Jack's with pad thai and spring rolls and even a pint of vanilla ice cream to go with the dessert. But he didn't look like himself, his skin ashen and his brow furrowed. He appeared uneasy and frazzled, like a man who had bitten off more than he could chew.

"Are you okay?" I asked Jack when we sat down to eat, but I already knew he wasn't. He was distracted and distant.

"Yeah, it's been a long week." When he talked, he was noticeably shorter with me than he had ever been before.

"Well, how was your first week? Did you love it? How were the students?" I was eager to hear what his first classes were like and how his students responded to the syllabus he spent so much time preparing.

"I'm just a little overwhelmed," he said between bites. He shoveled the food into his mouth like he hadn't eaten in days, and I wondered if he had.

"That's normal with a new job. There's a certain pressure to perform. I'm sure the students were super nervous, especially the freshmen." I tried to reassure him, but I noticed him shaking his head back and forth as I spoke as if to say, *No, you don't get it.*

"I don't know if I didn't do enough prep work. I feel underprepared with my curriculum. In my intro-level classes, nobody talked. I got through my agenda, and I left time for questions and a discussion at the end, but then, no one said anything. Class was over after twenty minutes because I didn't have anything else to do. I should have been prepared for every possible outcome, but I wasn't. I looked like an idiot, like I had no idea what I was doing up there."

"You'll get better with practice. Those intro kids are fresh out of high school. They don't know what it's like to be in a college lit course yet." I stopped, waiting for Jack to agree with me, but he didn't say anything, so I kept going. "And I could never stand in front of a class of people the way you do. I'm sure it's nerve-racking, but I know it probably went better than you think. We're our own worst critics."

"Yeah...maybe." He didn't seem convinced.

After dinner, we turned on a movie. I tried to cuddle up next to him on the couch, but he kept his arms crossed over his chest, his body turned slightly away from me. Just enough for me to notice.

"It felt really weird not seeing you for an entire week," I said, nuzzling his shoulder, but I swear I felt him flinch, like my touch was the last thing he wanted.

"Yeah, I guess we're used to seeing a lot of each other these days." Jack's tone was flat, and his eyes stayed fixed on the television.

I tried to lighten the mood. "You know, there's this new Indian restaurant down the street from my place. I heard the lamb korma is to die for, and I know that's your favorite. We should go next weekend."

"Sure." He nodded his head just barely.

I leaned into him more, craving some sort of affection, but he pulled away. "Sorry, I have a headache," he said.

"I'll rub your neck. That always helps me when I get them. I have one of these self-massage things at home I use whenever I sense a migraine coming on." But as soon as my fingertips touched his neck, he brushed my hand away, wanting nothing to do with me.

I quickly stood up and studied him for a moment, trying to see any emotion in his cold, heavy eyes. "I should go."

He yawned. "That's a good idea. I should get some sleep."

I slipped on my shoes, and we walked to the door where he kissed me goodbye, but it didn't feel like it usually felt when we kissed. His lips were taut and dry. The whole thing was awkward and forced, like he wanted to get it over with.

Jack was a version of himself I hadn't seen before that night, self-conscious and exhausted, so I went home to give him the space he clearly wanted. I tried my best to cast it aside. *It was a one-off, a bad day,* I told myself. But the next morning, I awoke to a message on my phone I didn't anticipate:

Thanks again for dinner and dessert. I hate to say this, but I think I need to take some time for myself right now. I need to focus on my career because I don't want this past week to set the tone for the entire year. I'm not feeling good about the way it all started. I hope you understand.

But, I didn't understand. How could everything change so abruptly? How could he go from sleeping in the same bed with me and holding me all night to wanting to take a break? And how did he think it was okay to text me something like that rather than tell me in person? The only thing I did understand was that this man who seemed so perfect, who I was falling so hard for, suddenly seemed like a coward.

When Jack tried calling a couple of weeks later, I cold-shouldered him, sending him straight to voicemail. A few days later, he sent a casual text message asking how I was, but I responded snarkily, letting him know he couldn't turn me on and off like a light switch. We had a brief conversation over text where he said I was not understanding of his situation and that his career isn't established in the way that mine is. However, I refused to waste time arguing with Jack about why he didn't want to spend time with me anymore, so I told him to stop checking in with me, that whatever we had was over.

That same evening, probably out of spite, I downloaded a dating app just to convince myself it was all for the best, to prove I was ready to say goodbye to him. I never even made a profile on the app, but the very act of downloading it made me feel liberated from the back and forth of Jack Keller's commitment issues.

It's been weeks since the last time we spoke, and with or without Jack, I still have my own life to live, a reality that's difficult to wake up to most mornings. But I keep doing it, day after day, because what else is there to do but trudge through the muck and try to survive it all? I'm beginning to think that's what adulthood is. Trudging through the muck until it's all over.

Recently, dinners with my parents, which have always been a source of comfort for me, have turned into a sort of weekly gauge to see how Dad is doing, to help me decide whether or not he is getting better or worse. Not that there's anything I can do either way. The forgetting, the repeating, and his newly developed temper are all so much more noticeable now compared to a few months ago.

"He is worse in the evenings. Early in the day, he is more like himself," Mom tells me, and that eases my anxiety a bit, like even when dinner is bad, I can remind myself the Dad I know is not completely gone. At least not yet.

"Maybe we switch to Wednesday brunches then," I joke.

And the truth is, the weekly dinners are getting harder to sit through. Every time Dad asks me the same question for the third or fourth time, I watch Mom's body tense up and her teeth grind into one another as she makes a mental note to write it down in her journal. Sometimes I can laugh it off, pretending it doesn't bother me when he asks me if he left his drill at my house for the tenth time in the same dinner conversation. Other times, I become frustrated, losing my patience when I respond curtly, "Yes, Dad." And when I do this, I go home and berate myself for being an awful daughter, a horrible person, one who doesn't deserve a dad as great as him.

"It's okay, Maddie. I get that way too sometimes. He understands, and he loves you," Mom tells me on the phone after a particularly difficult evening when I call her crying, apologizing for acting the way I did.

"But it's not okay, Mom. It's not his fault," I say through sobs.

"I know it's not his fault, but it's a natural reaction. It's to be expected actually." She sounds like she's quoting someone from the support group she's been going to for the last few weeks. Dad's doctor recommended one to her, and Mom started attending when she began to notice a lack of patience in herself, the same abrupt and unsympathetic tone I'm crying to her over.

"I don't know how you do it every day, watching your husband of thirty-three years become someone you don't even recognize anymore."

"Maddie, I promised in sickness and in health. Your father never blamed me for not being able to have more kids. He told me it was okay. He told me he loved me no matter what. And all the while, I cried myself to sleep every night wondering if I was ruining the future he dreamed of for himself, wondering what I did to deserve a husband with such patience, such unrelenting support. It's my turn to show him the love he showed me thirty years ago." I can see she hurts, and I can see she is struggling to keep it together. But she's doing it for me, the way good parents always do, holding it all inside until their kids are tucked in tight.

One of the most difficult parts of Jack's absence from my life is that he had been the only light when everything else was dark. Now the world is pitch black. Alone in my bed every night, I say prayers to the Man in the Moon for Dad to remember, for Mom to be strong, for Mike to recover by some grace of God, and for Sarah to survive if he doesn't.

At this point, Mike has completed six rounds of radiation and oral chemotherapy. It's been made clear to everyone the purpose of these treatments is simply to prolong his life and to not get any hopes up for a cure. The goal of the radiation was to kill whatever cancerous cells remained after the tumor was resected by Dr. Huber. However, subsequent scans have shown the remaining part of the tumor, though it has become slightly smaller, is still there. In addition, one of the reasons glioblastomas are so fatal is because the cancerous cells don't simply stay in one place but have a tendency to bury themselves in other parts of the brain. Dr. Huber has presented the option of experimental treatments in other facilities with other doctors, all of whom are far from Cincinnati. While there is hope that comes with these clinical trials, the side effects are risky. They could result in losing Mike even sooner and would also involve uprooting Sarah to a new place in her third trimester of pregnancy, an option Mike is not willing to consider.

"He's accepted that his days are numbered, and so I'm just grateful for every day," Sarah told me the last time we discussed his treatment.

She is finally adorned with a magical pregnancy glow, eager to meet her baby, the one who has been through so much before even taking a single earthside breath. I have spent my Saturday afternoons for the last few weeks helping Sarah to prepare a nursery for the new baby. She and Mike wanted the gender to be a surprise, so we've decorated in yellows and light grays with zoo animals as the theme. A six-foot-tall stuffed giraffe stands in the corner of the room watching over the crib, with black and white sketches of a baby gorilla, elephant, and zebra on the wall above the dresser.

Mike is always in bed or on the couch when I am over. Sometimes, he is upbeat and telling jokes, though other times he is hunched over a wastebasket from the nausea or lying down with a sleep mask covering his eyes, the soundtrack of heavy rain emanating from his phone. He is noticeably thinner, and his skin is a muted yellow, a distinct difference from his naturally tan complexion. I tell Sarah I don't want to intrude or invade his privacy, especially if he's not feeling well, but she assures me, "Don't worry, you're family. Besides, he wants you here. He knows you're helping me get ready for the baby, and he feels horrible that he can't."

The day Sarah goes into labor, it's as if all of the sadness we've faced fades away for a short time, if only to remind us of how beautiful life can be. She asked me to be ready when the time came, so I could drive them to the hospital. Mike isn't permitted to drive due to the possibility of seizures. She also requested that I take pictures during the labor and delivery the same way I did with Ace. I told her I would be honored.

The call comes unexpectedly, two full weeks before her due date, and at first I am worried. *Is it too soon? Will the baby be okay?*

Her water broke, "just like in the movies," she says on the phone. It is quarter past seven in the morning, the sun is beginning to creep through the darkness, and the cool morning air is the perfect temperature to enjoy the hot cup of coffee she has waiting for me. When I see Sarah, she is so calm, my worry fades. As we pull away from her house, Ace and Mike's mother wave to us from the front window. This is a monumental day for Ace. For all of us.

Mike looks better than I have seen him in weeks, wearing a flannel shirt and a Cincinnati Reds baseball cap that hides his bald head and surgery scars. He dotes on Sarah, sitting in the back seat of my car with her, holding her hand through each contraction, coaching her through the pain.

"You can do it, babe. You are so strong," he tells her. Mike says he's happy that for once, it's not about him. It's about his wife and his new baby. "Finally, something to celebrate," he says.

I hope Sarah will love each photo I capture in the hospital room. Mike kissing her forehead as she winces in pain. Her face scrunched tight as she pushes, Mike holding up her leg. And my favorite, Mike raising his arms in the air in victory as the doctor suctions fluid from the freshly born baby's mouth and nose.

Atlas Mae has the picture-perfect birth at exactly thirty-eight weeks. There are no nail-biting moments during her delivery, the ones where heart rates drop and everyone worries about mom and baby. Perhaps Atlas knew our hearts and our nerves couldn't handle anymore, so she arrives drama-free after only ten minutes of pushing, with good strong lungs and "a wail you can hear all the way down the hall," one nurse peeks in the hospital room to tell us.

Sarah cries, and Mike cries, and the nurses who hear their story cry. I take hundreds and hundreds of pictures, capturing every single moment so Sarah will be able to transport herself back to this perfect day whenever she needs to. So she will have these photos to show Atlas long after Mike is gone, a reminder of how much her daddy, the one she'll only remember in photos, loved her.

Chapter 12

In the spring, when the world outside my window becomes vibrant again, when rain brings new life to everything that's been dead, that's been hibernating, that's been hiding from the cold and the darkness, we say goodbye to Mike Campbell. It was a goodbye we had been anticipating, a goodbye we had already been grieving for nearly a year, but the forewarning didn't make it any easier. In fact, it might have made it even harder to finally lay him to rest.

Everyone in Mike's life had gotten used to his sickness. Over time, we all reluctantly accepted this new reality, understanding he was going to be thinner and less active but would still have the silly, easy-going personality we'd always loved about him underneath it all. I think I became so used to this new normal, it felt like he might hang on forever, never actually having to look death in the face. After all, how does one do such a thing with a wife and two children so young? It's too cruel to take him from them. Life isn't supposed to be like that.

But then the signs of the end all reared their ugly heads, feverish and turbulent, like a mad dog too far gone to try saving. Mike started sleeping twenty hours a day. It was rare to even see him awake, and when he wasn't asleep, he was uncomfortable, with barely enough energy to speak a few words. I spent more time at their house during these final days, helping Sarah with diaper changes and nap times while pretending it wasn't as bad as we knew it was.

Sarah was in constant contact with Mike's doctors, and one morning when his fever reached 103 degrees, I went with her to take Mike to the hospital. Somewhere deep down, I think both Sarah and I knew he wouldn't be coming back home. It was only a matter of time before swallowing and talking became incredibly difficult for Mike, so he was put on a feeding tube. Every word he said took every ounce of his strength. As a result, he spoke very little at the end of his life, simply nodding his head to respond to yes or no questions and telling Sarah he loved her when he could manage. His body blew up like a balloon, swollen from all of the medications. So much so, he was almost unrecognizable. And soon enough, he was unconscious for the majority of the time, unaware of who was with him or what was happening around him. That's when Sarah knew it was time for hospice.

"He wouldn't want anyone to remember him like this," she said. "He told me many times that if it got to this point, not to prolong it."

Sarah told me she didn't think she could cry anymore, that she didn't have any tears left, but when Mike passed only two weeks after being admitted to hospice, she did cry. She cried for so long I worried she would never stop. I reminded her of her kids. I reminded her she is their entire world, and they are half Mike after all. Most of the time I am with her, I worry I'm not saying the right thing. Sometimes I wonder if I should keep my mouth shut and not say anything at all, just be a shoulder, a warm body, if and when she needs it. There is no right answer for any of this, though, because none of it should be happening at all.

At the funeral, I turn around in the pew at the front of the church to survey the crowd. I have never witnessed a funeral the size of Mike's, a true reflection of the person he was, a kind and generous role model (and often even a stand-in father figure) for thousands of students and baseball players over the course of his career. The enormous church, the same one where Sarah and Mike got married and I stood next to them in a coral, floor-length bridesmaid dress, is so full that people are standing shoulder to shoulder in the back, on the side aisles, and even in the foyer to pay their respects. His brothers are the pallbearers. Sarah looks so young, too young, to be a widow, in a simple black dress and flats, a baby on her lap and a toddler by her side.

The high school where Mike taught for the past eight years hosts a service afterward for all of the students, teachers, and community members who want to pay their respects. A smaller reception for close friends and family is held in a banquet room at the local country club where Mike's parents are members. There are hot prime rib sandwiches and chicken salad on croissants and platters full of fruit and cheese.

All of the young nieces and nephews swarm to the dessert table because at a funeral reception, no one has to wait for dessert. They fill their tiny hands with little tea cookies and run out the door to the patio overlooking the golf course where they can play hopscotch and talk the way kids do, blissfully unaware of the struggle life can become when you reach a certain age.

I excuse myself from the table where I sit with Sarah, her parents, and her grandmother. I need a break from the cordial conversation, the forced smiles, and the obligatory eating when I have absolutely no appetite. This has always been the hardest part of funerals for me, the "party" afterward, the celebration of life, when we are supposed to talk about the good times and tell all the funny, lighthearted stories. In reality, we are all still mourning the loss, less than a week from the death of the person we loved so deeply. Today, *this funeral,* is by far the hardest of them all.

After some deep breaths and an extended handwashing session in the restroom, I prepare myself to return to the reception hall. *Only another hour or so until I can drink wine in my pajamas,* I tell myself. But when I leave the bathroom, Jack is standing in the hallway, his hands stuffed into the pockets of his gray suit pants, pacing back and forth as he peers at the framed art on the walls, paintings of lush landscapes and vibrant flowers and other happy, pretty things.

I stop in my tracks when I see him, tempted to run back into the restroom to hide. My mind has been so consumed with a million other things, and Jack has never been all that close to Mike or Sarah, so I haven't accidentally run into him or heard

Sarah mention him since I told her our *little fling,* as I innocently put it, was over. She was too busy and overwhelmed to protest it, and I was admittedly grateful for that. Not to say I haven't thought about him. I have, and I do. Most of the time it's at the end of a long day when I want someone to read next to, someone to decompress with, someone to complain about my toothpaste globs in the sink.

Jack and I haven't spoken in months, not since the last time he called, and I told him I moved on, that I'd started dating again, and he needed to respect that. I didn't tell him I was exclusive with any one person. Jack can interpret the words "dating again" however he wants. In all honesty, I have only been on three dates in the past six months. One was a setup arranged by an old friend, Taylor, from college. She is married with kids and occasionally gets bored and tells me she has the perfect guy in mind for me. They are almost never my type, and this one was no exception. Another I met at the Farmer's Market where he had his own stand featuring his woodworking hobby, and besides being physically my type, he turned out to still be "technically married" which is a big fat no for me. The last guy had promise.

I met Nick at Red Eye, a different coffee shop I began frequenting when I felt the occasional urge to get out of my house and watch strangers do ordinary things around me. I haven't been back to Sully's since I told Jack to stop calling me. Nick and I happened to be sitting diagonally from each other at separate tables. I was reading a Fredrik Backman novel, I don't remember which one because I've read four of them this year, and Nick was sketching on a drawing pad. He had full sleeve tattoos and an eye patch, both of which I found intriguing.

"What happened?" I asked.

"Bicycling accident," he said, and I liked that it wasn't a motorcycle. I've never liked motorcycles.

We went out for dinner the next week, and I thought there might be something there, but then, he ghosted me, never calling again or responding to the text messages I sent. I still think about what I did wrong on our date even though it was weeks ago. Maybe it was my high-waisted jeans. Those can be polarizing I think. Or it could have been that I ordered the pork tacos. A lot of people have strong opinions about pork. But I guess I'll never know. I haven't stepped foot into Red Eye since.

Now, in the hallway of the country club, Jack catches my glance, undeniably handsome, his hair perfectly messy as usual. In the way he's lingering, I can tell he wants to talk to me. Jack and I are the only ones in the hallway, and he waits for me to say something first. I give in.

"Long time no see." My voice echoes in the empty corridor.

"Hey." His mouth draws out the word, like there's more he wants to say. He's just not sure how to. I wait because I can't pretend not to care. So I stand there, turning my gaze to the wall, a sea of red and yellow marigolds on canvas.

"How's Sarah?" he asks.

"Not great. I don't know how anyone recovers from something like this."

"I don't either." His eyes move to his feet. We both sound frustratingly helpless because we are.

Helplessness is a feeling that's debilitating to me. I'd rather feel any other way. I remember taking one of those psychology quizzes in a college seminar that measured my Locus of Control.

I had the highest Internal Locus of anyone in my class, which essentially means, I believe I control my own destiny. I can make decisions that impact where I end up and what happens to me. That mentality is what gave me the courage to leave my nine-to-five job that provided health insurance and security to start my own business. But I've learned there are things that happen in life that can rock your entire world, that can turn everything upside down and sideways in an instant. Mike's death is one of those things. Dad being sick is one of those things. And for the first time in my life, it's like I have no control over anything that matters. I'm standing on the edge of a cliff with high winds on my back. The universe is trying to push me over the edge, and I'm just fighting not to fall.

"If there's anything I can do… for Sarah or you—" Jack says, but I stop him there.

"I don't think there is. Sarah is leaving soon. She's selling her house and moving to Florida. Her parents are retired, so they can help her with the kids." When I say this, I can see sympathy in Jack's eyes. He knows how close Sarah and I are and can probably guess how devastating this will be for me. I don't want pity from anyone. I'm not the one whose husband just died after all.

When Sarah came up with this plan, I tried everything to get her to change her mind. I offered to move in with her and help with the kids. I extended an invitation for her to move in with me. We have never lived so far apart, and frankly, putting a thousand miles between us right after her husband died is the worst-case scenario for me. But, she told me she's been thinking about it for a long time.

Sarah said when faced with the thought of life after Mike, she'd known two things. First, she would need full-time help with the kids. She didn't want them to spend nine hours a day in daycare while she worked, only to come home to an exhausted and depressed single mom. Second, Sarah didn't want to stay in her house. While there were so many happy memories under that roof, the one she and Mike fell in love with because of the big front porch with the rocking chairs and the finished basement perfect for a house full of kids, the fact that she watched Mike die in their home would never escape her. She wanted to remember Mike the way he was before the headaches, the seizures, and the cancer. In that house, she knew it wouldn't be possible. So the best option, she decided, was to move to Florida, to lean on her parents, and to start a new life, not one where she forgot about the past, but one where she could try to thrive again one day.

"When is she leaving?" Jack asks.

"Next week. She's flying back to Ft. Myers with her parents. I offered to drive the moving truck down with all of her things, so she doesn't have to be away from Ace and Atlas."

"Let me come with you," he says abruptly, and then, once the words exit his mouth and he has a moment to consider them, he adds, "You know, unless you already have someone going with you."

"I don't, but that's really okay. I was looking forward to some alone time. I have some audiobooks to listen to on the drive."

"That's too long of a drive to do on your own, especially after the past few months you've had. Let me come, and we can split the drive. You don't even have to talk to me if you don't want to."

I wonder if he's offering because he feels guilty for how things ended between us, like he owes me something for breaking up with me over a text message. The truth is I don't want him to think he owes me anything. He doesn't.

"Really, it's just—" I start to say, planning to tell him it's not that far of a drive and that I actually love road trips, but he stops me before I can begin my *please-don't-feel-sorry-for-me* rant.

"Please, Maddie," he begs. His eyes are fixed on mine, his shoulders hunched a little.

"Okay," I agree, not in the mood to belabor the request any longer. If he wants to sit in a truck next to me for fourteen hours while I listen to books, then so be it.

"We leave on Sunday," I tell him, turning to walk back into the reception hall, but then his hand is on mine, gently turning me back around to face him.

"I wanted to tell you I didn't mean for it to end like it did. I didn't want it to be permanent," Jack says, his face so close to mine I can smell the peppermint on his breath. He looks like he might kiss me, like he wants to kiss me, but for the first time, I don't want him to.

"Okay," I say, and I turn back around and walk away.

Chapter 13

In a rented moving truck filled to the brim with all of Sarah's possessions, I pull up to Jack's condo complex just after dawn on Sunday morning. Mike's brothers loaded it last night, occupying every square inch of the back with furniture, clothes, toys, dishes, and miscellaneous sentimental items.

"How do you plan on fitting all of this stuff into your parents' condo?" I asked her, as we sorted through everything she owned a few days earlier, organizing it into three piles: keep, donate, and throw away.

"My dad is renting me one of those storage lockers in Florida," she told me, "until I can figure out what I need to hold on to and what I'm willing to part with."

And it actually makes a lot of sense. How can you make decisions about what parts of your past to keep when you are in the thralls of grief? I can just imagine Sarah dropping off boxes to Goodwill full of things she never thought she'd need again. But then, on a pensive, rainy morning, she'll think of something small, a coffee mug perhaps. One she donated. It will be the cup Mike used the morning he proposed, and she'll suddenly want it back, to hold in her hands and remember. She would catch the first flight back to Cincinnati and desperately root through every thrift store in the tristate to try to find it.

I text Jack from the parking lot to let him know I'm here. I'm not interested in going into his place where I know my mind will return to that last night we had together before I was blindsided. Jack must have been ready and waiting because almost as soon as I put the truck in park, he is out the front door, equipped with one of those fancy hiking backpacks that probably cost a couple hundred bucks at REI. He has on a buffalo plaid flannel hanging open over a white t-shirt and dark denim jeans. I wish I wasn't so attracted to him. It would make the next day and a half of driving much easier.

As he walks towards me, I can't help but wish I had declined his offer and done this drive alone. At least then, there would be no pressure to talk about the way we ended things. I'm not up for hashing out the past right now. I need to keep this drive light. No tears.

I'm in joggers and an old New Found Glory t-shirt from high school with no makeup and natural hair, which for me means a frizzy, unkempt mane on top of my head. I throw it into a messy bun and then turn down the volume of the pop-punk I've been playing unnecessarily loud. Blasting music in the car still makes me feel like a newly licensed teenager rocking out on her first solo drive. I craved that sense of innocence again when I hopped in this moving truck this morning.

Jack steps up into the passenger side, and upon hearing Something Corporate playing through the speakers, the first thing he says is, "Woah, blast from the past." Sometimes Jack talks like a nerdy dad, and I can't help but think it's sweet. I give him a small smile and then sing the words to the interlude while he situates himself in the seat, his backpack at his feet.

The song takes me back to fifteen years ago when I wore fishnets to my winter formal. I went with a boy named Andy who painted his thumbnail black and couldn't go to any after-parties because he had Saturday detention the next morning (something about throwing a desk out the window in his math class). I thought he was so cool.

Jack starts laughing at my performance, and I proceed to ask him, deadpan as can be, "What? Am I not a good singer?"

"I didn't say anything like that," he swears, clearly worried that I think I am (and also that I thought he was laughing *at* me). But I don't make him sweat it for too long.

"It's okay. When I was eight, I told my parents I wanted to be a singer, and my mom politely informed me that I'm basically tone deaf and have zero rhythm."

"Woah, tough break. Aren't parents supposed to lie to you about stuff like that? That's what mine did when I told them I wanted to be in the NBA."

"Hell no. Parents are supposed to make sure you don't end up on the audition episodes of *American Idol* completely embarrassing yourself on national television."

"Well, my mom must have missed that memo, along with a bunch of others." He flashes me a playful smile. "So, do you want to take the first leg, or should I?"

"I'll take it. I'm already behind the wheel, and to be honest, I'm not great at being a passenger." I shift the truck into reverse and pull out of his complex parking lot and onto the street. The directions to Florida from Ohio are about as simple as directions get. Basically, find 75 South, and then keep driving for approximately nine hundred and seventy miles.

Tension hangs in the air as neither of us speaks, and I try to ignore it. I think Jack does too. We're both pretending everything is fine, that there wasn't a six-month hiatus from speaking to one another. I don't necessarily *want* to have a normal, casual conversation with Jack the way friends do, but I realize if I choose to continue to give him the silent treatment, this is going to be a very, very long road trip.

"So why aren't you a good passenger?" Jack finally asks, and I'm thankful he broke the silence.

"When I was in the first grade, I rode the bus for exactly one week, and I threw up every single day. The worst part was when the driver hit the brakes to stop at a red light and then accelerated again, all of the puke slid down the floor to the seats behind me, getting all over everyone's shoes and backpacks. By the end of the week, all the kids knew to keep their bags on their laps and lift their feet at stoplights and stop signs."

Both of Jack's hands cover his mouth. "That sounds… traumatizing. How long have you been in therapy for it?"

"I still have nightmares." I laugh. "So as my road trip partner for the next two days, you should know I get major motion sickness if I'm in the back seat of a vehicle for a long ride or if I try to focus on something other than looking out the window, like reading or staring at my phone. Basically, the only surefire way I won't get carsick is to drive, so I'm going to stay right here until I can't anymore." My hands grip the wheel at ten and two.

"Alrighty then, I guess I better get comfortable over here." Jack adjusts his position in the passenger seat and pulls a giant hardcover book from his backpack along with a gallon-sized bag full of snacks.

"Trail mix?" he asks, holding the open bag out for me.

"I'm good," I say. He grabs a fistful for himself before closing up the bag and stuffing it back into his backpack.

"What are you reading?" I ask him, catching a glimpse of the massive book on his lap. It reminds me of one of those print copies of encyclopedias I used to look through in my elementary school library.

"*IQ84,*" he says. "The only Murakami title I've yet to read. Never had the time."

"You were just waiting for a really long road trip where you didn't have to drive?" I joke.

"Well, the road trip was a happy accident. It's Xavier's spring break this week, and this has been on my to-do list for far too long."

"Ah." His immediate offer at the funeral to take this trip with me finally makes sense. "I was wondering how you were able to take the time off work to do this with me."

He opens the front cover and lets his gaze rest on the title page. "Have you ever read any Murakami?"

"Only his nonfiction one about running," I reply. "I listened to the audiobook of it when I was training for a half marathon a few years back, but I haven't read one of his novels. Isn't he obsessed with cats or something? I think he's a little too *out there* for me, if that makes any sense."

"I'm not usually into surrealism either," Jack says, "but Murakami, man, the guy's a genius. *Kafka on the Shore,* read that one if you only ever read one of his. It'll change your life if you let it." I make a mental note to order the book when we return home. Whether I like Jack or not, I'll always trust his book recommendations.

Once we're on the freeway heading south, there is nothing but highway signs and other cars to look at for the foreseeable future. I put the windows up and opt for air conditioning because even though the temperature outside is mild, the scent of fresh morning air has now been replaced by the smell of rotten egg and pollution.

Jack must sense my hesitation to get too deep into a conversation because his chattiness dissolves into quiet. The only sounds for the next fifteen miles are the reverberation of the engine and the occasional rattle of the contents in the back when I drive over an unavoidable pothole. That is, until I get out of my head for long enough to realize there's no music on, so I turn the volume back up.

"Brand New," Jack says, recognizing the song on my road trip playlist. I threw one together in case our dynamic didn't seem fitting to listen to an audiobook together, and I'm glad I did.

"Did you listen to them back in the day?" I say, and I immediately cringe. God, now I sound like a nerdy dad. *Back in the day?* Is that even a phrase people still say?

"Not really, but I had some friends who did. Too much angry breakup music for me. I never had a breakup, remember?" He smirks, and his comment only serves to irritate me. I don't really know what point he's trying to make here.

"Yeah, I do remember." My jaw is clenched tight and my eyes are on the road, with my right hand on the top of the steering wheel and my left hand resting on my lap. Over the course of the next thirty or so miles, I get lost in my playlist. Dashboard Confessional, The Postal Service, Taking Back Sunday, each song transporting me back to my bedroom in my parents' house where I would lie on my back for hours at a time, staring at the glow-in-the-dark stars on my ceiling and thinking about boys who made me cry and didn't care.

Jack doesn't know that over the past two seasons, a part of me has changed from the girl he knew in the summer, the girl who would dive headfirst into a relationship with him, lifejacket or not, if he said the word. I recognized this change in myself in the winter when I watched my mother make her mental notes, write in her journal, and kiss my dad on the forehead when his eyes looked empty. I felt the change when I witnessed Sarah spend every second caring for her children and her dying husband, torn by the people she loved most in the opposite directions of life and death. I saw the change when I stopped caring about finding someone to spend my life with, no longer concerned with dating, now content and even comforted by the time alone with only myself to worry about.

When I glance over at Jack now, taking my eyes off the road for a split second to see him so deep in his book he doesn't even notice me looking at him, his pointer finger resting on his bottom lip the way it often does when he reads, I don't feel the way I used to. I don't have that yearning to know him on a level no one else does or ever will. There's no denying my attraction to him. I still think of his perfectly toned chest and arms with no shirt on and the way his scruffy face felt against my skin. I suppose you can't erase physical attraction. It's just science. But the emotions, the act of falling in love, the intention and everything that comes with it, you can stop that. I can stop myself from loving him. It's not because of my pride or the fact that Jack ended things in the fall but because I don't want that for myself anymore.

My mom suffers every single day as she watches Dad slowly slip from her grasp, from his own consciousness. She can't do anything but stand by as he becomes someone entirely different, a man who we sometimes can't even recognize. Then there's Sarah, who endured a loss so great, she'll never fully recover. While the pain may lessen with time, turning from an electric shock to a dull blade, she will always feel that agony. She'll feel it every night when she goes to sleep alone. And years from now, when she wishes Mike were there to watch Ace play in his first baseball game or see Atlas's first dance recital, Sarah will disguise her aching heart with a smile for her kids, saying, "Daddy would have loved this," but she will still hurt so badly. This is what love does to people. It makes them miserable.

Chapter 14

Right outside Richmond, Kentucky, only about two hours into our trip, I see brake lights and a long, stagnant row of cars ahead. I instinctively slam on the brakes of the U-Haul, realizing this truck won't stop as fast as the Subaru I'm used to driving. My right arm stretches out in front of Jack's chest so he doesn't jerk forward, and I get flashbacks to my mom dramatically doing the same exact thing every time she had to hit the brakes in her boxy purple minivan. The one she purchased despite only having one child because she'd hoped there would eventually be more.

With the jolt of the truck coming to an abrupt stop, Jack's head bounces up, looking away from his book for the first time in about an hour. There is an endless line of cars in front of us filling three lanes of highway for as far as we can see, traffic completely stalled. No one is moving. A guy in sporty sunglasses and a Ralph Lauren polo even gets out of his car to walk his energetic Labrador on a leash up and down the shoulder of the highway.

"Well, that's not a good sign," Jack says, giving a small wave to the guy as he passes by.

"What should we do?" I ask, dreading the inevitable stop-and-go traffic, which only exacerbates my car sickness.

"Let me see if I can figure out what's going on." Jack pulls his phone from his backpack pocket and opens up a traffic app. In a matter of seconds, he is zooming in on a road map, one with a seemingly endless red line indicating the stopped traffic. This is the first time he has picked up his phone since we have been in the car. There are not very many people today, especially under the age of forty, who can go more than thirty minutes without checking work emails or text messages. Just as I've suspected, Jack is an old soul through and through.

"It says here there's a forty-minute delay. Oh, wait, now it's forty-five minutes," he says.

"Grrreeeaaattt." I roll my eyes, a bad habit I've never been able to completely rid myself of despite Dad's incessant warnings that eye-rolling is akin to gum chewing and fingernail biting.

Jack continues examining the map. "But look, there's a detour we can take. It could save us some time if we get off at the next exit." I sense a little hope in his voice as he points to an alternate route on the map, one with squiggly lines like a snake.

I let out a small sigh. "That looks like one of those one-lane backcountry roads. I can't drive those."

"You *can't* drive them?" He's wondering what makes them any different than a freeway.

"Nope." I shake my head. "I get nervous on the curves,

so I drive slow, and then before I know it, I have a line of pickup trucks riding my ass, irritated that I'm a scaredy-cat driver. They'll all be honking their horns and cutting us off, and, yeah, it's bad."

"Why don't we trade seats? I'll drive," he suggests.

In spite of my apprehension for relinquishing the sense of control I have from the driver's seat, I agree Jack should take over. My hope is we'll be able to continue straight through to Florida without having to stop anywhere to sleep tonight, but this traffic has the potential to put a wrench in my plans.

"So, how do we do this? Get off at the exit and switch seats?" I ask.

"That, or we could switch right here. I mean, it's not like we're going anywhere."

"Okay, then." I put the truck in park and hop out onto the freeway at the same time Jack does. The road vibrates under my feet, and we awkwardly shimmy past one another in front of the truck. Jack smiles at me and does a little wiggle of his arms asking if I, "Wanna dance?" My cheeks flush as I pass him without a reply. I pull myself up into the passenger seat and buckle my seatbelt. Jack adjusts the seat and mirrors to make up for our height difference before leaning over me to retrieve his sunglasses from the front pocket of his bag, which is now at my feet.

"Let's rock 'n' roll," he says as he slides them over his ears and shifts the truck into drive.

I push my sunglasses to the top of my head. "Has anyone ever told you that you talk like one of those midwestern sitcom dads sometimes?"

Jack starts laughing so hard he throws his head back and holds his stomach. When he finally catches his breath, he replies, "No. No one has ever said that to me."

"Well, you do," I say, a smirk on my face, admittedly proud I was able to make him laugh like that.

We are in the far left lane of a three-lane highway, but it takes Jack no time at all to maneuver the truck in the small spaces between slow-moving traffic and make his way over to the right lane. He is proving to be the kind of driver I usually can't stand. The driver who slips into the spaces cautious drivers like me leave in front of us for safety, not so impatient assholes like him can weave their cars in and out of traffic. But, I am actually grateful for his reckless driving right now because the last thing I want to do is sit on this highway for what is, according to the app, now a sixty-minute delay. We make it to the exit ramp way faster than we would have if I were the one driving.

"Take a left off the exit, and then you're going to take a right at the second stoplight," I tell him, consulting the app on his phone.

At the end of the exit ramp, there are two gas stations on either side of the road, though one of them appears to be vacant. A rundown, one-story motel boasting rooms for $49.99 a night along with a restaurant attached that is simply called "Restaurant" sits next to one of the gas stations. The final attraction this exit has to offer is a sex shop, and the fact that there are cars in the parking lot on this sunny Sunday morning grosses me out. I can't help but notice there is a towering billboard right next to the freeway which seemingly looks over this exit. The billboard is black, with huge, bold white letters that read, "HELL IS REAL."

I act as Jack's copilot, helping him navigate through the next five minutes of multiple turns down winding roads, a half-mile on one, a quarter-mile up another, leading us deep into the country. I start to wonder whether this detour is really going to be worth it if we end up lost in the middle of nowhere with no cell phone service to find our way out. However, Jack assures me it's for the best.

"Road trips are so much better this way!" he says excitedly once we are finally on a long stretch of road, cornfields on either side of us and not another car in sight.

"Road trips are better when there's a lot of traffic that makes the trip way longer than anticipated?" I ask.

"They're better when you're not stuck on the highway the entire time staring at white lines on the road and trying not to get pissed off at every car that's going too slow or too fast," Jack clarifies. "I like this stuff." He gestures to the miles of fields and farms ahead of us.

"I like seeing the land, the calmness of the rural roads, and seeing houses like that..." He points to a gorgeous two-story, white farmhouse surrounded by green pastures. There are horses enclosed in a split rail fence on one side of the home and a red barn out of a storybook on the other side. "...next to houses like that." Now, he points to the other side of the road, where there are three neglected shacks right next to each other with wrecked cars in the front yard. They all look like they belong in a junkyard. A barking pit bull is chained to the tree, and an overweight man with leathery skin smokes a cigarette on the porch.

I understand what he means. I recall road trips with my parents as a kid, imagining what kind of people lived in the houses we saw. *Who can possibly live in this tiny cottage on the side of a mountain or in a trailer on the bank of a river?* I would wonder. *Are there kids? How far away is their school? How many students could possibly attend a school in an area so remote? And how far away is the grocery store? Do they have to keep coolers with ice packs in their trunks so their ice cream doesn't melt?* I forgot about that game I used to play until now.

"Do you think you could live somewhere like this? The kind of place where you say things like, *I'm going into town,* when you are actually just going to fill up your gas tank or to the grocery store?" Jack asks.

"With no neighbors and only one restaurant within driving distance? Yes, without question. But I'll need a chicken coop, a cow, and a riding lawnmower." The idea of it excites me.

When I was in high school, I imagined my adult life in the big city, New York or Chicago, working in a high-rise office building and being so busy I couldn't think straight. That was my dream when I applied to Fordham and Vassar and the University of Chicago, but then my parents suggested the University of Cincinnati as a more economical decision. They encouraged saving big-city life for graduate school or my first career. I wanted my life to be like Anne Hathaway's in *The Devil Wears Prada.* However, at the ripe age of eighteen and as an only child completely pampered by my loving parents, I also couldn't imagine getting dropped off in New York in August and not seeing Mom and Dad again until Thanksgiving. So, I took their advice.

I'm thankful I did because after a few weeks of dorm life at UC, I realized I am much more of a homebody than I ever knew. It's easy to daydream about a completely different life, but to live it isn't quite the same. I got my bachelor's degree and started my entry-level office job, but after a few months of cubicle life, I was so grateful my parents helped me make the decision to stay in Cincinnati for college. Now, big-city life was the last thing I wanted. Instead, I dreamed of a quiet existence in a big white house on several acres of land. Perhaps my parents knew me better than I knew myself. I think all good parents do.

"I could live out in the country too," Jack says. "I would read and write and walk around the house naked."

My eyebrows raise as I peer over at him. "You know, you either have a naked window neighbor, or you *are* the naked window neighbor."

"I am most definitely the naked window neighbor," he confesses. "Look at that, you're learning new things about me. I bet you're happy I invited myself to come along."

"Ecstatic," I reply sarcastically, even though I have to admit, this is better than being in my head contemplating all of the sad things I'd be bound to think about if I were alone.

Jack's smile fades, looking more serious as he gazes at the road ahead. "I really have missed you, Maddie. The only reason I haven't called you all this time is because you told me not to, and I wanted to respect that. I meant it when I said I didn't mean for any of it to be like this."

I don't know what I'm supposed to feel when he says he misses me. My immediate thought is that he must just be lonely. "I appreciate you respecting my wishes," I reply, and I leave it at that.

Jack looks over at me briefly and then moves his eyes back to the road. "I wasn't completely honest with you, and I want to come clean." My stomach jumps a little, like when you drive too fast down a steep hill. He clears his throat and then continues, "It's true that my new position was stressing me out. That wasn't a lie or anything, but I was also scared. I've never let myself get romantically involved with someone because I was afraid of all the bad things that might happen, of all of the ways I would be limited or my life would change into something I never wanted it to be. But then you came along, this perfect, beautiful person who makes me laugh and makes me think, and I couldn't help but start to fall for you. And that scared the shit out of me, so I ended it before I became this other person I didn't recognize anymore."

I shift in my seat. He's not telling me anything I didn't know. I could feel Jack falling for me, the same way I was falling for him. But he ended it before either of us could say it out loud or see what came of it. And maybe that's why it hurt so bad when it was all suddenly over. In hindsight though, he spared both of us when he ended it in the fall. It would have been more painful to lose him if it would have gone on any longer. A nasty breakup, a horrible accident, a debilitating disease, I can count a million ways it could have gone worse the longer we stayed together.

It's impossible to pick up where we left off. Everything is different now. *I'm different now.* How do I explain I don't feel the same way I used to about love, that the risk isn't worth the reward? The pain and the struggle and the inevitable loss aren't things I'm sure I can emotionally deal with. I see Mom and Sarah, and I don't know that I can be as strong as them or that I even want to try to be. So, instead of attempting to explain this to Jack in a way that it makes sense, in a way that doesn't make me look like the same coward I thought he was, I take the easy way out.

"I'm seeing someone," I say, and then I watch the hope drain from his face, realizing he thought he might win me back on this road trip. That's the reason he came after all, the reason he offered to spend his hard-earned spring break in a U-Haul truck. To try to get me back.

Jack and I don't speak for a while. My lie lingers in the air, and the radio fills the silence. The off-freeway detour takes longer than I imagined it would, and I'm anxious to get back on track. When we finally make it to the highway again, we are greeted by a sign that reads, "Tennessee, the Volunteer State, Welcomes You."

I close my eyes and place headphones in my ears. It's difficult to pay attention to my audiobook at all because I'm trying not to get sick and also weighing whether the lie I told Jack was a bad idea. *Should I have just been honest with him?* I could have simply told him I want to focus on my career, traveling, experiences, and being comfortable doing all of those things alone. He would have to understand that, right? In fact, that is almost exactly what he told me he wanted a year ago.

I try to think it all through, but I keep getting distracted because the inside of the truck's cab is sticky and hot even though we have the air conditioning set to sixty-eight degrees. I periodically put my window down a couple of inches to get some fresh air, wondering if I'm having a hot flash or if something is wrong with the truck.

The stifling heat finally becomes too much. "Are you hot!?" I ask Jack, almost desperately. It's the first thing we've said to each other in an hour.

"I am. It's like a sauna in here." I can see the sweat beads on Jack's upper lip and forehead. "I think there's something up with the air conditioning. It keeps going in and out. It feels good, and then it feels bad. Really bad. Plus, I'm getting hungry. Should we stop for food?"

I nod. "I think I'm always hungry." I was originally hoping to grab fast food and eat in the truck so we could reach our destination faster, but I need to get out of this muggy sweatbox if only for a thirty-minute meal.

I pull on the neckline of my shirt, dying to get out. It's getting worse by the second. "Let's stop at the next exit," I say.

We both look to the blue highway sign to our right with only one restaurant option. "Waffle House it is," Jack says.

Chapter 15

Jack parks at the end of the lot outside Waffle House next to a blue Ford pickup truck that looks like it's half-rust. We walk side by side past a wrinkly woman smoking a cigarette in the signature Waffle House uniform, a blue button-down with a full black apron, both of which display the yellow logo of the restaurant. She is on the sidewalk near the dumpster, and her age is hard to tell. She could be fifty, or she could be seventy. When we pass her, she gives us a head nod, as if she's telling us, *I'll be right there.*

Jack and I sit at one of the booths on the far end of the galley-style restaurant. There is only one other patron in the place, a brawny trucker-type with a knotted beard sitting at the bar. He has a cup of coffee and an impressive spread of breakfast food in front of him. He shovels the food into his mouth like it's fuel, filling his own tank like he fills his truck. Almost as soon as we sit down, the cigarette-smoking waitress from outside sets two water glasses in front of us and says, "Be right back," already heading in the other direction.

Jack looks to the side and then turns to peek behind him, taking in the familiarity of the restaurant. "Anywhere you go, I swear there's always a Waffle House, and it always looks exactly the same inside."

"I don't think I've been inside a Waffle House since high school. My friends and I used to sit for hours and drink coffee until we felt sick, then we'd order toast with apple butter to soak it all up. Come to think of it, I don't think I've ever actually had any food here except toast."

"Worst waffles you'll ever eat. Best hash browns, though. Get 'em smothered and covered." Jack talks with a little twang in his voice. I can't tell if he's joking or if Waffle House brings out a country side of him I've yet to see.

"You're quite the Waffle House connoisseur," I joke.

"My dad loved it. Every time I came to Cincinnati to visit, he took my sister and me to Waffle House for breakfast at least three times."

"He loved it?" I ask, emphasizing the past tense. "What happened? Did he get food poisoning or something?"

Jack takes a long, slow swig of his water and sets the cup back down. "He died. Five years ago."

My eyes widen at the shock of his statement. "You never told me."

"I know. I don't talk about it." He shrugs and twists the straw wrapper around his finger.

It's not like Jack had to tell me his dad died or that I even had a right to know, but I also would like to think if he was falling for me the way he said he was, he would have revealed something so monumental about his life, about his past.

"Howdy," a voice standing above us interrupts, and I look up from Jack's stoic face to see our waitress. Her entire mouth looks kind of gray. It reminds me of my former boss who used to have a "cigar hobby," as he referred to it. I bought him a nice one every year for Christmas to suck up. Whenever he talked, I could never stop staring at his mouth, which didn't look pink or red like a normal mouth. It was always an odd shade of gray that made me think of what a decaying body might look like.

"My name's Darlene, and I'll be takin' care of y'all today. Can I get you started with some coffee, orange juice, or sweet tea?" She talks like she's reciting a script, like none of these words are her own.

I give Darlene a polite head nod, but I'm still preoccupied with what Jack told me. "Umm, coffee would be great, with some cream please."

"Make that two," Jack adds. I watch the smile lines on his face get deeper when he talks.

"Comin' right up." Darlene heads behind the counter and returns seconds later with a half-empty pot of drip coffee and two mugs. "Where y'all comin' from?" she asks as she pours us each a cup and sets a little saucer of cream between us.

"Ohio," Jack says. "Just passing through."

"Of course you are." Her voice is thick and raspy, and her words come out slow like molasses. "That's all anyone's doin' round these parts, just passin' on through," she adds. Her eyeglasses have grease spots all over the lenses, and I have no idea how she can even see us clearly. I resist the urge to take them off of her face and wipe them with my shirt.

"I saw y'all pull up in a U-Haul. You movin' south?" she asks, and I'm surprised at how curious she sounds. I was a waitress at a breakfast restaurant in high school and never thought to ask any questions to my customers beyond, *How do you like your eggs?* or *Do you want bacon or sausage?*

"No, we're helping a friend move," I say.

"Ain't that nice a y'all." I try to decide if she's actually being nice or if she's milking us for a decent tip. "Well do yas know what you're gonna have?"

Jack looks to me to order first, but I realize I haven't even looked at the menu yet.

"You go, and I'll decide." I scan the convoluted menu, looking for the simplest thing I can find. Jack orders some combo meal that consists of a waffle, eggs, bacon, and hash browns.

"Sounds good to me. I'll take the same," I say, relieved I don't have to look anymore. There are too many options for such simple food.

"Gimme a few minutes," Darlene says, before turning around and yelling, "Ralph, I got one!"

A scruffy, heavy-set man walks through the double doors in the back of the restaurant. His shoulders are hunched over, and he moves at a snail's pace, picking up his metal spatula and practically throwing a handful of shredded potatoes onto the grill as Darlene spouts off our order in restaurant lingo. He's one of those guys who looks slender from the back, but when he turns around, he has an enormous beer gut that hangs over his pants.

"I thought the waffles aren't any good?" I say to Jack.

"They're not." He gives me a half-smile and leans back, extending one arm along the top of the booth.

Before we know it, our food is sprawled out in front of us on way too many dishes. My bacon is on a separate plate from my eggs which is on a separate plate from my waffle. "Why didn't they put it all on one plate?"

Jack shakes salt onto his eggs. "That's not the Waffle House way, my friend."

To my surprise, the food tastes better than I ever imagined Waffle House food could taste. It's salty and greasy, and I wonder where it's been for every hangover I've ever had.

"This," I say to Jack between mouthfuls, pointing to my plate with the fork clutched in my hand. "Am I just hungry, or is this really good?"

"Probably a little bit of both. I think it's good though." He smiles as he douses his waffle in imitation maple syrup. "It tastes like my childhood."

I smear the enormous scoop of butter over my waffle. "I'm sorry about your dad," I say, and his smile dissipates. "There I was, whining to you about my own problems, and I never asked about yours."

"You weren't whining, Maddie. You know it's okay to have people to talk to about the hard stuff in your life, right? That's a good thing. I've never been good at that, which is why I never mentioned my dad's death." Jack takes a bite, syrup dripping from his fork. He washes it down with the burnt coffee.

"So what happened, if you don't mind me asking?" I take a drink from my mug and add, "This coffee sucks by the way."

"It's exceptionally bad coffee," Jack agrees. "And, my dad drank himself to death." He says it so casually, the way you might say, *See you at seven,* like it's just any other thing to say.

My mouth opens, like I want to speak, but I'm speechless as I take in his words.

Jack sets his fork on his plate and leans back into the booth. "After my mom left, he was a mess. He wanted her to stay. I remember him telling her he would do anything she wanted if she would stay, but her mind was made up. She didn't give a shit about him at that point."

"Why not? Did something happen?"

"I never fully figured that out." He softly shakes his head. "She said Dad never cheated or hit her or anything. I think my mom is just selfish, to be honest. She always has been. If it's not about her, she doesn't care." Jack holds on to the handle of his coffee mug but leaves it resting on the table as he talks. "After she moved my sister and me out west, my dad was alone for a long time. When we would visit, he always asked about her, and he seemed hopeful that maybe she'd come back someday, that we all would come back, and we could be a family again. But I knew that would never happen. Mom never even mentioned him unless it involved discussing when we would go visit him next. I never had the heart to break it to him that we weren't ever coming back."

Jack doesn't seem to be overtly sad when he tells me all this, just a little solemn, the way you tell a story that happened a long time ago. One you've had a lot of time to let settle in and grapple with, so now it's merely a retelling.

"We didn't see Dad often, but I do remember noticing there was more alcohol around when we'd visit. More beer in the fridge and bottles of liquor on the counter. I don't remember him ever drinking around us, but I do recall seeing it. That was the extent of it though. I noticed it was there." Jack's eyes aren't focused on me. They rest on the wall behind me, like he's daydreaming. "After a few years, he met a nice lady named Allison. She wasn't as beautiful as my mom, but she was really nice, and she had two sons of her own. She and Dad got married, and I went to the wedding. He loved to talk about her on the phone to me, about what a great cook she was and how she kept the house so clean, and she was always making different crafts. He even set up a whole little craft room for her. But she died in a car accident."

"Oh my god." My palm instinctively covers my mouth.

"They were driving home from seeing a band play, some band of old dudes my dad knew who were playing at this restaurant on the river. Their car got hit by a drunk driver, and she died."

"That's so awful, Jack. I don't even know what to say."

"Dad said it was his fault because he convinced her to come with him to the show. And after that, I could tell he was drunk whenever we talked. His speech was slurred and slow, and he always sounded like he was falling asleep. When I saw him after that, he didn't hide the drinking either. He always had a beer or some mixed drink in his hands, and so when I got the call that his liver was failing, that he was in the hospital, I wasn't surprised. I was mainly just sad I wasn't around more, that I didn't get to know him as well as I should have."

"That's not your fault, Jack." I reach across the table and rest my fingers on his forearm. "You weren't the one who chose to leave. You were only a kid when you left."

"You're right." He looks down at his plate. "But at some point, I became an adult, one who could make my own decisions, and I didn't see him or call him like I should have. I never thought much about calling him until it was too late, and now I think about it all the time."

"What was his name?"

He looks back up at me. "Everett. Everett Keller."

Conversations like these, the tough ones that leave me speechless, seem to come along more often with each passing year. When I was younger, I'd hear people say that life is hard, but it never really resonated with me. Life hadn't been so hard for me. School always came pretty easily. I wasn't popular by any means, but I always had a few friends to eat lunch with and got invited to sleepovers on the weekends. And I was lucky enough to have the kind of doting parents who never missed a game, a show, or even a practice. Hell, I'm still one of the only people I know whose parents are still married to each other. Sure, bad things happened from time to time but nothing that changed me entirely or made me question anything about the way I lived my life.

I remember my high school English teacher assigning us a personal narrative to write. "Tell me about something that happened in your life that changed you," she had said. "And no writing about grandparent deaths or parents getting divorced. Those may have impacted you, but I want you to think deeper than that. What is something that's happened to you that not everyone else has experienced?" I recall thinking that my parents aren't divorced, and I've never experienced the death of a grandparent or even been to a funeral for anyone other than my fifth-grade teacher, Mrs. Benson, who had breast cancer. I felt guilty that I had it so easy, and I worried something bad would happen soon. It was bound to be my turn to experience turmoil. That's when I started saving heads-up pennies and wishing on stars, an attempt to have some control over the things I might not be able to control. I don't know how I would have survived an upbringing like Jack's. That takes a kind of strength I don't have.

Darlene walks by our table, and instead of asking how our food tastes, she places a quarter in front of each of us.

"Have at it," she says, nodding to the jukebox against the windows, parallel to the bar stools. "I need some tunes to make this shift go by a lil faster," she adds with a wink.

"You first," I say to Jack.

"You don't have to tell me twice." He scoots out of the booth and walks over to the antiquated jukebox, definitely not one of those new digital ones. I can hear Jack's Converse sneakers sticking to the floor with each step he takes. He peruses the catalog, leaning against the curved glass, taking his sweet time considering the options.

When it seems like he might never pick a song, I call to him, "Just go with your gut."

"You might regret telling me that," he says, laughing but never turning his gaze from the jukebox. I can see he is torn. After all, having to choose a single song can say a lot about you. It's like choosing an anthem.

A few minutes later, he walks back to the table as I hear the opening chords to *Glycerine* by Bush. "First song I ever learned to play on guitar," he says, sitting back down. "I don't think they've updated that thing in twenty years by the way." He lifts his fork from his plate and begins eating again. All that's left are his untouched hash browns. He's one of those people who saves the best thing on his plate for last.

"I didn't know you played guitar. This is turning out to be a very revealing Waffle House trip."

"I'll have you know you are talking to one of the members of the first runner-up in the 2007 Sedona Battle of the Bands." He pulls on the collar of his flannel shirt. "We lost to these nerdy prep school dudes who literally just pressed a button on a keyboard and then did some silly rap over the music. They weren't even a real band."

"You don't sound bitter at all."

"Not nearly as bitter as you are about, what was that guy's name who made you spell Saturday with an *O*?"

"You're hilarious, you know that?" I roll my eyes, but I'm laughing on the inside. He got me there.

When Jack's song is almost over, I saunter over to the jukebox. I peek back at him and notice he is softly singing the lyrics to himself, his eyes looking to my empty seat on the other side of the table. I watch him until the song ends, and silence washes over the restaurant.

"What do you think I'm going to pick?" I call to him when he turns his head to catch my glance.

"I *know* what you're going to pick," he says, confidently.

"Oh you do, do you?"

"I most definitely do." He nods.

"Care to make a bet?" I ask, walking back towards the table now.

"Sure thing. I need my *Scrabble* revenge. What's the bet?" He wipes his hand on his napkin and crumbles it onto his empty plate.

"If I win," I say, "you have to confess your most embarrassing moment to me. You already know mine, puking on the bus obviously, and I could use a good laugh."

"Okay, but *when* I win, you have to make a whole pan of your delicious tiramisu for me when we get back home. No funny business when you pick your song though. Go with your gut." He repeats the same words I said to him. I nod in agreement. Then, he stretches his arm out, and I shake his hand with a firm grip.

"But how will I know—" I begin to ask.

But Jack calls out, "Darlene, can I please borrow your pen?"

"No problem, honey," she says, tossing it to him from two booths behind us where she is sitting and eating a waffle of her own.

Jack jots something down on a napkin, carefully shielding the letters with his hands and folding it up so I can't see. "Now you know I can't cheat."

I return to the jukebox and take a quick look through the twenty or so pages of music. There's quite a variety ranging from Frank Sinatra to Elvis Presley to Britney Spears, but Jack is right, nothing after 2005 or so. When I see it, I know. This song makes me think of walking through the mall with Sarah at fourteen years old, buying cheap jewelry at Claire's that turned our skin green, daring one another to walk to the back of Spencer's where the sex toys were.

Standing in front of the jukebox and listening to the first verse of my song, *Mr. Brightside* by The Killers, I peer out the window and daydream of a time when life was so much more simple than it is now. This song came out the year I had my first French kiss. His name was Scott, and he went to one of the all-boys schools near mine. I didn't know him all that well, but I liked that I didn't have to be self-conscious about the whole thing, that my first kiss wasn't with a boy I was in love with. The same night, I poured gin from the back of my parents' liquor cabinet into a water bottle and took it to a party. I was too scared to have more than a few sips, but I felt so guilty over the whole thing, I've never had gin again to this day.

I turn my glance to see Jack's head dropped down in disappointment, and I return to the table and take my seat across from him.

"I was so wrong," he says, pushing the folded napkin over to me. I open it and see, *I Want It That Way* BSB, scribbled in messy letters.

"Hey, I love that song too," I tell him.

"It's a classic," he says, like he is convinced it is impossible not to like that song. And come to think of it, I don't think I have ever met anyone who doesn't.

By the last verse, a frumpy old man pulls up in a light blue Buick LeSabre and shuffles into the restaurant. I would guess he's in his eighties. He has on gray dress pants with a striped button-down shirt, but the buttons are all messed up. A few of them are in the wrong holes, leaving these awkward lumps of fabric down his chest and portly belly. The top of his head is bald with freckles, but the white horseshoe of hair that connects his ears is disheveled, poking out every which way. All I want to do is go up to him and fix his shirt and comb his hair.

"I think I'm going to cry," I whisper.

"Why?" Jack asks, confused.

"Old people make me weak. I think they are just the cutest

and the sweetest, and when I see them out alone, I want to cry. I think if I didn't do what I do, recipes and blogging, I would work in a nursing home. I would be an emotional mess, but I think I might love it."

"But why do you want to cry?" he asks, still not understanding.

"Because I start to get all in my head about how they are probably widows or widowers with grown kids and grandkids who don't visit enough, and this outing, whatever it is, is probably the highlight of their day. Maybe even their week. The whole thing is even worse when they're alone like he is."

Darlene walks over to the old man, and I hear him talk to her, chuckling, a couple of teeth missing and a thick accent, German maybe. They talk back and forth for a minute, and then she looks to the cook, who is sitting now in the same booth where Darlene was eating her waffle. His eyes are glued to his phone screen.

"The usual," Darlene says, and the cook looks up and nods but waits another couple minutes before actually getting up from his seat.

I am watching so intently, I almost forget Jack is there, until I notice him staring at me out of the corner of my eye. "What are you looking at?"

"Just you," he says, gently and without explanation.

A few seconds later, Darlene slips to the employee-only back of the restaurant briefly and emerges with a balloon that says *Happy Birthday* along with a small, round cake that looks like she picked it up from the grocery store. A single candle is lit in the center. She brings it over to the old man's table, cupping the flame with her palm, and sets the cake in front of him.

She ties the balloon to the napkin dispenser. His eyes light up, and he claps his hands together, a giant grin across his face.

"Oh, no," I say to Jack or maybe to myself. "Now I think I really might cry. I'm not trying to turn into an emotional mess in the middle of Waffle House. I'm ready when you are." I place my napkin onto one of my empty plates, only smears of syrup remaining. Jack takes the check sitting on the end of our table and says, "On me."

"You don't have to do that," I protest, honestly not wanting him to pay for my meal. This isn't a date, and I don't want him to think I expect this from him.

"I insist," he says, standing and walking to the register with the check. I don't argue, but instead, I tell myself I'll pay for the next meal we have to grab.

I use the restroom, and when I walk back out, I notice Jack is still at the register talking with Darlene. He sees me approach, and says, "Are you ready?" I nod. Jack gives Darlene one of those goodbye head tilts without actually saying the words, the one handsome men always do in the movies. Then, we walk out together.

"My turn." I snatch the keys from his hands and climb up into the driver's seat.

"What were you guys talking about?" I'm being nosy, but I can't help but be curious. It did seem like they were deep in a conversation.

"It was nothing."

"Was it about the old man?" I ask, unable to let it go.

"I just told her I wanted to pay for his food. No big deal." I can tell he didn't want to tell me. He wanted it to be some secret. I think it's so sweet, and his kind gesture is enough to put my emotional state over the edge where it's already sitting, but I hold it together for the sake of Jack and the long drive we have ahead of us.

"You really make it hard not to like you," I say.

"I'm happy to hear that."

Chapter 16

A few hours later, outside of Atlanta, we are cozy in the cab of the truck. Well, Jack is at least, reading his book with a cute little light that clips onto the cover and arches over the page. I, on the other hand, am growing increasingly tense in the driver's seat as I watch the sky turn dark in the distance. Soon, thunder rumbles causing the truck to vibrate with its roar. Torrential rain begins to pour down from the clouds, and even with the windshield wipers on high speed, I can barely see a few yards in front of me.

"Can we switch?" I ask Jack, gripping the steering wheel so tight my knuckles are white. "I hate driving in the rain. I'm like an old woman. Sorry for being so damn difficult."

"Sure." Jack is unbothered by my request, closing his book and shoving it into his backpack. "Turn your flashers on, and pull over to the shoulder."

We decide to climb over one another instead of getting out of the truck cab so neither of us has to get drenched. At one point, his hands are on my waist and mine on his thighs, and the awkwardness is only heightened by the lightning bolt I feel inside when he touches me, the fact that I want him to keep touching me. *It's not love. It's science. A chemical reaction.* That's what I tell myself.

I like watching him drive, calm and collected, confident in his complete control of this enormous vehicle. The opposite of how I felt in the same seat minutes prior, like a scared puppy afraid of the storm.

"Hopefully we just drive through it, and it's over soon." Jack sees I'm uneasy, though much better now that I am not the one behind the wheel. The rain is relentless, pounding on the windows, loud and wild. Lightning strikes on all sides of us, and it's evident we are in the center of the storm, moving with it rather than away from it.

It isn't long before my stomach starts to gurgle, and there's a buzzing inside my head I can't seem to drown out with other thoughts. I clench my eyes shut as a sorry attempt to ease the discomfort, but my brain is like a spinning dreidel instead of the stillness I crave. Usually, I open my window and get some fresh air to help when the car sickness starts, but I can't do that now. So, I rock back and forth in my seat, changing positions every few seconds. I bend my knees and sit on my feet. When that doesn't help, I lean my shoulder against the door and rest my head on the windowpane. I sit criss-cross applesauce like a preschooler, but nothing eases the growing wooziness.

"Oh no," Jack says, noticing how restless and fidgety I am. "Do you need me to pull over?"

"It's okay. Just keep driving." My self-imposed deadline for our Florida arrival is running through my head.

"Do you want to switch spots again? Didn't you say you don't get carsick when you drive?"

My hand clutches my forehead as I stare down at my lap. "The rain. I'm nervous driving a vehicle this big as it is, let alone in a downpour. I'll stay where I am." I've turned into an entirely high-maintenance mess of a person I've always prided myself on not being. "I'll be fine," I add a few seconds later, though I worry I won't be. I'm afraid Jack is going to join the long list of people on Bus #4 who have witnessed the very worst of me. Holding back for as long as I can, I breathe in and out slowly and deliberately, going back and forth between opening and closing my eyes because I can't decide which is worse. But there's no end in sight. According to my phone, we have a little less than half of the drive to Fort Myers remaining.

"Hey, uh, Jack..." I hesitate because I don't want to do this, but I have no other choice. "I think I need to get out for a second."

We aren't near an exit, and the highway isn't very crowded, so Jack pulls over right there on the side of the road. My hand is already gripping the door handle before the truck is completely stopped. By the time I jump out of the cab, I'm gagging, trying to stop myself from getting sick until I can at least get out of Jack's line of vision. I run through the overgrown grass to get as far away from the truck, from Jack, as possible. But my body won't let me resist any longer. I start vomiting beneath a Denny's billboard in the pouring rain. The water drops are colder than I would have imagined them to be in the Georgia heat.

I twist my head, glancing behind me to see if Jack is still sitting in the cab of the truck or if he followed me out here. It's too dark and there's so much rain, so I yell to him, "Don't come over here please!" between bursts of vomit. My skin is crawling with those cold, clammy sweats that make me feel like I'm having a hot flash and the chills simultaneously. I have no control as my body empties everything in my stomach onto the ground. The waffles, the hash browns, the coffee. It's all laying there in the grass, unrecognizable now. My body shudders at the taste on my tongue, and just when I think I might be finished, that there's nothing left inside of me, I begin to dry heave, which is almost worse, like I'm convulsing. My abdominal muscles contract and release in painful repetition. I squeeze my eyes shut, and white oblong ovals swim slowly in a black sea.

It feels like forever before I am finally able to stand up straight from my hunched-over position in the long grass. Before I turn around, I wipe my mouth with the back of my hand, inspect my shoes and pants to see if they are covered in vomit, then pull my soaking wet hair back into a ponytail with the spare hair tie I always have wrapped around my wrist. The rain is still falling heavy and fast. I pray Jack stayed in the truck, but when I turn around, I see him through a thick haze of raindrops standing about fifteen yards away with a polka dot umbrella over his head. I instinctively run over to seek safety from the water pellets pummeling me.

"I wanted to come over there and hold your hair back for you." Jack is inches from me now, his clothes and hair still dry. "But I wanted to respect your wishes, so I stayed back here."

So he had heard me yell to him. Thank god he didn't come over there.

"Thank you," I mutter pathetically. All I can think about is how I want to keep distance from his face because of the way I probably smell right now.

"I went ahead and made a reservation on my phone for a hotel tonight while you were… you know… over there. We still have a long way to go, and there's no way you can sit in the truck for that long tonight." Instant relief washes over my body. I desperately wanted to get this drive over in one day without having to stay overnight anywhere, but I know I can't spend any more time in that cab tonight.

"What did I do to deserve a driving buddy like you?" I ask, accepting his proposal. I'm already looking forward to pillows and blankets and getting out of this god-forsaken truck with the broken air conditioning.

"You deserve much better than me." Jack wipes away the rain that falls from my dripping hair onto my cheeks with his hands. He is warm, and I am freezing. His touch sends goosebumps down my arms and legs, like my body knew I wanted him to touch me even though my brain didn't. My reflexes have always been a step ahead of my crowded and often chaotic mind.

Huddled close under the umbrella, we turn and walk back to the truck together. Jack still manages to smell amazing even after spending eight hours in a truck, like dark coffee and shaving cream. I, on the other hand, am a hot ass mess, soaking wet from head to toe, vomit on my breath with rogue remnants likely in my hair. Jack opens my door for me, and I climb back into my seat. He runs around the front of the truck to the driver's side where he closes the umbrella and shakes what water he can off of it before placing it on the floor behind our seats. He climbs in, wet now, though not as soaked as I am.

"I can't believe you thought to bring an umbrella. Did you check the weather or something?"

"No, but I've been on a lot of road trips, and it's one of those things I always wish I'd brought when I forget it." I can tell he's proud he could save the day.

Back in the truck, my body feels much better now that it has been completely emptied of everything other than my organs, but all I can think about is how badly I want to take a long, hot shower and brush my teeth. Every inch of me is self-conscious about the way I smell and look as I sit so close to Jack. He starts the truck and merges back onto the highway, leaving my Waffle House dinner and all of my remaining dignity in the wet grass beneath the billboard.

"I made the reservations with an app on my phone while you were over there, two queen beds in one room. I hope that's okay. The hotel is just an exit away." Jack peeks over at me to gauge how I'm feeling.

I give him a crooked smile. "That's perfect. Thank you so much for thinking of it. I'm so stubborn I would have jumped back in the cab and told you to keep driving if you didn't do that."

"I know you would have. That's why I didn't ask."

It strikes me at this moment that Jack knows me better than I realized. He is able to sense how I will react to certain things, and he's not at all wrong in his predictions. Even though we haven't talked in some time before this trip, I let him in a long time ago. It's not like all of that just disappears. The truth is he knows more about me than most people do. And I know Jack, too. I know that when we get to the hotel, he is going to make decaf coffee with one of those tiny coffee makers they have over the mini-fridge. I know he's going to let me shower first, but then he'll shower too because he always showers at night. He's going to turn on the television because he likes the noise, but he'll sit on the bed and read his book, not paying any attention to what's on the screen.

When Jack pulls into the hotel parking lot, I'm so appreciative he chose a decent place instead of one of those cheap motels where you can rent the rooms by the hour. A decade ago, Ben and I used to go to concerts in cities a couple of hours away, and he would always book us these cheap motel rooms where I couldn't even sleep because I was paranoid about bed bugs and dirty sheets and mysterious stains on the carpet. I would even bring those cheap two-dollar, foam flip-flops to wear in the shower, and then I'd pitch them on the way out. I always wanted to tell Ben I would rather bring a tent and sleep at a campground because then at least I know my own stuff is clean, but I never complained to him about it. I was always too afraid when I was with him that if I did something wrong, said something wrong, he would suddenly stop loving me.

"Let me pay for this," I say to Jack, as I anxiously turn around to grab my duffle bag behind the seat.

"My credit card is already on file. I paid on the app. It's on me, Maddie."

"But this was my trip, and you're here helping me. I insist."

He looks me square in the eyes. "Maddie, I'm a grown-ass man, and I want to pay for this, okay?"

"Okay. Thank you."

Jack checks in on his phone so we get to bypass the front desk, and he can use his phone as a virtual key to get into the room. We are in room 214, his birthday he tells me. I follow him around the corner to an elevator.

"How did I not know your birthday was on Valentine's Day?"

"I guess it never came up. We weren't talking on my birthday." He flashes me a flicker of a smile.

"I feel like that's something I should have known. Do you love or hate having your birthday on Valentine's Day?" I ask, as someone whose birthday is on an incredibly ordinary, not at all special day, though my parents threw me parties every single year. Some of my friends growing up who had siblings only got to have parties every other year, but big annual birthday parties were one of the perks of being an only child.

"Loved it as a kid. We got to have parties at school every year on my birthday, so it always felt special. As an adult, I have to admit it's kind of lame. The restaurants I want to go to are always booked, and friends can't go out because they've got plans with their significant others. I've considered picking a different day to celebrate."

Saturated, my clothes stuck to my body, I plod down the long hallway, our room at the very end of it. While Jack fiddles with his phone trying to figure out how to get in using the app, I stare out the window. It's dark outside, but I can still make out the shadows of construction vehicles and massive mounds of dirt just beyond the hotel parking lot.

When we enter the room, it resembles every other three-star hotel I've spent the night in, only a little more updated than the ones I used to vacation in with my parents as a kid. There are modern light fixtures, fancy textured wallpaper, that sort of thing. It's comforting, the way some things don't change very much because they don't have to.

Jack takes off his shoes, leaving them in the middle of the floor. Then he plops down onto the bed closest to the window. He's a little messy, but I always liked that about him. The way he can be careless in ways I can't. He takes the remote control off of the nightstand between the two beds and turns the television on. Jack looks cozy and comfortable, like he's lounging in his own living room. I, on the other hand, am self-conscious about everything right now, uncomfortable in my own skin.

I set my duffle bag on the other bed, but jittery and awkward, I quickly pick it back up. "I'm going to hop in the shower," I mumble.

Jack nods, and I carry my bag over my shoulder to the bathroom where I spend the next fifteen minutes slathering my body in those little tubes of hotel body wash and shampoo. After my shower, I brush my teeth for quite possibly the longest amount of time I've ever brushed my teeth. Though I don't intend on being as close to Jack again as we were under the umbrella, it's the only way I can try to erase what happened under the Denny's billboard. I throw on a pair of cotton shorts and a tank top, and when I finally leave the bathroom, I feel like a new person.

My hair has only been towel dried. Slightly damp, it settles into these loose waves that look sort of pretty, the way I wish it would always stay. Unfortunately, my natural hair insists on drying into straight-up frizz that looks like I've applied a layer of Aquanet to it. I admire the current state of it in the mirror, making a mental note that I have approximately forty-five minutes of good hair in my future before I need to pull it back, maybe an hour if I'm lucky.

When I finally leave the bathroom, I find Jack sipping on coffee in a paper cup reading his giant Murakami novel with one of those true crime documentaries on in the background. Keith Morrison is narrating the twisted plot of some upper-middle-class suburban mom turned murderer. There's a love triangle. There's *always* a love triangle. Jack doesn't look up until I dig my own book out of my bag and lie on my bed, back against the headboard and legs extended, in prime reading position.

"If you're all finished, I'm going to take a quick shower." Jack sits up so his feet are on the floor. He sets his cup and book on the nightstand.

"I am. Thank you for letting me go first. I feel so much better."

"Good." There's satisfaction in his eyes. "Now rest, because we have to do this all over again tomorrow."

"Don't remind me," I groan.

I open my book and stare at the jumbled words on the page for the next fifteen minutes, never processing what they mean. Instead, I listen to the sounds of Jack's shower, so much more gentle than the pounding rain. The scent of lilacs permeates the room as steam from the bathroom seeps beneath the space where the door meets the floor. The pale lamplight provides the calm I need right now to simply sit and be. By the time I see Jack again, a towel wrapped around his waist, I haven't even turned the page.

"Sorry. I forgot to bring my clothes into the bathroom with me." He pulls a pair of plaid boxers and a plain white t-shirt from his bag and returns to the bathroom to change. I wish this didn't have to be so awkward, but I don't know how it wouldn't be. Two single people who were once romantically involved now sharing a completely platonic hotel room, apologizing for things like wearing only a bath towel in front of the other.

"Are you feeling okay? Are you hungry or anything?" Jack asks when he returns, now fully dressed.

"Yeah, much better now. Sorry about all that. It's been so long since I've been on a road trip like this. I kind of thought maybe I'd outgrown the motion sickness."

"I want you to feel better. That's all I care about." Jack resumes his reading position in bed with his book on his lap.

We sit quietly for a brief moment, but then I turn to him. "By the way, don't think you being all sweet and charming is going to make me forget you have to share your most embarrassing moment with me."

He laughs. "Damnit, I was hoping you would forget about that."

"No way, I can't wait to hear this."

Jack closes his book and scoots down on his bed so he is lying on his side facing me now, his head propped up with his hand.

"Honestly, I don't know if it's that great of a story," he begins, "but I'm still haunted by it. I was in middle school, and I joined the track team. Usually, I played baseball in the spring, but my best friend decided he wanted to do track, so I did too." Jack's eyes light up. They always light up when he tells a story. "The thing is, we never really practiced. We walked around the track, hung out under the bleachers talking to girls, and there were only two coaches for like fifty kids, so no one paid much attention to what we did. On the day of our first meet, I signed up for two events. The first was the two-hundred-meter dash because I figure, hell that's easy, and I'm skinny. Skinny guys can run fast, right? And then shot put. I was most excited about that one because I didn't even have to run. Stand there and throw a ball, how hard could it be?"

"Oh boy…" I say as I tip my cup of water to my lips.

"Let's just say, when I did shot-put, every other dude was twice my size. I couldn't even reach the line where you got on the board. So I literally didn't get a score. My friends were giving me shit about it and everything, but that's not the most embarrassing part."

"This is going to be good."

"Well, when it came time for the two-hundred-meter run, everyone bolted out in front of me, and I didn't realize how slow I was or that I was even slow at all until that very moment, and I panicked." Jack jolts his hands to either side of his head, like he's back in the moment, reliving it. "Those narrow lines got blurry, and my feet got all tangled up. So I tripped and completely face-planted. But then, here's the fucking kicker. I was too embarrassed to admit that I tripped, so when all of these adults started running over to me to see if I was okay, I told them I blacked out, that everything went dark and I didn't know what happened."

I fall forward, clutching my stomach as I laugh.

"So all of the sudden, these EMTs are up in my face checking my vitals right there on the track, holding up the entire meet, and hundreds of people are watching me from the stands to see what happens next. The worst part is I'm pretty sure everyone could see right through my bullshit, but you can't just call a kid a liar when he says he fainted. There's too much liability there, so everyone went along with it."

"I can't believe you ever went back to school after that!" A tear falls down my cheek. I can't remember the last time I cried from laughing so hard.

"I rode the waves of my lie forever," he pronounces confidently. "Even when my friends tried to call me on it. You're actually the first person I've ever admitted it to."

"Wow, I'm incredibly honored." I bring my hand to my chest.

"You should be. You won the bet fair and square, and I'm a man of my word. That's also the last time I put my money on the Backstreet Boys."

"*Fair and square?* You really are Danny Tanner."

Jack tilts his head. "Danny Tanner?"

"Yep, from now on, I'm going to refer to you as a cheesy TV dad every time you use one of those 'dad' phrases like *fair and square*. That's straight out of an episode of *Full House* circa 1989."

Jack immediately begins humming the theme song with a giant grin. One of the things I've missed about him in the time we've spent apart is the way we can tease each other. The way we can call each other out, and we never take it personally.

I think back to a date I went on a few months back. It was with this guy, Noah, the one my friend Taylor set me up with. I told him he had some mannerisms that reminded me of Toby from *The Office,* and *he did.* Noah was soft-spoken, super calm, and wanted to avoid any slightly controversial topic of conversation.

He also had the same hair color and receding hairline as the guy who plays Toby, so to me, it seemed like a fun and light-hearted comparison, not at all malicious. Who doesn't love Toby from *The Office?* But the guy lost it. He turned out to be a very big fan of the show and took complete offense to my joke. Apparently, Noah sees himself as a Jim (he was most definitely *not* a Jim), and then he proceeded to accuse me of calling him "a pansy," and the date was over. I remember thinking of Jack that night when I went home, wishing there were more guys like him who could have the kind of back and forth banter we had.

"I seriously never realized I talk like a middle-aged dad until you said something. How weird is that, to live your whole life without knowing one of your very own quirks?"

"Tell me one of my quirks I don't know about," I say. "I mean, I know I've got to have something weird, unique, whatever you want to call it, about myself that I don't even realize."

While Jack ponders my eccentricities, I brush my hair out from in front of my face where it always seems to find its way. I say a silent prayer that I don't look like one of those Siberian cats with the staticky-looking fur enveloping its entire body. That happens to be exactly what my hair looks like without a blow dryer and straightener, but it is not nearly as cute as a Siberian cat.

"Has anyone ever told you that you have a million different laughs?" Jack asks. He sets his book on the nightstand now, indicating he no longer has any intention of reading. I do the same.

"No," I reply immediately, shaking my head. "I have never heard that in my life. What do you mean?"

"You have a different laugh for every occasion and mood. Sometimes you're unbelievably loud, and it bursts out of you like a balloon just popped. But sometimes, you laugh and there's no noise at all. It's completely silent. I can see you laughing, but I can't hear anything, like you're on mute. And then there's the snort."

"The snort!?"

"Yes, The Snort." He says it like that is now the official name he has given to one of my supposed laughs. "Sometimes you laugh with your nose instead of your mouth, and there's this really cute snorting noise you make. Not like a giant hog or anything. More like one of those little teacup pigs. It's sort of subtle, but it's definitely there. I've never heard anyone laugh like that in my life."

"Sort of subtle!? As in, not at all?" I cover my face with my hands. *How am I a snorter?* And even more importantly, *How did I not know this about myself?*

"You're right. It is very weird to be told something about yourself that you never even had any inkling of before. I seriously have never thought twice about the way I laugh."

Jack's expression gets a little more serious now. "Maddie, please don't change anything about it. I love the way you laugh."

I suppress the flutter of butterfly wings in my stomach, shoving it down deep somewhere I won't be able to find it. A hiding place in my own body even I won't be able to uncover. I'm not interested in butterfly wings anymore.

"I'll try not to," I say.

I don't even know when it happened, but we are both sitting up in our beds now, knees parallel to one another.

We're a nightstand apart. His gaze overtakes me, and I feel the need to come clean. "Listen, I want to be honest with you, because I've always been a person of my word, too." And it's true. Every time I've told a lie in my life, even over the most trivial of things, I've felt a weight, a pressure, that's difficult to bear. Anxiety mounts inside of me from having to remember my story and from realizing I might have to continue lying to this person in order to keep their trust. So, I decide I want to tell Jack the truth.

"When I told you I was seeing someone, I lied. I'm not seeing anyone. I've been on dates, but there's no one person I'm seeing exclusively," I confess.

Jack's facial expression looks like a mix between confusion and disappointment as he lets his eyes fall to his hands that are now clenched tightly together on his lap. "Okay, why would you lie to me about that?" he asks, trying to make sense of it all. He picks up his paper cup of coffee and takes a prolonged gulp, closing his eyes as he drinks.

"I just, I didn't…" I stop to take a breath, before starting over. "It's harder to explain than I imagined it would be. I didn't want you to think there was any chance you and I could be something, you know, more than friends." I wish I hadn't ever told the lie in the first place. *It's always better to tell the truth from the beginning.* That's a lesson both of my parents have instilled in me for as long as I can remember, from the time I broke my mom's favorite ceramic flower vase as a kid and blamed it on my imaginary friend because there were no other siblings to pin it on.

"Oh… okay." His face folds into a frown as he runs his fingers over the space between his eyebrows. I'm not *his* anymore, and quite possibly, I never was, so there isn't much more for him to say. But everything about the way he looks is so utterly and undeniably handsome that even when he's frowning, I have to resist the urge to pull him in and kiss him. *It's all chemical,* I remind myself. That's all it is.

"It's not you," I tell him, wanting him to look at me the same way he was a few minutes ago when we were laughing, when there was no tension. He rolls his eyes a little, but I continue. "I mean, yeah what happened in the fall was shitty, and it took me a long time to get past that because I really, truly was falling for you, and I thought you felt the same way—"

He interrupts me, almost urgently, his hands moving earnestly as he speaks. "But I did. I do. I got scared because I have never felt the way I feel about you with anyone else. I've never felt so completely out of control of my own mind, my own body, my own will, when I'm with someone before. I would do anything for you Maddie, and that's fucking crazy for me to say because I've always made falling in love not an option." He said that word. *Love.* And he said it about me.

He leans forward, and a deep wrinkle forms between his eyebrows. "But you changed all that for me. You made me the kind of person who sees love as something I could do, something that's not going to be a chore."

There is a longing in his eyes that tells me he has envisioned this moment a hundred times before, the one where he would tell me all of this. He's lost sleep over it. Here it finally is, and it's not at all how he imagined, me telling him I don't want him anymore.

"You and I, together. It's not something I can do." My eyes shift downward, avoiding his gaze. "I thought it was something I always wanted, love that is. But you ending things, well, I didn't like the way you did it, but it was the right thing to do."

"No, it wasn't the right thing to do. I was being a jackass." His elbows are on his knees, his head in his hands.

"But it was, Jack. Over the past six months, I've realized love isn't something I want anymore. I think life will be so much better, so much more enjoyable, without it. I can't be hurt the way Sarah was or the way my mom is. I don't think I can be as strong as them."

Jack stands up now and takes one giant step towards me. He wraps his fingers around my forearms to pull me up from the bed so I'm standing too. I look up at him, breathe in his familiar scent, the one I never got the chance to properly say goodbye to, the one I've dreamed about even when I haven't wanted to. He stares down at me and leans his face into mine, his lips as close as they can possibly be to my lips without actually touching them. My body wants him to clutch my face in his palms and kiss me for so long that I can't think straight, that I forget I don't want this anymore.

His eyes are dark and his tone is resolute when he says to me, "Don't you ever doubt how strong you are, Maddie."

Chapter 17

Jack lets go of me, but as soon as he does, I crave his touch again. *It's chemical.* An intense attraction I can't ignore. His eyes are an inch from mine. His lips even closer. He doesn't step back after he utters those words. *Don't you ever doubt how strong you are.* I don't step back either. It's a standoff, like the Wild West. Someone needs to retreat, to step back and put an end to the tension between us before we act on it, but neither of us concedes.

"What do you want, Maddie?" Jack asks in a raw and desperate attempt to make sense of everything I've told him. He needs answers, but the problem is my mind is telling me one thing, and my body is telling me something completely different. I don't know what the right answer is. All I know is I want his skin on mine, his body on my body, his lips on my lips. I want him to take control here, the way I can see in his face he longs to. Most of all, I don't want to have to think about desiring every part of him anymore. I want to know what it's like to finally have him, to no longer resist what my body is begging me for.

Standing there in front of him, my arms dangle at my sides and begin to shake. "I want you, Jack," I whisper.

As soon as I speak those words, he grips my hips with his hands and pulls me in close. I feel him, his waist pressed into my abdomen, ready to do what we've both been waiting so long for. He kisses my lips first, but then he moves to my neck and glides over it with his mouth, a million tiny wet kisses across my shoulder blade, gently grazing my skin. His delicate touch causes my heart to race as a tingling sensation overtakes my entire body. Without warning, he lifts me up, gripping the back of my legs and wrapping them around his waist. My hands grasp his biceps, and I flip my hair out of my face so I can kiss him again. I am burning hot from the inside out when he lays me down on the bed, our lips still pressed together.

He pulls away, taking a step back as I lie on the bed, and he looks at me with hungry eyes. I raise my arms over my head so he can undress me, but he takes his time, admiring me. I've never felt so impatient in all my life.

"What are you waiting for?" I pant breathlessly, eagerly waiting for his body to be on mine. I want his face buried in my neck, my chest, kissing me everywhere. He steps forward, standing over me, and slides my top up over my head. His hands run up and down the sides of my body, from my shoulders to my knees, gentle massages along the way.

"Maddie, I have been waiting for this for so long." His voice is deep and a little raspy. "Let's not rush it. I want this to take all night." He climbs on top of me, positioned like he's ready to do a push-up, and he slowly lowers himself down. He smiles against my lips before tasting my mouth, my tongue, slowly and deliberately. I forgot how much I love the way he tastes.

"Espresso," I whisper.

"Vanilla," he whispers back, a flirtatious smile on his face.

My limbs writhe beneath him, yearning for him to undress all of me and take me fully, but he continues to tease me, sliding single fingers one at a time under my bra straps and then letting go. Slipping his thumbs into the waistband of my shorts and then back out again.

"You're going to make me crazy if you go any slower."

"Good. That's exactly what I want." His smirk is mischievous, and I hate that I love it so much. He works his way down my body, drawing a line with his mouth from my chest to my hips and then to my inner thigh, kissing that now.

I focus on my breathing, trying in vain to slow it down, but my body is on fire. "Oh my god, you are seriously going to kill me."

"I never knew you were so impatient." He laughs between kisses, his tongue running across my skin. I let my fingers play with his hair, but when it becomes too much, I clench his shoulders tight.

"I didn't either." I am barely holding on to any self-control I have left. But when I know I can't last another second, he sits up and pulls his shirt over his head.

"It's getting kind of hot in here." I watch the corners of his mouth raise, his abs glistening with sweat, his arm and shoulder muscles bulging. He clasps either side of my shorts with his fingers and pulls them down so slowly I want to rip them off myself. But I hold back, taking a heavy breath when he finally tosses them to the floor. He kisses me between my legs, over my neon pink underwear I didn't foresee him seeing tonight. If I did, I would have probably gone with something more subdued.

"These are so hot," he says. "It's a shame I've got to take them off." His thumbs slide into either side of the lace, pulling them down gently, so leisurely I start to squirm. I feel the build-up of every nerve in my body with his magic hands and electric tongue. I am on the edge and then over it, rising and then sinking. I groan because it's so good and because I want more.

"Get inside of me," I demand, because I want him to experience this with me. I don't want to be alone in this.

Jack smiles and kisses me before he says, "I was hoping you would say that."

He sits up on his knees, and I slide his boxers down quickly, with a fire under me, when I remember, "Do you have a condom?"

"No." He hesitates, his eyes apologetic. "I didn't know this was going to happen."

"I'm on birth control," I say quickly, and then add, "and you're the only person."

"You're the only person too." He lets out a sigh of relief and lowers himself back down, pressing into me.

"Okay, good," I say as I wrap my arms around his back, relieved this doesn't have to stop. But now I try to take my time, attempting to savor every second. I reach for him with my hands before guiding him in. His hips slide up and down, in sync with mine, first deep and slow until I can see he is dancing on the edge of a cliff too. My hands cling to his back, my nails sinking into his skin, and he speeds up, pounding and pressing into me while gripping the back of my thighs.

He moves my body as he pleases, pivoting my legs, turning my torso as he moves inside me. I didn't know it was possible for a man to hold on for this long, but Jack is different. I always knew that about him.

There's a scorching inside of me again before I finally surrender to it, just as Jack lets go too, both of us shuddering in unison. He collapses on top of me, catching his breath. Then he kisses me softly and rolls off to lie on his back next to me. I'm a puddle. Pure liquid. Drained and warm and wonderful all at once.

My mind drifts for a while, maybe a minute, maybe longer. I have no idea. But when I turn my gaze to him, his eyes are closed, sweat beads resting on his face.

"When can we do that again?" I ask, only half-joking.

He opens his eyes and turns his head to look at me. "Give me ten minutes, and I'll meet you in the shower."

A grin forms on my face that I can't wipe away. "That was… so good." I'm a little embarrassed I can't think of anything better to say, but my body and my brain are like mush.

Jack stares up at the ceiling and rests his heavy, tired hand on my bare stomach. "I always knew it would be with you, but that was better than I even imagined."

He stands up from the bed, and I watch him walk across the room, his perfect body resembling a work of art. He returns with a cup of ice water for each of us. I sit up and chug it, unaware of how thirsty I was until it touches my tongue. When I finish, he sets our cups on the nightstand and lies down next to me on the bed. He pulls my face to his and kisses me hungrily, sending my entire body into overdrive yet again.

"Sorry," he says, releasing his lips from mine. "I could do what we just did forever."

"I know what you mean." I nudge his shoulder so he rolls onto his back, and then I climb on top of him to do it all again.

It isn't until later when we are lying in bed next to each other, our clothes in little piles on the floor, laughing and talking and touching one another's undressed bodies, that he brings up what I said earlier.

"You said you don't want all of the other stuff, the feelings that come with a relationship." He pauses, swallowing hard. "But I do. I finally want that. I tried to move on and forget about you when you told me to, but it's impossible. I love you, Maddie."

My breath stalls as my hand instinctively moves from his thigh where it was resting onto my chest. Jack telling me he wants me as more than a friend, as his person and his partner, is everything I wanted and needed to hear from him six months ago. But now, in the middle of this Georgia hotel room, I try to let him down easy.

"I can't do it, Jack. I'm sorry, but I can't put myself in that kind of situation." I shift onto my side to create some space between us, our bodies disjointed for the first time in hours.

"But, Maddie, you're—" he begins, but I don't want to hear anymore. I know it will only make this harder, so I stop him.

"Sex is one thing but a relationship? I can't. I'm too afraid, Jack. I just can't." My voice is gentle, however, purposeful and unwavering. I am adamant about this decision I made weeks before this road trip, long before I ever saw Jack again at Mike's funeral.

He doesn't say anything as he stares at me with wistful eyes. The silence forces me to explain, to make him understand why this isn't an option anymore. Why *we* aren't an option anymore. I sit up in the bed, my legs crossed. Jack sits up too, his body facing mine, legs stretched over the edge. I choose my words carefully.

"You should see Sarah. Like *really* see her. Not how she was at the funeral when she had makeup on and looked beautiful and put together the way she always does. You should see her when there's no one around but me and Ace and Atlas. She's just barely hanging on, and everyone's offered everything they can give to help her, but there's nothing that fixes the kind of pain of losing your soulmate."

My eyes well up with tears, but I hold them in. "And my mom, when she's not with Dad, watching him like a babysitter or driving him to doctors' appointments, she's at support groups where other people try to help her keep it together for him because he's still alive. But what happens when he's not anymore? We have to face it's going to come soon, and she's going to be exactly like Sarah, only worse because she'll be alone in her house with no little kids to help fill the space in her mind with something happy or hopeful."

If I were twenty-five and carefree and hadn't faced these tragedies yet, everything might be different, but I'm covered in calluses now. No matter how much I like Jack, or maybe even love him, I can't set myself up for that kind of pain.

He doesn't realize how sure I am though because he pleads with me. "But you are the person who changed me, the one who made me believe there's something bigger than living and working and dying. You're the one who made me believe in love. There's something I've been missing. Something big. Something fucking huge that can make every day better." He is earnest and sincere and so hopeful. I hate that it has to be like this.

"I'm not her anymore." I cover my face with my hands to hide the tears that force their way out of me, but Jack weaves his fingers with mine, gently pulling them from my face.

He leans down to force me to look into his eyes. "But you are, Maddie. What we did tonight, it wasn't just sex. We did something I've never done before. I've never had sex that felt like that before." He's right. What we did was so much more than that.

"I haven't either," I admit.

"So what does that tell you?" He is steadfast, but I'm just as stubborn.

"It tells me that I've let myself get too attached."

"Please, let me love you. The way that you deserve to be loved," he begs, looking deep into my eyes, but he can see they are tired and hollow. I wipe away the wetness on my cheeks and rest my head on his chest. My eyes stay fixed on the pattern on the curtains while I let him hold me this last time.

Chapter 18

The next morning, Jack and I sit across from each other at a continental breakfast. He has Raisin Bran, and I have oatmeal. We both drink the acrid hotel coffee because we agree it's better than nothing. I make every effort to avoid the inevitable awkwardness, consciously trying to keep the conversation going to avoid the possibility of silence. I ramble on about my favorite Cincinnati breakfast spot. Then, he tells me about this place in Arizona that serves deep-fried Spam and eggs, and he insists I stop there if I ever make it to Phoenix. We go over the logistics of the drive: how long it will take, when we will need to stop, and when we should arrive at the condo. That sort of thing.

But there are moments throughout the morning when we slip, when we say and do things that aren't at all casual. Jack tells me I look beautiful as I sip on my coffee. As soon as the words leave his mouth, he shifts in his seat, and I can see he wishes he wouldn't have said it out loud. Beneath the table, my legs are crossed, and my ankle brushes against his calf. I keep it there because I like the way it feels.

If I could freeze time, I would let myself love him in this moment. I'd savor every second of it too. But I can't keep us from getting old, nor can I stop all of the horrible things that happen in this world, car accidents and cancer and disease and murder and everything else that turns the lives of unsuspecting people upside down. Loving him would come with predestined and unbearable pain. I can't do it.

Out of Atlanta, I drive the first leg of what's left of the trip. The sun is out, the traffic is light, and the day is so beautiful. It doesn't seem right that I am on my way to say goodbye to my best friend of over a decade, the one who has never lived more than a twenty-minute drive away from me until now. When Jack takes the wheel, I don't look at my phone or a book, but instead, I focus on the road ahead, everything in front of us. The trees and the billboards blur together with my thoughts creating jumbled mayhem in my head. I think about the mess I've made with Jack. I think about how different life will be when I get back home without Sarah to drink wine with, Ace to make me belly laugh, or Atlas to help me remember perfect things do exist in this world. I think about how fast Dad is changing. Day by day, he loses more of himself, and I don't know how much of him will be left when I return or even how much time I'll have with what remains. I've heard so many people say to cherish the time you have with the ones you love, but I'm already grieving him. The process of goodbye has already begun. It's difficult to cherish moments with anyone when all you can think about is that they will be gone soon.

We pull into the condo complex where Sarah's parents live in the late afternoon, tan stucco surrounding us and neon beach towels hanging over every balcony rail. Sarah runs to the truck to greet us, Atlas on her hip and Ace waddling like a chunky, little blond penguin behind her. I can't help but notice how bright she looks. Her skin is tan and healthy, and her eyes are rested, hinting she has slept more than her average three-hour stretches. I smell jasmine and oranges when I hug her. She looks like a version of herself I haven't seen in a year.

"Thank you so much!" she says when she hugs me. "You are the greatest, you know that?"

"Only to you, girl," I reply.

Sarah's mom, Beverly, welcomes us with tart, homemade lemonade and a platter of freshly cut fruit when we walk inside. She is dressed in a floral romper that is way more stylish than anything you'll ever see me wearing on a Monday afternoon.

"You two are a godsend," Beverly tells us.

Sarah's dad, Greg, has on one of those full-brimmed straw hats old men wear on the beach. He's also wearing his signature khaki shorts, the only thing I've ever seen him wear other than dress pants at weddings. His hat matches his shorts perfectly, like they came as a set. Greg may be in his sixties, but he goes to the gym every morning and golfs nearly every afternoon, so he is well-equipped to help Jack unload the moving truck. They drive together to a storage locker he arranged for Sarah and empty the contents of the U-Haul, all that remains of Sarah's life in Ohio.

I snuggle Atlas, who I've missed so much in only a few days apart, and I help put her down for a nap. Ace watches a cartoon with Beverly while Sarah and I sit on the balcony of the second-floor condo looking out at miles of colorful beach umbrellas poking out of the sand, gentle waves rolling onto the shore.

"You honestly look so good," I tell her. "I was worried you were making the wrong decision by leaving, but I realize most of that was just me being selfish and wanting you to stay."

Sarah smiles and looks relieved. "Leaving you and the house Mike and I bought together were the hardest parts of moving, but I knew if I stayed there, I would cry every day for the rest of my life thinking of the way he was in the end, lying in bed lifeless. He was nothing like the man I married in those last months."

"Mike wouldn't want that," I say, but I know she has already thought of this. She's considered everything, and that's why she is here now.

Sarah's eyes are on the ocean ahead. "No, he wouldn't. And Ace and Atlas don't deserve a sad mess of a mom. They already lost their dad."

"You're right. They don't, but I'm still going to miss you so damn much."

She laughs at me. "Don't be so dramatic, Maddie. I'm still here. Just a little farther away, but I'm still here. There's FaceTime, and you can get round-trip plane tickets to Cincinnati for pretty cheap. You're my best friend. I won't let you miss me, believe me."

"I know all of that, but I'm going to be lonely. I might need to find someone to hang out with me in Cincinnati."

"It looks like you already have." She grins, and I know she is referencing Jack without her even saying the words. Half of our conversations are left unsaid.

"No, I'm not interested in that," I pronounce, perhaps too adamantly.

"Why not? I can tell he's crazy about you. I mean he has to be to drive a moving truck down to Florida for no other reason than to spend time with you."

"I don't think a long-term relationship is in the cards for me after all. I want to focus on my career. I haven't been putting in the time I should be lately."

Sarah shoves me so hard in the shoulder my chair almost tips backwards. "You've got to be fucking kidding me. You focused on your career for all of your twenties, and you have the job of your dreams, but you're still not happy. Do you know why?"

I shrug. "Because I've been too worried about finding a man, and it's not worth my time. Because I haven't realized there are other ways to be happy that don't involve finding a husband," I reason.

"No, Maddie. It *is* worth it. Every single person on this planet deserves love. Everyone deserves someone to share their life with, if only temporarily, because it is the greatest thing you can ever feel. Listen to me." She leans in close and looks me square in the eyes like she is about to let me in on a secret. Her voice is low, almost a whisper. "Even if I knew what the future held, I would go back and marry Mike and have Ace and Atlas a million times over because the time I had with Mike was worth every ounce of the pain of losing him. He gave me everything I ever wanted, and I'll love him forever."

She doesn't cry when she tells me this. I've learned you can only cry for so long when you grieve before you have to move on to the next stage, the one where the daily tears dissipate, and you figure out your new path. You find a way to keep living while still holding on to the memory and the impact of whatever or whoever you lost. That's where Sarah is. Just because she's not crying doesn't mean losing Mike hurts any less than it did yesterday or last week.

"So what's the deal with Jack?" Sarah asks, wanting to know where he and I stand now that we've spent two days in the cab of a truck together after not speaking for months. "Do you love him?"

I hesitate. "I don't exactly know the answer to that," I mutter, pondering the depth of the question and what my answer might mean.

"Yes, you do."

I shake my head. "It's not that simple. He told me he didn't believe in love and that he didn't want a relationship. And now all of the sudden he changes his mind? People don't just change like that."

"Sounds like the same way you decided to change your mind about the same damn thing." She makes a point I feel foolish not to have realized before I said it.

"But, it's different because—" I attempt to defend myself, to explain why I'm not a hypocrite, but Sarah knows me better in many ways than I even know myself, so she stops me.

"It's not different. You are making this more complicated than it needs to be. In the end, it's all so simple. If you love him, be with him. Don't you see what you're doing?"

"I'm protecting myself, Sarah."

"You're not protecting anyone. For so long, you acted like you wanted love, but you were too scared to let yourself be with anyone. That's why you went on a million blind dates, and it never turned into anything. It's because you didn't let it. You've been doing the same thing Jack did. You were afraid, the same way he was. And now he's finally ready, but you're still running."

When she speaks those words, something clicks inside of me. I'm not sure if she is right, nor do I know how to figure out if she is, but I do know I need to reflect on what the hell I have been doing and what I want. "I think I need some time."

"I get it. It's a lot. But don't think for so long that you lose him."

The squeak of the glass patio door opening behind us interrupts our conversation. Jack is standing there, like some sort of sign from the universe. The problem is I don't know what it means.

That night, Sarah's parents take all of us out for dinner to one of those typical Florida seafood spots where the place looks like a dive from the outside. Those tacky miniature umbrellas come in every drink, but the food turns out to be so fresh and amazing, especially for a couple of people who are accustomed to Cincinnati seafood (frozen then thawed).

I've had hundreds of meals with Sarah and her parents over the years, but this one is so different. First, I notice a void, an emptiness in the conversation. The parts where I know Mike would have jumped in and made a joke that would have made us laugh until our cheeks burned. I hope I always remember that about him. Dinners like these may be where I will miss him the most. And then there's Jack, who seems to fit right in like a missing puzzle piece. He sits next to me and joins the conversation so naturally, the same way he did on that first night we had lasagna at Sarah and Mike's house, the night of our setup. Jack is likable and sincere and funny, and I can tell Sarah and her parents love him being there. I think I might love him being there too.

Greg drives Jack and me to the airport at eight the next morning. The truck will stay at a rental facility in Florida, and Greg bought us two plane tickets to fly home. Before we leave, I hug Sarah for what seems like an eternity, and she tells me, "Stop being a drama queen! I will literally talk to you tonight. I love you, best friend."

"I love you too, best friend. Good luck in your new life." It feels like the end of some sort of chapter, and I wonder how the next one will go. I hope it's a happier one.

On the flight, Jack and I don't sit next to each other since Greg bought Jack's ticket after he bought mine. Jack is five rows in front of me in the aisle seat on the left, and I am seated in the aisle seat on the right. A young mom and her wild little boy sit next to me. He's a little older than Ace, and she keeps apologizing when he nudges me or asks me a question. I assure her I am not bothered, but she doesn't believe me. I can't help but look at what I can see of Jack when I'm not talking to "Theodore James Parsons," which is the response the little toe-headed toddler gives me when I ask him his name.

"What a handsome name," I say, and then I turn to continue watching Jack's messy hair peek out over the seat, the back of his muscular arm idle on the armrest. As passengers continue to board the plane, my phone buzzes on my lap, and I see Jack sent me a picture. It's an unflattering selfie from a horrible angle making it look like he has three chins and a miniature forehead, and it instantly makes me laugh. Theodore and I take a selfie of our own to send to Jack. We lean into one another making peace signs with our fingers and duck faces with our lips.

"Let's take another one! Let's take another one!" Theodore begs, while his mother repeats, "I'm so sorry."

"I love kids. He's adorable," I say, but she still doesn't believe me.

Both of my parents come to pick us up from the airport. While making arrangements, Mom offered to drive Jack home. It sounded like a good idea at the time, but now I have flashbacks to my preteens when my parents chauffeured my friends and me around, except it's worse now because this is a friend I've had sex with.

On the drive to Jack's condo, Dad asks us how the trip was a few times, obviously forgetting he already asked. He also asks Jack what he does for a living twice. It makes me sad, but Jack answers the same questions again and again with pure patience and grace.

When we arrive at Jack's place, Mom honks her horn as soon as Jack gets to his front door on the second floor. "Mom!" I yell, "Did you seriously just honk at him?"

"What?! That's how you say goodbye in a car. Didn't you know that?" I shake my head like I'm embarrassed, but I'm actually thinking about how adorable my parents are. Both of them. I don't know when exactly your parents go from being these power-hungry rule-makers to cute, lovable humans, but at some point they do, and they don't have the ability to embarrass you anymore when that happens.

"By the way," Mom says, turning the oldies radio station completely off so she can be sure I hear her, "Jack is very handsome."

"I know he is, Mom." I'm also aware her comment is a clever way of fishing for information about whether Jack and I are dating, and if so, she wants to let me know she approves. However, I'm not spilling anything right now, so I leave it at that.

Chapter 19

In the weeks following the road trip, I let my work consume me in hopes I won't miss Sarah too much or fall into something I'm not ready for with Jack. Luckily, I have a number of sponsored features coming up on my blog and social media platforms featuring Fourth of July and Labor Day picnic ideas. Most of my clients are requesting recipes featuring the latest food trends like microgreens, gluten-free and vegan options, and eco-conscious ideas to eliminate food waste. It requires a lot of research and an exhausting amount of recipe testing, which keeps me in my kitchen most days from dawn until dusk. I let myself focus on my work in a way I haven't done in a long time, fully immersing myself in this separate little world and enjoying it as much as I can.

In my free time, I'm making an effort to really think about the things Sarah said like I promised her I would. However, I made a promise to myself then as well. I swore I would not jump into anything with Jack when we returned home from Florida. It would be so easy to get caught up in the physicality of it all after sleeping with him, but I want to know I really and truly want to be in love if I decide to let myself fall again, especially for a man who has hurt me once already.

Sometimes Jack texts me or sends me silly pictures or memes, and I do the same, but it's not every day, and he never asks to see me. Any communication we have is virtual. I know where he stands, and for now, we are not in the same place. Jack is in this newfound space he's confident in, and I'm somewhere new too, except I'm unsure and wary. He is giving me the time I need. That's what I am assuming at least. Whenever I have the urge to call him and ask him to come over, I do yoga or go for a jog, and it helps to put my own wants and needs into focus. But in the back of my mind, I hear Sarah's emphatic voice telling me, *Don't think for so long that you lose him.*

Nearly a month after returning from Florida, it's 5:30 a.m. on a Saturday when all of the answers come to me. Recently, I have gotten into the habit of going for morning runs, anywhere from five to eight miles most days of the week. In my early twenties, I ran a couple of half marathons but didn't stick with it for long. This new running routine began after the road trip because I was having trouble sleeping. While my blogging and cooking occupied my mind during the day, at night I had this chaotic movement in my head jumping from one thing to the next. I would think about Dad and then Mike and then Jack. Before I knew it, I'd end up down this rabbit hole in my brain thinking back to some regrettable night in college or an awkward conversation from years ago that never found its way out of my head. I figured physically exerting myself might help me sleep better, and it did. After a couple of weeks, running became something I looked forward to each morning. It was a way to clear my head and plan for my day (as well as an excuse to indulge in daily poppy seed bagels smeared with cream cheese as my post-run fuel), all while unintentionally fitting into my favorite pair of jeans I haven't worn in six years.

On this particular Saturday morning, though, I don't start my day as energized and ready as I usually do. I wake up before my alarm, half an hour earlier than usual at 4:30, but there is no point in trying to fall back asleep. I drag a little in getting myself dressed, my knees and ankles aching. I make a mental note to ice them when I return from my run. Then, I waste time sipping on iced coffee and scrolling through social media feeds on my phone before finally forcing myself out the door. I'm in an inexplicably bad mood, grumpy for no reason, the way you sometimes just wake up on the wrong side of the bed.

The first mile of any run is always the hardest. My body is tight, sometimes it even hurts, and my breathing has yet to find its natural rhythm. After that first mile, I eventually forget about the uncomfortable parts and start to enjoy it, the cool breeze on my skin and the lullaby of my sneakers hitting the pavement while the warblers sing their morning songs. This morning, though, every mile feels like the first. Every step is forced, and every breath is a gasp for air. All I can think as I plod down the road, my shoes full of cement, is, *When will this be over?*

Then, it is over, suddenly and unexpectedly, when I hear the sound of squealing tires, the broad shadow of a car fast approaching. There isn't any time to react, to save myself. Everything goes dark.

I wake up in a hospital room, surrounded by white, the incessant beeping of mysterious machines coming from all directions. I try to piece what happened together, remnants of the accident floating around my brain. There are glimpses of a middle-aged woman standing over me as I lay on the ground. She was screaming, "Oh my god!" and crying uncontrollably as she frantically called 9-1-1. There is an EMT strapping me onto a stretcher and wheeling me into the ambulance, flashing lights all around me. There is that feeling, that emptiness, when I wished Jack was there.

The remainder of my day is spent in the hospital, every inch of me poked, prodded, and inspected by doctors and nurses who keep telling me how fortunate I am. It turns out a Chevy Malibu swerved into the bike lane on the side of the road where I was running. The driver hit the brakes, but not in enough time to stop before I rolled up onto the windshield and then onto the pavement. I have a concussion, a broken left arm, and my body is well on its way to becoming a giant, achy bruise. However, my injuries are minimal compared to what they could have been. It turns out the lady who hit me was a nurse on her way home from a twelve-hour shift at the same hospital where I am now. She was exhausted, overworked, and checking a text message from her husband when she saw me too late.

The irony of the whole incident is that as I lie here in the hospital after being hit by a car only hours ago, I have never felt so lucky in all my life. If it had been some drunk person driving, they would have never hit the brakes, and I would be dead. When my parents walk through the door to my hospital room, I am so utterly grateful to see their faces. And more than anything, I am thankful for the clarity I finally have. The answers to the questions I have been seeking for weeks came to me this morning like a bolt of lightning, or, like an unexpected car crash.

Lying in the uncomfortable hospital bed attached to monitors and covered in bandages, I consider the life I'm living. While I love my job and the career I've been able to create for myself, I know work alone is never going to be fulfilling enough on its own. My job won't comfort me when the madness of life seems unbearable. I need my tribe: my parents, Sarah, and now, Jack. I don't simply want a warm body to fill the empty space in my bed, and I wouldn't risk the pain of love for just anyone. But Jack isn't just anyone. I am certain I want to be the one by his side through the good and the bad and the ugly. Because I love him.

When I am discharged from the hospital fourteen hours after the accident, I have a very clear image in my mind. The final scene in *When Harry Met Sally,* a movie I've watched with Mom countless times over the years, when Billy Crystal runs up to a stunning Meg Ryan in that iconic green velvet dress with those gloves at a New Year's Eve party. Frank Sinatra plays in the background, as Harry finally admits he's in love with Sally. It couldn't wait another second. Nothing about their love story was perfect, but I've learned few things in life are.

Now, I'm no Meg Ryan, and Jack is way sexier than Billy Crystal, but all I want is to find Jack and tell him I am ready to let myself love him. That I'm sorry it took so long. So when I limp into the back seat of my parents' gold sedan, every inch of me sore, I ask them to drop me off at Sully's, the place where it all began.

"I have something I have to do," I tell them.

"Call me when you need a ride home," Mom says. "You're not allowed to drive with that concussion."

"I'll get an Uber."

"Remember, nothing good happens after midnight," she says.

Dad nods his head stoutly in agreement. "Your mother is right, Madeline."

"It's seven o'clock. Most people haven't even eaten dinner yet." But it doesn't matter because those are the exact words Mom has said to me every single time she's dropped me off anywhere since I was thirteen years old.

I'm wearing a pair of my mom's leggings and one of my dad's Ohio State University crewneck sweatshirts. I asked them to bring me some clothes to change into because all I had was my blood-stained running outfit. I am positively disgusting, and I'm sure I smell and look dreadful. This isn't exactly how I imagined ever telling the man I want to spend my life with that I love him, but if I've learned anything this past year, it's that there is no time to waste.

When I step inside Sully's, Jack is standing behind the

counter, back to me, talking to a customer. He told me he was picking up his old Saturday shift during the summer semester, so I knew exactly where to find him. I sit down at the cat table and wait for him to notice me. For several minutes, I admire the way he moves, making espresso drinks and opening craft beer bottles while being his charming and outgoing self. As soon he spots me, he smiles, though it quickly fades when he realizes my condition. He rushes to me, concerned.

"Are you okay? What happened to you?" he asks frantically, placing a soft hand on my cheek as he examines the scratches on my face, the bandage on my head, and my left arm resting in a sling.

"It's been a day, but I'm okay," I reassure him, and I am suddenly hesitant. *Should I just blurt out the words or ease into them?* Jack is at work after all. "I wanted to talk to you about something," I finally say.

"I wanted to talk to you too." His eyes are wide and alert as he speaks. "I was going to call you later tonight actually. I'm happy you're here. Let me make sure Lucas has the bar under control."

Jack walks behind the counter where he has a brief conversation with the other barista, and then he returns, moving his chair from across the table so he is sitting next to me.

"Okay, I'm good. Tell me everything. What happened?" He rests his hand on mine on the tabletop.

"You go first. Mine's a long story, remember?" I wish we were at his place, kissing on the couch and undressing each other.

"If you say so." He wets his lips, and then his words come

quickly and all at once. "I got a job offer. A tenure-track position at Syracuse. Positions like that are basically impossible to come by, especially for someone as young as me. I have to take it." A huge grin rests on his face.

I instinctively reply the only thing it makes sense to say right now. "Congratulations!" I throw my free, unbroken arm up in the air and wrap it around his back. The way his body feels against mine for the first time since Florida affirms what I came here to tell him. *I love him.*

"Thank you! I just found out this afternoon. I haven't been keeping it from you or anything. It's so surreal, and when I applied, I thought it was such a long shot. Like, no way in hell, right? It's the kind of position I've dreamed of getting, and it's happening."

I try to disguise my disappointment with excitement and acclamation, but the words that exit my mouth, "You earned it. You're amazing. I'm proud of you," are much different than the other looming words, the ones I won't say out loud: *Syracuse. As in New York. As in five hundred miles from Cincinnati.*

For a moment, I wonder how he can just get up and leave what he has here, but of course it won't be hard for him to go. He's only been in Ohio for a year after all. How deep can someone possibly plant their roots in three hundred and sixty-five days? Jack has moved lots of times in his life. Not like me, born and bred in the suburbs of Cincinnati and still here. Not to mention, there are countless other women just like me in Syracuse. In a couple of short months, maybe less, I will be merely a memory.

"What did you want to tell me?" he asks, still beaming from sharing his news with me.

"I... well, I..." I pause, unable to go on because I know I can't tell him what I came here to say anymore. My future flashes before my eyes. Long-distance phone calls while lying alone in my bed, lonely plane rides back and forth, a million frequent flyer miles. Then there's the inevitable heartbreak in the end because long distance never works. Everyone knows that. There's also time, patience, money, and jealousy to consider, and none of those will be on our side.

So in that moment, I decide not to tell Jack what I came here to say. It will only hurt us both. "I just wanted to tell you about the day I had." I force a more casual tone as I fill Jack in on all of today's unexpected events, except for the one that matters the most. He puts his hands on mine and holds them. When he touches me, I am safe, like nothing in this world could break me.

"I'm so sorry that happened to you," he says, stroking my fingers with his thumb as he eyes every scratch, visibly worried even though it's all over now. I want to tell him what happened today changed my life. I want him to know all I could think of as I was rushed to the hospital, while I was waiting on x-ray and MRI results, was how badly I wanted to see him.

But instead I say, "It's fine. I'm okay. I have a crazy story to tell now, that's all. And since Sarah's not here, I thought I'd come and tell you." I act like there is nothing else, and I don't know if he can see right through me or not, but he kisses my forehead and wraps his arms around me. *This,* I think to myself, *is my favorite place to be.*

Holly, the blue-haired barista, is hanging out off the clock towards the front of the shop. Jack asks her to take over his shift so he can drive me home. I told him I'm fine with an Uber.

"It's not a big deal," I say, but he assures me Holly is always looking to pick up extra shifts, especially since one of her two roommates has moved out, and her hip downtown loft rent is now being divided two ways instead of three.

"Of course I'll take over!" she says, showing off her perky personality that doesn't quite match her all-black attire and deep burgundy lipstick in the dead of summer. "I'm already here, and I could use the cash."

Jack thanks her, and he pours us each a fresh cup of decaf in Styrofoam cups before holding my hand as he walks me to his car. He finds every excuse to touch me, brushing my hair out of my eyes with his fingers, resting his right palm on my thigh while he drives. He suddenly can't keep his hands off of me, and I don't do anything to stop it because his touch is everything I need right now. I don't want to say goodbye to him tonight after a short car ride home, or ever for that matter.

"Let's go to your place," I say. Jack doesn't even blink before he taps his turn signal, hanging a left in the direction of his condo.

"Whatever you want."

And I really believe Jack would try his best to give me whatever I want if I let him, and I believe he loves me the way he says he does. If I asked him to stay, to work another year or five as an adjunct professor in Cincinnati, I think he would give up this opportunity in Syracuse to stay with me. It's the kind of guy he is. But because I love him too, I can't let him.

When we walk into his condo, the one I haven't seen since the fall, almost everything is the same as I remember it.

Alphabetized books all in a row, a lone potted aloe plant in the front windowsill, and the scent of pumpkin spice in the air even though it's June. He told me once that each fall, he buys enough candles to last an entire year because he loves the scent of pumpkin spice year-round.

"I can't do all that floral and citrus crap in the spring and summer," he said.

"I've never met a guy so dedicated to a candle scent," I joked with him, but I have to admit, I love the smell of pumpkin spice too, and now it makes me think of him. I inhale the scent and let my eyes wander around the room to see what, if anything, has changed in all this time.

"You got a new couch." I glide my hands along the brown suede, watching the streaks my fingertips leave in the fabric.

"Yeah, well, when I started sinking into my old one like I was drowning in quicksand, I decided it was time for a new one." He tousles his hair with his hands. "Would you like a glass of champagne?"

"After the day I've had? Yes, please. When did you get so fancy?" I'm well aware Jack doesn't stray far from his taste for sour craft beer from the brewery up the street unless he happens to be sharing a bottle of wine with me. If that's the case, it has to be dark and red.

"I just knew you loved it, so I bought a couple of bottles to have on hand a long time ago. They're all still in my refrigerator."

"That *was* very sweet of you." I emphasize the *was* because he obviously did that before he dumped me.

While I linger in the living room, eventually taking a seat on the newest furniture addition, Jack walks into the kitchen and returns with champagne for each of us in two stemless wine glasses. "Sorry, I don't have those skinny champagne glasses."

"Those are too uppity for me anyway. This is perfect." I take a sip and melt into this incredible couch. I feel cozy in his apartment, almost like I'm home.

He sits down next to me and gently squeezes my shoulder with his free hand. "I can't believe you got hit by a fucking car this morning, Maddie."

"*I* can't believe I got hit by a car this morning! This has seriously been the longest day of my life."

"I'm sorry it happened, and I'm sorry I wasn't there." Jack did nothing wrong and has absolutely nothing to apologize for, but I can tell he really wanted to be there for me. I can also sense he is aware it was more serious than I'm making it out to be. My head shakes back and forth, brushing away the weight of it, the fact that I could have just as easily died this morning instead of sitting here now next to him.

I lean into him and place my lips on his, like it's the only thing to do right now, the only thing that makes any sense in this crazy, unpredictable life. He kisses me back, long and passionate, his hands on my back, and mine in his hair. It's like he has been waiting for this moment, the one where I finally come to my senses and realize how perfect we are. But I keep Syracuse on my mind as he eases me onto my back.

I tug on his jeans with my unbroken arm, telling him to take them off.

"Is this what you want?" he asks.

"Don't make me beg for it, Jack." I let out a small laugh before he pulls my leggings off and tosses them behind him.

He positions his body horizontally over mine, his torso supported by his palms on either side of me. His gaze moves over every inch of my face.

"God, you are so beautiful," he finally says. My body shudders beneath him as he kisses my forehead and then my cheek and then my neck. I have no makeup on, and I am wearing my parents' clothes, and there are two inches of bandage wrapped around my broken arm, but I believe him. I feel beautiful in his presence.

Every move Jack makes is gentle and unhurried, careful with me in my fragile state. Maybe it's the extra strength Tylenol they gave me at the hospital, but I don't hurt quite as bad now that I'm with him. We move from the couch to the floor to the bed, exploring every angle and every experience available to us. We catch up on the weeks and the months and the years we lived without one another. We make love. The kind of head-over-heels, crazy, maddening love they write songs about.

Chapter 20

"Come with me," Jack says the next morning in his bed, his warm body enveloping mine, the peach sunlight barely beginning to peek through the gaps in his bedroom blinds. I've only gotten to hear his gruff morning voice a handful of times now, and I love it more each time I hear it.

"Come with you?" I ask, still trying to register everything that happened yesterday, reminding myself it wasn't all a dream. I have a sling on my arm, an aching body, and Jack spooning me in his bed to prove it.

"Yes, to Syracuse. Come with me," Jack repeats.

Here it is, the moment I knew was coming. *He'll want to know where this is going. He'll want to know if I love him too.* Last night, I thought this to myself when we were making love, when he was pressed against me from behind, massaging my shoulders and kissing the back of my neck. But, the heat and the passion helped this thought to dissolve as quickly as it arrived. Now it's here again. Jack wants to know, and he deserves to know the truth. I roll over to face him, my hips pressed against his, our feet twisted together. His ruffled hair is poking out in a million different directions, and his eyes are bright. He is hopeful and happy.

"I love you." I utter these words to him for the very first time. I am certain of them. However, what I say next has the power to unravel everything. "But I can't go to Syracuse with you."

I don't think Jack even hears the second part though because he grabs my face and pulls me in, giving me the most profoundly beautiful kiss of my life. It's the kind of kiss you dream of when you picture being in Paris in front of the Eiffel Tower surrounded by a million twinkle lights face to face with the love of your life. Only I don't need any of that. I just need Jack.

"I love you." He is soft and sincere. "I never saw this coming. I never saw *you* coming, but Maddie, you are the best thing I never knew I wanted."

I run my fingers through his hair and let my palm settle on the back of his neck. "Yesterday, when I got hit by that car, I was foggy and in pain, and I had no idea what had even happened to me. I didn't know if I was alive or dead, but the one thing I remember thinking when I was lying there on the pavement is that I wished you were there. That's why I came to see you last night. That's what I wanted to tell you," I confess.

He lights up. "So come with me to Syracuse. Let's create a life together somewhere new." He makes it sound so easy, so simple.

"What about my life here? I own a house. I just renovated that house. My job is here."

"We can buy a new house together. You work in your kitchen and online. That's one of the perks of the job you have. You can do it anywhere," Jack argues.

"My parents…" I pause to try to fathom what it would mean to leave them, a thought that hasn't crossed my mind since I was eighteen years old dreaming of New York City. I take a deep breath and try to put everything into words he will understand.

"It's been the three of us since the beginning, Mom, Dad, and me. I'm their only child, and that means I'm the only one who can help take care of them. My dad is sick, and he's never going to get better. He's going to keep getting worse until it—" I break to breathe, taking in as much air as my body will allow. "Until it finally takes him. I can't leave and miss the end of my dad's life. Let's say I did. And then what? My mom is left here to grieve alone with no help to pick up the pieces of the life she built with my dad? And then I feel guilty and grief-stricken for the rest of my life?"

The expression on Jack's face shows he didn't anticipate the weight of the question he asked, how loaded asking me to come with him really is. He was imagining the fairytale, but that isn't real life. He sits up in his bed, back against the headboard. I do the same. We both stare ahead at the mirror over the dresser, the reflection of the two of us sitting side by side.

"Then I won't go. I'll stay here." Jack is resolved in his statement, and I soak in his willingness to sacrifice for me, but only briefly.

"I won't let you do that. A tenure-track position is what you've been working towards for so long. There's no way I would ever let you give all that up to stay here with me."

Jack turns his eyes from our reflection to look at me now, the real me. "But what if that's what I want? There will be other positions, Maddie. It just may take some time"

I shake my head. "That's not happening. You're not giving up this opportunity."

"Then what about long-distance?" he suggests. "Just for a while until we figure out the rest. We can drive or fly to each other on the weekends and talk on the phone every day."

And here we are. It is the last possible suggestion to save us. The last resort before the inevitable.

"Until we figure out phone calls and text messages aren't enough to sustain a relationship? Until we figure out long distance makes both of us miserable? You know we can't do that to ourselves, Jack."

He stands up, his body rigid, and he begins pacing around the room. I stay in bed, holding the sheets up over my naked body. Jack steps into a pair of boxer shorts and throws me a pair along with a clean t-shirt from his drawer. I pull the t-shirt over my head and let the sheet fall so it's only covering my legs.

"So what, Maddie!? What do we do?" He tips his head back to look up at the ceiling. His frustration floods the room, enough to drown us both, and I can't blame him one bit. I'm frustrated too, not with him but with life. The way something so good has finally happened after a long string of horrible things, and I'm not even in the position to enjoy it. Neither of us is. Instead, we have to give each other up. It's the only way to spare us both the pain that will come with loving one another. Jack is unwilling to give me up though, so it's my job to make him.

"When do you need to leave?" I want to know the deadline to our story, when the clock will strike midnight, and he will vanish.

"Classes start in early September, but there are some things I'll need to do before the first day." Jack sounds unsure. Everything happening is so new, so sudden. "I mean, I need to find a place to live first. There are always a bunch of meetings and professional development seminars before the new school year starts too. Maybe a month?"

Maybe a month, as in, maybe even sooner. Regret engulfs me as Sarah's words replay in my mind: *Don't think for so long that you lose him.* Would this all be different if I told him weeks ago in Florida or right after we returned home? What if I didn't take that time away to think, but dove in, headfirst? Would we even be in this position right now? I know I have no other choice than to accept the consequences of waiting too long, of taking him for granted.

"Well, we have until then… until you leave."

"And then what?" Jack asks, his arms crossed over his chest. He's rocking back and forth on his feet, looking at me intently.

"And then we say goodbye." I turn my gaze away from him, back to the reflection in the mirror where I'm all alone in the bed now.

"Maddie…" Jack sits down next to me, gently touching my chin, rotating it so I have to look at him. He's ready to argue, ready to change my mind, to talk some sense into me. But I know I am sparing him regret by not letting him stay. Jack has been working towards this position, this career, for almost a decade of schooling now. He has only known me for a year. He made it very clear a long time ago how important his career is to him, more than love or anything else, and I could never be the one to ask him to sacrifice that. So, I interrupt him before he can try.

"Do you ever believe the universe sends you signs? Four-leaf clovers and heads-up pennies and broken mirrors and special numbers. They all happen when they're supposed to, at exactly the right moment to help guide you in the right direction. Think about it. Maybe this job and the fact that you were offered it on the exact same day I got hit by a car and told you I loved you is a sign. It's the universe telling you to get out while you can before you get hurt."

"I don't believe any of that." His face is so close to mine now I can feel his balmy breath on my skin.

"But I do." I look him square in the eye, unwavering. Jack's face is serious and solemn, and now, he is the one who turns his gaze from mine. I'm staring into his eyes, and he's looking right past me. "So what do you say? Do you want to do this thing for a couple more weeks? We can thoroughly enjoy it while it lasts and then have a cordial goodbye at the end."

His expression softens. "Maddie, I don't agree with any of this." He hesitates and swallows hard. "But I will love you for as long as you let me."

Then, he gently leans me back on the bed, and we kiss as if the end is right now, long and fervent, like lovers leaving one another at an airport. We are saying goodbye to the potential of forever while embracing what we have in the here and now. And I am seeing for the first time that the present can be even more beautiful than the future.

Chapter 21

A few days after the accident, I have an appointment to see an orthopedic surgeon to replace the bandage on my broken arm with a cast. I've never even had so much as stitches before, so I'm probably more nervous than I need to be. As I sit rigid on the examination table, my heart is thumping, and my palms are sweaty. I have no idea what to expect. So when the technician asks me to have a color for my cast picked out when she returns to the room, I get way too in my head about it.

I text Jack, *Quick, what color for my cast? I can't make a decision.*

By the time Jack replies, I'm already in my car on the way home. The whole ordeal was much less dramatic than I imagined.

Sorry, I was in a Zoom meeting. What did you go with?

While I sit at a red light, I send him a picture of the hot pink cast stretching from my palm all the way up over my elbow. *I'm already having color regret.*

Jack quickly replies, *No regrets. That's a statement piece right there.*

His response makes me smile, and I don't give my color choice another thought. That night, when I go to his house, I ask Jack if he'll sign it.

"Are you sure? That thing is going to be on you for like six weeks, right?"

"More like eight, but I'm sure. It's not like I have an office job to go to or anything. And even if I did, who the hell cares?"

"Well, in that case..." he says and disappears into his kitchen. I hear him rustling through a drawer, and he returns a minute later with a black permanent marker. "Where do you want it?"

I point to my forearm. "So I can always see it."

I notice right away he isn't writing his name. He draws short, careful strokes with the marker, the tip barely touching the cast, like he's using a paintbrush. He chews on his bottom lip as he draws, so focused he doesn't even speak. A few minutes later, Jack's drawing is complete, a crescent moon with a little man cradled inside, a few stars around it.

"The Man in the Moon," I say.

"I don't know why, maybe it was that date we went on, but whenever I see the moon now, I think of you."

In the days that follow, Jack and I spend every second we can together. When I am not working and when he is not tying up loose ends in Cincinnati or making arrangements for Syracuse, we are visiting a local burger spot, sitting on my patio gazing up at the stars, or eating takeout while playing board games. The topic of when exactly Jack is leaving is not one we address. I assume he'll tell me when he knows for certain, and neither of us wants to let thinking about that inevitable day ruin the present. So we act ignorant of it, pretending a happily ever after is in our future. And the truth is, I do hope I have a happily ever after, and I hope he does too, even if it's not with me.

One Wednesday evening a couple of weeks into our new normal, I decide to invite Jack to join me for my weekly dinner with my parents. Mom is hosting this week. She found Ora King salmon at Findlay Market on Saturday and doesn't want to freeze it.

"It's the Wagyu beef of the ocean," she told me.

I playfully rolled my eyes and asked her what food magazine she was quoting. "Probably *Bon Appetit.* If you ask me, they try way too hard to be trendsetters."

"I'm not hip enough for *Bon Appetit,* Madeline. It was probably from that Pioneer Woman. What's her name again? Ree? I love her."

Then, I asked Mom if it would be okay if Jack joined us.

"Certainly!" A wide grin formed on her face.

"Jack's moving soon," I felt the need to add, completely unprompted, so Mom didn't jump to any conclusions. I'd like to avoid the embarrassing questions she might ask if she suspected Jack has husband potential.

"Okay," she replied, but in the signature way she says *okay,* where her voice goes up an octave on the second syllable, insinuating there is much more to her response than she lets on. It's an age-old Mom trick, and I don't fall for it, moving on to a new topic entirely.

Conversations like this one with Mom, where I skirt around the topic of a relationship, help me begin to see what

Sarah meant when she told me I was the same as Jack, when she said I was running away just like he was. I realize I've been running from love for the past six years. After Ben, I didn't want to get hurt again. I let myself fall too hard only to watch him move on like I never even mattered at all. When we broke up, I cried for hours every day, lost weight from not eating, and avoided having any sort of social life out of fear I might see him out at a bar or a party. Meanwhile, he moved on so easily with the girl who started hanging around right after our relationship ended. I spent hours upon hours comparing myself to her, scrutinizing pictures of her online and wondering what she had that I didn't. Sometimes it made me feel crazy, like I was losing my mind. But, Ben was the first person I ever truly fell in love with, and at some point, he chose not to love me anymore, to just stop. I wasn't good enough, and the girl who happened to stroll down his street a few days later apparently was *good* enough.

That relationship took so much longer to heal from than I ever imagined it would. In the years that passed, when I finally felt ready to move on, I set my heart on forever, a husband and kids, the whole shebang. But while I was surfing the tidal waves of internet dating, I was oblivious to the fact that I was playing games myself, self-sabotaging any true chance at happiness. I wasn't actually willing to let myself fall in love again, and that makes all of this even more difficult to digest. Jack is the only person I have let myself love since Ben.

That evening, Jack and I go to my parents' house together. He holds my hand as he drives, the fingers of his other hand curled around the top of the steering wheel. I haven't brought someone home for my parents to meet in years, and I keep catching myself biting my lip and picking at my fingernails, the nerves catching up with me.

"I want all of the embarrassing childhood pictures. Give me missing front teeth and bowl haircuts," Jack says through laughter.

He is charming and funny the way he always is. If Jack is nervous at all, I can't even tell because he doesn't exude a hint of it. His hand holding on to me is dry, not clammy like mine. I have to admit I'm often envious of how good Jack is at interacting with other people. He is so naturally charismatic, not at all like one of those extroverts who is loud for the sake of being heard or who always wants to be the center of attention. Jack asks people questions about their lives and actually listens to their responses, avoiding commonplace conversational platitudes and really attempting to get to know whomever he meets. Coming from the perspective of a girl who often responds to restaurant servers and retail workers who ask me to, "Come again!" with "Thanks, you too," watching Jack interact with anyone is truly captivating.

We arrive just after six to my parents' house, a signature Cincinnati Tudor on "the West Side," as it's referred to by locals. Jack presents my parents with a box of fancy truffles from a local chocolate shop, mentioning to me he almost brought wine but remembered I told him Dad can't drink alcohol anymore due to his medications. *I love him,* I think to myself when he tells me this.

During dinner, Jack hears my slow, deep breaths when Dad forgets Jack's name and again when he stumbles over his own stories, unable to recall the basic details of who, what, when, and where so the whole thing ends up jumbled and senseless. Jack takes my hand under the table and gently squeezes it to remind me he's here. *I love him.*

When Dad begins to lose his temper (an inconceivable notion prior to his diagnosis) because he can't find the Babe Ruth signed baseball he wants to show off, Jack helps Dad dig through old shoeboxes in his closet until they find it. *I love him.*

"He is very handsome," Mom tells me when Jack and Dad are on the other side of the house sifting through stacks of baseball cards safe in their plastic sleeves. Mom and I are still at the kitchen table sipping on our iced teas.

"You already told me that, Mom."

Her eyes light up. "Well, he is! He seems like a real keeper, Maddie."

"I already told you he's moving... to New York, like, really soon. He got a really great job offer there." I'm curious why she is digging like she is. My mother has never done this with anyone, not even Ben. She didn't like Ben much though, and I never knew why.

"Well, what does Jack moving have to do with anything?" She stands and begins stacking our empty dinner plates to carry to the kitchen. I follow her lead and gather the stray utensils and napkins in my hands.

"Considering I live in Cincinnati, it has a lot to do with everything, Mom." I follow her from the dining room to the kitchen, patiently waiting for her to make her point. This is what she does. Usually, it's not relationships we're talking about but something else big in my life, some huge career decision or whether or not to get the beagle I've been toying with adopting for the past five years. She plays a little game like this, pretending she's not about to make a point, and then *BOOM,* there it is.

"In my opinion..." she pauses, weighing her words carefully before she says them.

"Please share, Mother." I'm sarcastic, but I can't help it.

"I think two people who love each other are lucky to be so close in a world this big. Even if he is going to New York, that's not so far." Her words sound so poetic. I wish it could be that simple.

"How do you know we love each other?" I lean against the counter while Mom stands at the sink rinsing dishes.

"Please, that boy is smitten. And you? I've never seen you glow like this in your entire life."

It takes me a moment to process what she says, and then my lips spread into a smile. "Really?"

She dries her hands on a towel and places them on my shoulders. "Really. Watching you two together reminds me of the way your dad and I were when we were young. When we were together, there was nobody else. Other people existed of course, but they were blurry in the background. They didn't even matter. It's still kind of like that actually. That's how you know you've found your soulmate."

"Well, Dad never moved five hundred miles away."

"I would have followed him if he had," Mom adds without missing a beat. "When you meet the one, that's what you do."

She hugs me, and I let the weight of my chin rest on her shoulder as I breathe in the familiar coconut scent of her shampoo. "Are you telling me I should move to New York?"

"I'm telling you that if you are in love with Jack the way I think you are, you don't just give that up. Besides, you're not locked down here. You can do your job anywhere."

"That's what Jack said too, but—" and that all too familiar pit drops in my stomach. I swallow hard. "I can't leave Dad, and I can't leave you. Especially not now. Dad gets worse by the day, and I don't want you to be alone taking care of him. I should be here to help you."

"I'm not alone, Maddie. I have lots of friends, my support groups, and your father of course. We can fly to see you, and you can do the same. Not to mention, if I told your dad you were staying here for him, he would have a cow. We raised you to follow your dreams and chase down happiness. And while you're doing that, I'm going to take good care of him."

"I don't think I can leave you guys," I mumble as my shoulders hunch and my chest begins to cave in. The person I trust most in this life is suggesting I do the exact opposite of what I've already decided.

"I'm not telling you to stay or go, Madeline. That's a decision you need to make for yourself. What I am saying is you need to do what makes you happy. Don't make a decision based on Dad and I. We'll be just fine."

Jack drives us both back to my house that evening. We've been splitting the time between my place and his, but every night since I told him I loved him we've spent together. I am quiet and pensive on the drive, and by the time I'm brushing my teeth and applying my night cream at the bathroom counter, anxiety is racing through me. The pro-and-con list continues building in my brain, and I'm so inside myself that when Jack places his hand on my thigh as we lie next to one another in bed, I flinch.

"Two weeks. I'm moving in two weeks," he says.

Chapter 22

The fourteen-day deadline to Jack's departure makes it feel too late to change my mind and go to New York with him. When Mom and I spoke, she made moving seem like something I should do, a very real possibility to consider, but now it is so far away from any reality I can imagine. Everything is happening so fast, it doesn't even seem like an option. I didn't realize the end of my relationship with Jack would be so abrupt, so painfully sudden. The older I get, the more endings seem to happen like this.

Jack has been renting his condo in Cincinnati, and the subletters he found to take over his lease need to move in two weeks. He's already found a place in Syracuse, a one-bedroom townhome far enough away from campus, he won't be constantly running into students.

"That's worth a twenty-five-minute commute," Jack assures me when he tells me about his new place. We sit in his bed combing through pictures of the area on his laptop. I nod my head, only vaguely listening when he goes on about the used bookstore and coffee shop within walking distance, Oneida Lake in his backyard.

"I've actually had this place for a while. I found it online a few days after accepting the job, and I couldn't pass it up." There is excitement in his tone, and I don't blame him. The prospect of an entirely new life is exciting.

Jack turns his gaze from the computer screen, catching me staring down at my lap next to him. He tilts my chin up to his. "I stayed in Cincinnati these past few weeks because of you. I'd rather be with you." I think he tells me this so I will feel good or special or something, so I will see how much he loves me, but it only makes me sad, like I have been holding him back.

I wonder if this is how it would be all of the time if I moved to Syracuse, like I'm preventing him from reaching his full potential. I think back to the fall when he told me he needed space because he was overwhelmed. *It was all too much at once,* he had said. It's even higher stakes now. Much higher stakes in fact. He has another new position, a more important position, one sought after by so many in his field. Tenure-track positions aren't easy to come by. And as for me, choosing to go with him would require abandoning my parents, selling my house, and leaving the only city I have ever called home. Love shouldn't have to be *all* sacrifice, right? The timing just isn't right for us.

I flash a shaky smile to conceal the tears when I tell him, "I'm going to miss you." He closes his computer and sets it on the nightstand. We lie in bed talking until our blinks become long and slow, and neither of us can keep our eyes open a second longer.

The next day, I help him start to pack, placing book after book into cardboard boxes, "vertically only" Jack insists, clearly a bit uptight about how his books are packed, but I think it's adorable.

"Do you want me to keep these in some type of order so it doesn't take forever to organize them when you get to Syracuse?"

Jack stands a few yards away in the next room wrapping his dishes in brown packing paper. "Neh, it'll give me something to do in a place where I don't know anyone. Plus, I might try something new. Maybe I'll do them chronologically or by genre. Gotta keep things interesting, you know?"

"Okay, I'm feeling your *High Fidelity* vibes."

He looks at me confused, but I don't bother explaining. Jack and I have completely different movie tastes. I'm a sucker for any romance, blockbuster or indie, but Jack exclusively watches documentaries or anything with Arnold Schwarzenegger. I actually love that about him. It reminds me of my dad. When I was a kid, I used to watch these endlessly boring *History Channel* documentaries with him and pretend to be interested so he wouldn't have to sit there alone. I'd even ask questions too, but I always thought Dad might like a son to watch his macho action movies with.

"Anyways," I continue, "I think you should organize by the color of the spine. You can create an ombre work of art with your books. Imagine dark to light in every color across an entire wall."

"That sounds really cool actually, but I think I might need you to help me with that. Art was the only class I ever got a C in back in high school. I'm also color blind, just a little. Can't tell the difference between blue and purple."

"Are you serious?" My eyes narrow. Sometimes I still can't tell whether or not Jack is joking with me.

"Yep, I didn't even know until I was twelve and went to get glasses for the first time. My teacher sent a letter home because I couldn't see the board."

"So do you think my eyes are purple?" I smirk.

I am sitting cross-legged on the ground, and Jack walks over to me, squatting down so his eyes are level with mine. He peers into them. "Those are the most beautiful ocean purple I have ever seen." He throws his head back and laughs at himself, and I playfully push him away before he kisses me on the forehead and stands back up.

"Well, I'm sure you can find some artsy chick in a coffee shop in Syracuse who can help you."

And with those words, Jack's limbs stiffen. The smile on his face melts away. "Is that what you want? You want me to find some other girl and bring her back to my place to help me organize my books?"

I falter over my words trying to answer his question as the mood of the room shifts suddenly and without warning. "No… I mean, yes. Eventually. Maybe not right away. It would be okay if you missed me for a while, but I want you to be happy."

Jack sits down on the couch, resting his elbows on his knees and cradling his head in his hands. I get up from the floor and sit next to him. I begin gently scratching his back with my fingernails.

He stares at the floor as he talks. "But you make me happy. I don't want some random girl coming to my apartment. Ever since I met you, now that I know what loving someone can be like, I don't see how guys can sleep with girls they don't care about. I'm not ready to let you go."

"I mean, maybe someday the stars will align in our favor, and we can do this. But right now, the universe has us in two different places, and—"

He scoots away, leaving miles between us. "Stop with the fucking metaphors, Maddie. You choose your fate. You decide where your life will go. You built an entire business off of that principle. The nine-to-five cubicle life wasn't for you, so you created something that was for you. I don't understand why that can't apply to me too."

"Because you want me to move a plane ride away from my sick father."

Jack stands, retreating to the other side of the room. "Don't make me out to be a bad guy in all of this," he shoots back. "That's your excuse, Maddie. I offered to stay. I offered to do long distance. You don't want any of it!" His voice is raised, close to yelling. It's the loudest and angriest I have ever heard him.

"I'm sorry. I should go." And suddenly, I'm struggling for air. A fish out of water, floundering around for my bag, my keys, and my composure. I only find the first two before I am practically running out the door, already worried this might be the last time I will see Jack, already wishing it would have gone differently. Our conversation plays on repeat in my head as I descend the stairs, race to my car, and turn the key in the ignition. *How did it all get so out of hand so quickly?* We were laughing, and then we weren't.

I stall for a moment in the driver's seat, my eyes locked on his door, watching and wishing he would come running after me. But his front door is sealed shut. I shift my glance to his window, but the curtains are closed. He's not even watching me leave. Jack isn't going to chase me. He's done. I reverse out of my parking space and stop to look back once more before I turn out of the lot and go home alone.

I stay up late waiting for him to text me, or even better, to show up at my door and make everything right again. He never comes, and I end up wine-drunk on my patio listening to whiny emo bands and eventually calling Sarah.

"Do you know what time it is?" she says when she answers.

I squint at my phone, but the time doesn't jump out at me right away. "I don't know, like eleven?" I guess.

"More like 2:30, as in bar closing time. I have two children who will be awake in roughly three hours. This better be good," she gripes, her voice hoarse.

"Jack's leaving in thirteen days. Well, I guess twelve days now since it's already tomorrow," I mutter.

"Well, best friend, it sounds like you've got a big decision to make."

"As in?" I squint to make the blur of shapes around me more clear.

"You need to decide if you stay where you are or if you go with him, obviously."

Rather than respond, I close my eyes and rub my temples with my fingers. For my entire friendship with Sarah, I have always been the one who overthinks things, making everything more complicated than it has to be. One of her most complementary qualities is that she can boil things down to their simplest and easiest-to-understand form.

"How can I leave my parents when my dad is sick and somehow be okay with that?" I finally ask, attempting to show her the layers to this decision she's telling me to make. It's a decision everyone else seems to think is so simple, but it's not in the slightest. The trouble with life is it's almost never black and white. There's always a little gray.

"I'm not saying you can or you should. I don't think that's a decision anyone can make but you," she says. "Why don't you talk to him?"

"Talk to who? Jack or my Dad?"

I wonder how many questions I have to ask before she'll give me the answer, until she tells me what she would do. All I want is to not have to be the one to make this decision.

"Now that you mention it, probably both. I'm talking honest, completely open and unguarded conversations. Lay it all on the line. What have you got to lose?" Now Sarah's the one asking the questions. This isn't quite working out how I wanted.

"I've got a hell of a lot to lose, Sarah. The worst part is I'm guaranteed to lose something either way."

"All the more reason."

"I miss you like hell, girl."

"I miss you too. Now go to take four ibuprofen and chug a bottle of water. Hangovers are so much worse in your thirties."

I stumble inside and pour out what's left of my wine glass before swallowing all four ibuprofen in one gulp. Then, I lie down on my bed, not even bothering to get under the blankets, and I fall asleep fast for the first time in a long time.

The next morning, I stay burrowed in the dark of my room until I feel ready to emerge from my lair and face the rest of the world. I have a fuzzy blanket wrapped around me like a cape, and my hair is in a fantastically messy bun on top of my head. The thought crosses my mind to put on a pair of sunglasses, that it might make the light less abrupt, but I talk myself out of it. That would be way too pathetic. Sarah was right about the hangover thing, though.

The only thing motivating me to get out of bed is my craving for coffee and air-fried pizza rolls, but just as I press the button on my espresso machine to prepare a double shot, I hear a *tap, tap, tapping* on my front door. There's a familiar rhythm to it, and my stomach jumps a little. I peek at my reflection in the front of the stainless steel refrigerator, attempt to wipe away the smoky remnants below my eyes with my thumb, then shed my blanket cape and drift in the direction of my front door.

When I open it, I am instantly safe and warm. That's the effect he has on me. "Dad," I say, stepping onto the porch and wrapping my arms around him. He smells like my parents' house. I want to bottle up his scent and save it forever. "I hope you didn't drive yourself here." My instincts are to worry about him, to protect him as much as I can for as long as I am able.

"Mom dropped me off," he says, a soft smile smeared across his face. "She's running an errand, and then she'll be over. I wanted some time with my little girl." He is wearing a baseball cap and a t-shirt that is two sizes too big. My mom buys his clothes like she is shopping for a growing child. "He's not getting any bigger, you know. I'm pretty sure he's finished growing," I always joke with her.

"He likes his clothes loose. He's not one of those hip young guys," is her standard response.

Dad meanders his way into my kitchen, the heart and soul of my home, shuffling his feet a little as he walks. He glides his hand along the countertops he installed himself, watching his long, slender fingers as they move. His hand stops suddenly, and he glances at me.

"Sorry, I'm a mess," I tell him, reaching for the monstrosity on top of my head. "Did you tell me you were coming?"

"No, no, it was a last-minute thing. We were in the neighborhood. You know how it is."

Except I don't know how it is because my parents, who live on the other side of town, are incredibly loyal to *their* grocery store, *their* bakery, *their* Target. I happen to love all Targets and never discriminate against one over another, but my parents prove that apparently you can be loyal to one specific Target and refuse to frequent any others. In addition, having lived on the West Side for most of their lives, all of my parents' friends live on their side of town as well. Basically, they only leave to come to my house or to meet me at a restaurant. So, the fact that Dad claims to have "been in the neighborhood" is suspect at best.

"Yeah, I know how it is." I accept his explanation even though I don't believe it. I wonder why he's lying to me, but I'm also too afraid to call him out. "Can I make you a cappuccino?"

"How about some regular coffee?" He's always been a no-frills kind of guy. I got my frills from Mom.

"Coming right up."

As I reach into the cabinet for the coffee grounds I never use, I see him looking up at the ceiling, eyes moving along the crown molding from one corner to the next, inspecting everything. My dad, the handyman. He's always looking for a project, something to fix or improve with a tool bag, a couple of two-by-fours, and a trip to Home Depot. He lives for a weekend house project. Unfortunately, his doctors won't allow him to do them anymore, at least not by himself, since he forgets things he used to do regularly and requires pretty much constant supervision. It makes me sad to think his days are now spent mostly in front of the television watching golf until he dozes off. After retiring two years ago, he kept busy working at my house or in his garage on projects until Mom forced him to come in for dinner. I can only imagine how bored and helpless he feels now.

We talk about baseball until the coffee is ready. I hand him his favorite Ohio State University mug, and he carries it to the brown chair in my living room where he rocks back and forth slowly as he sips. I've never seen that man put a drop of anything in his coffee. Not cream or sugar or milk. He likes it thick and muddy, and because of him, I've always had the notion that real men drink their coffee black. I can remember a crush from college who I met in my Introduction to Psychology class. He had a slight lisp that I thought was cute, and when he finally asked me out for coffee after a month of flirty texting, he ordered some sugary beverage I don't even think had any coffee in it. I could never think of him the same way again.

Dad and I sit, our hands wrapped around our warm mugs, and we don't say much for a long while. He's always been a man of few words. An observer, if you will. But when he does talk, you listen.

Suddenly, Dad stands up from his chair, almost startled, and darts to the French doors that look out over the backyard, something out there sparking his interest.

"Come over here," he says, waving his hand at me as if I need to hurry. I get up from my seat on the couch and stand next to him.

"Blue Jays." He points in the direction of two birds perched on my fence.

"They're beautiful," I say, admiring the intricate pattern on their tail feathers, their sprightly color that stands out from all of nature's greens and browns.

Dad's gaze follows the pair of birds as they fly from my split-rail fence post to the white oak tree at the back of the yard. "When a Blue Jay finds its mate, they stay together for life. That's why you usually see them in pairs like this."

"Wow, that's fascinating actually," I say. "I think penguins are like that too. Most humans aren't even that loyal."

"You're right. They aren't. That's why when you find someone who is, you can't let them go." Dad glances at me now, and he gives me the same subtle look he used to give me when I was a little girl and he would sneak me a treat before dinner. His eyebrows raise as his eyes widen, and he tells me what he's thinking without saying anything. I don't see Dad in the mornings very often. Usually it's the evening time, but Mom said he's much more alert and "with it," as she put it, earlier in the day. I can see what she means. He doesn't seem overly confused or forgetful right now. He seems like my dad, perceptive and clear, not the stranger he turns into when the sun begins to melt into the sky.

"Mom told you?"

"All I know is I don't want you missing out on any part of life on account of me. You leave if that's what you need to do, and I'll be up there all the time to visit, Madeline. Your mother and I don't have anything else going on." Of course they do have things going on. They have a lot of things going on, but it's just like Dad to downplay the big things, to believe it's all going to be alright, even if it's not.

"Dad, I really don't think—"

"Let's leave it at that." He wraps his arm around me and takes another gulp of his coffee as we both watch the Blue Jays resting on a limb.

I remember when Dad seemed like a giant. When I was little and I would look up at him, it was like gazing up at a superhero. He was this tall, handsome man who would protect me from all of the dark and scary things in life. Now, his body feels frail next to mine compared to what it once was. I'm already grieving him. Moments like this will be fewer and farther between soon. The man I know as my father is slowly dissolving into the atmosphere and being replaced by a person I don't know at all. That won't make the ending any less agonizing, though.

"I love you, Daddy," I tell him.

"I love you too, Madeline."

Chapter 23

Despite the time I need, the countdown to Jack leaving doesn't stop, like sand in an hourglass continuously falling. There are eleven days until he is officially gone, and then there are ten, and then nine. Each day passes, and I don't hear from him. I can sense him drifting further and further away.

The people who matter to me most have told me not to let Jack go so easily. However, I can't shake the notion that saying yes to a life with him means I'm abandoning my parents when they need me most. I am their only child, the one who is supposed to take care of them in their old age. What if it doesn't work out with Jack? What if it ends up like it did with Ben, suddenly over with nothing but heartache to show for it? How would I deal with that kind of regret? How would I make up for the time lost with my dad I'll never be able to get back?

Jack hasn't contacted me since I ran out of his apartment. I imagine he's already created a completely new image of what

Syracuse will be for him, likely one that doesn't involve me at all. He may very well be looking forward to a fresh start in a new place without me being a cowardly, noncommittal pain in the ass. It's exactly what I wanted, isn't it?

So, I continue to ignore the advice of everyone who loves me, and I focus on moving forward without him. At this point, my decision isn't going to change.

That Sunday, after a full week of preoccupying myself with recipes for vegan cheesecake and "hidden veggie" meatloaf for two of my clients, the last place I want to be is my kitchen. I've spent hours upon hours standing at my center island, and I need a break along with a reason to get out of my house. So I decide to order dinner, saag paneer from the Indian place down the street.

I walk to pick it up. The August air is stifling, but I don't want to drive. I feel like moving my limbs, spending more than a five-minute car ride out of my house, and listening to the gentle sounds of the Sunday traffic, a stark contrast from the busy noise on Friday and Saturday nights. When I arrive, there are only two tables eating in the entire restaurant. The inside is adorably quaint with white tablecloths and stemmed water glasses at every seat. I pay with cash, and the bored teenage boy working behind the counter hands me a brown paper bag from the line of ten other carryout orders.

On the walk home, I think to myself that it's a shame there was barely anyone eating inside. Everyone wants to eat in front of the television and avoid real face-to-face conversations, I guess. Or, maybe most people are alone with no one to even go to a restaurant with. I think about the old German man from Waffle House. I think about how watching television is an easy way to make yourself feel like you're not alone. I think about all of the easy distractions like social media and email and podcasts. People today are so caught up in screens and media, they think they have a tribe of supporters they don't actually have. It makes me sad. I think I'd like to eat inside next time.

So tonight, I don't let myself turn on *The Office* reruns while I eat my dinner like I usually do. Instead, I sit at my dining room table. Usually, the dark-stained wood serves as a backdrop for pictures of my food, and I can't remember the last time I actually sat and ate something here. When my parents come over, we eat in the kitchen.

I sit at the head of the table, shifting in my chair until I'm comfortable in this unfamiliar seat, and then I proceed to eat my meal without the comfort of the television to occupy my mind, stopping myself before I get too full. Dad always told me it's important to leave room for dessert. I inherited my sweet tooth from him.

I reach into the refrigerator and pull out a small white ramekin of crème brûlée I made yesterday. Good crème brûlée always sits in the refrigerator overnight. With a small kitchen torch, I caramelize the top until it gets dark and bubbly, and then I take my seat at the table again. Out the window, I watch the trees and the birds and the neighbor who always mows her lawn at the oddest hours, like 7:00 a.m. on a Monday or on a quaint Sunday summer evening like this one after all the neighborhood kids are fast asleep in their beds. I only shift my gaze for a moment to watch my spoon crack the top layer, my favorite part. Crème brûlée isn't just a dessert. It's an experience, I always say. And when I spoon the heavenly custard into my mouth, I make sure to take small bites so it lasts longer.

As I eat, I notice one solitary Blue Jay land on my split rail fence. He sits there for a long while, his little neck twisting every which way. I start looking for his mate, peeking around my yard, a game of *Where's Waldo,* searching for another fleck of blue amidst all the green. She is nowhere, and I start to worry. I give it some time, but I don't stop looking. The Blue Jay seems restless, continuously rotating his head around and around, never stopping. He's looking for her too. But she never comes. Too much time passes, and he eventually flies off alone, and I have this weird feeling I get sometimes when I think about how big the world is and how small and insignificant I am in comparison. I could see a thousand more Blue Jays in my lifetime, but I'll never know if it was the same one I saw today, and I'll never know if he found her. That's when I know I have to go see Jack.

I dash to my car, leaving a half-eaten crème brûlée on the table and open takeout containers strewn about on the kitchen counter. After pulling my car out of the garage, I have to scurry back into the house to grab my phone and my purse before driving fifteen miles over the speed limit through residential neighborhoods like I have no time to waste. The radio is off. The only thing playing is my one-track mind: *Get there.*

When I pull into his complex, I take the turn so sharp and so fast, my car lets out a loud and searing, *screeecchhh.*

Considering Jack once told me I have the driving tendencies of an eighty-five-year-old woman, I have never heard my Subaru make a sound like that before. I park in two spaces, straddling the white line, and don't bother to correct it. My breathing is fast and heavy, like I've been sprinting, before I even exit my car and run up the stairs to his condo. I stop halfway to run back and grab the flip-flop that falls off of my foot.

Face to face with his navy blue front door, I stop for a brief moment to let my mind catch up to my body, now pumping with adrenaline and purely acting on instinct. "This is it. This is where it happens," I whisper to myself before knocking. I strike the door with my fist so forcefully his neighbors probably think a fight is brewing, but I'm not angry. Not at all. I'm just ready. I'm finally ready.

I knock incessantly for what feels like forever, but Jack never comes to his door. I try to peek into his window, but his curtains are closed, the slightest crack between them only revealing darkness inside. He could be in his bedroom listening to music with headphones in his ears, a very likely possibility. So I run back down the stairs, clenching my toes as I move in an effort to keep both sandals on my feet this time, circling around to the back of the building where his parking spot is.

Please be here. Please be here.

My body halts when I see his spot is empty. No blue Honda Civic in its designated space, only a number seven painted on the blacktop in white. I walk over to the empty parking space anyway, moving slower now, like there are suddenly weights around my ankles. I squat on the parking block to process his absence. Do I sit here and wait for him to return? Do I leave and pretend this never happened? Yet another beautiful moment of clarity I've been waiting for, but he's gone. On the drive over here, it struck me that Jack might tell me it's too late, but I knew I had to try or I'd regret it forever. It didn't occur to me that he wouldn't be here. Love isn't like the movies after all.

Catching my breath now, I notice the moon starting to peek through the clouds as the late summer sun sets in a tie-dye pink sky. I wonder for a while where Jack could be, what he might be doing on a Sunday evening. This is the night he's usually home making himself boxed pasta with jarred tomato sauce. Sometimes he puts chicken on top, and other times he uses those store-bought meatballs you can get in the freezer section at the grocery store, but no matter what, Sunday is always pasta night at home for Jack. That is until now, apparently.

Unless.

And then it hits me. Jack already moved. He was only staying for me. There was nothing else keeping him here, he had said. When I ran out of his apartment that night, I took away every reason he had to be in Ohio, every reason he had to put a hold on his new life in Syracuse. I could try calling him to confirm, but I know I don't have to.

This must be my sign. It's time to move on.

Chapter 24

In no rush to fall asleep alone or to tell Sarah over a pathetic, tear-filled phone call Jack is gone, I take the long way home, driving down winding back roads with the radio blaring. By the time I turn into my neighborhood, the pink sky has transformed into an ominous black. There are so many clouds, I can't even see the stars. Raindrops begin to fall on my windshield one by one, so slowly I can count them. A thundercloud roars in the distance, the first of many. I usually look forward to a good thunderstorm when I'm cozy in my house with a book on my lap and a cappuccino by my side, but this one is fast and furious like it has something to prove.

By the time I'm on my street, the rain is falling so hard I can barely see a foot in front of me, even with my windshield wipers on full throttle. I think about the storm in Georgia, the Denny's billboard, and Jack. I want to be in my house hiding beneath a fuzzy blanket from whatever rage Mother Nature is trying to release tonight, but first I have to make it inside.

With my car parked safely in my driveway, I make a plan, bracing for the impact of a million water pellets pummeling my skin. I have no umbrella and no jacket. In fact, I'm even wearing my glasses, which makes this situation even worse (rain is the bane of every glasses wearer's existence.). But my biggest concern is the hot pink cast covering almost my entire left arm. I've been ordered by my doctor to keep it dry, and I have about fifteen yards between me and my front door.

I pivot to peek in my back seat for something to shield it with, but my car is spotless, nothing but seats and seatbelts. This is the only time in my life being uptight about having a clean car has not paid off. I check in my center console for something to cover my cast with, but there is only spare change, a tin of mints, and a green velvet hair scrunchie (Did I mention I'm really crazy about having a clean car?). Yet another quirk I got from my dad. So I sit helpless in the driver's seat strategizing about how I'm going to get into my house. The rain is pounding with a vengeance, with no inkling of letting up anytime soon. There's no way I am going back to the hospital to get a new cast because this one got drenched and has to be sawed off. The hospital is the last place I want to be right now.

After some thought, I come up with exactly one solution, and I don't feel great about it. My tank top is too thin to simply tuck my arm inside, but if I take off my shirt and wrap it around my cast a few times, I might be able to keep it dry. I've always been on the modest side, but I remind myself it's dark, almost pitch black, and with this amount of rain, the chances of someone seeing me are slim. So I take off my shirt and cover every inch of the cast as best I can, rotating my arm in my line of vision to be sure it's completely protected. I shimmy the scrunchie over the shirt to help hold it in place. I'm wearing a bra, but it's one of those see-through, lacy bralettes with barely any coverage. It couldn't even pass for a bikini top if I tried. I say a quick prayer none of my neighbors happen to be looking out their windows, and if they are, I hope they don't have their phones nearby. I do not want to go viral for this.

"Ready or not." I open my car door, and instantly a gust of wind and rain tries to shut it back on me. I have to force my way out, pushing the door with all of my might. I dart to the front of my house while trying not to slip in my two-dollar sandals and break another bone. I don't know how many times I have to tell myself to stop buying these shitty Old Navy flip-flops before I finally listen. The rain is relentless and painful, like I'm in a savage game of paintball, one I'm losing horribly. When I finally make it to the safety of the covered porch, I throw my arms up to celebrate, like I've won some sort of game. That is until I reach for my keys.

"SHIT!" I yell loudly, and now I am sure I'm on one of those dystopian Japanese game shows where everyone laughs at my misery. I'm also positive the neighbors must have heard me and are now watching me run around like a literal maniac in lingerie, but there's nothing I can do. Thank god for my car's keyless entry, I won't be locked out for long. However, I do have to run back out into the deluge to retrieve my house keys. I take my glasses off and set them on the porch swing. Then, completely drenched, I trek back out to my car.

It's not even worth it to run and take the risk of potentially hurting myself, so I go slower this time, cursing at the cold rain and the timing of it all. I even hold up my hand and do a little wave to whoever is watching me from their windows and getting a good laugh. Hopefully, there are no children.

I finally make it back to my front porch, dripping wet and concerned about the state of my cast. Just as my house key slips into the knob of my door, I hear someone yell my name.

"Maddie! Maddie! Wait!"

Startled, I quickly turn to see Jack sprinting towards me looking as wet and crazy as I do. His Civic is behind him, parked on the street, the headlights still on. I didn't even see or hear him pull up in the midst of the storm and my own misfortune. But here he is, running towards me. It feels like slow motion, every movement drawn out, every second an eternity. When he reaches my front porch steps, he stands at the bottom for a moment and looks up at me, his t-shirt plastered to his skin. He shakes his hair with one of his hands so it's no longer matted to his head, weighed down by the wetness.

"What are you doing down there?" I ask. "Come on!" I gesture for him to come up and escape the downpour.

Jack doesn't say a word but slowly ascends the stairs until he is right in front of me, both of us beneath the awning, protected now, though dripping wet and slightly traumatized from losing our battle with the elements. He peers down at me with tired eyes. He looks like he hasn't slept in days. Water droplets fall from the tip of his nose onto his lips as he comes closer, taking one of my hands in his. He pulls me in, wrapping his arm around my waist. His tongue parts my lips, and he kisses me urgently, like the world might end if he doesn't do it right this very second. I kiss him back, desperate for him. We're both out of breath from the running, but when my lips are pressed to his, everything is right in the world. Like this is how it's supposed to be. I break away for an instant to breathe and notice he's hanging on to something in his right hand, the one that isn't holding me. Something I didn't notice before.

"What is that?" I ask, pointing down to the black, bulky object suspended from his fingers. He looks down at it too.

"It's a boombox. I scoured through five thrift stores to find it. I wanted to come here and be your John Cusack," he says, with a smile. "I was going to hold it over my head like this and play music really loud until you looked out your window." He holds the boombox over his head with his feet shoulder-width apart and makes the exact expression of Lloyd Dobler in *Say Anything,* stoic and troubled.

"How do you know about that movie?" I ask, both curious and skeptical.

"Maddie, I spent the past two weeks watching every John Cusack movie of all time so I would know how to woo you."

My eyes widen in disbelief. "Really?"

He nods, so I test him. "What about *Serendipity?*"

"Watched it." Jack flashes me his signature smirk and sets the boombox down next to our feet.

"*High Fidelity?*"

"That was the best one of all of them." He links his arms around my waist.

I bite my lower lip as John Cusack's resume runs through my brain. There must be one Jack didn't watch. "How about *America's Sweethearts?*"

He pulls me in close, both of his palms pressed firmly on my back. "Yeah, that one was rough."

"You really are something, Jack Keller, you know that?" He grins from ear to ear. "What song were you going to play?" I ask, and I drape my arms around his neck.

"Well, I have a whole playlist actually. All your favorites, but the first song was my pick." He bends slightly, moving his face down to mine, his lips hovering over my lips.

"Oh?" I lean into him.

"It's really cheesy. I'm actually embarrassed and decided on the drive I would skip to the second song."

I playfully try to push him away, but he pulls me in tighter, unwilling to let me go. "It's too late now. Just tell me!"

"Savage Garden, *I Knew I Loved You.* It was my first slow dance ever in the seventh grade." Jack's cheeks turn a pale shade of pink.

"No fucking way. That was my first slow dance too! I danced with the same guy I lost the spelling bee to. I went to Catholic school, so there weren't many options."

"What a weird coincidence. It's like you and I were meant to be," he says, but the look in his eyes tells me he's not very surprised, like he knew all along. "Anyways, I'm sorry my romantic gesture was a complete failure. I didn't realize you would be running around your lawn like a maniac too." I can't help but laugh because he's right. I am a maniac. We both are.

"*This,* Jack, was definitely not a failure. We're soaking wet, and it's pouring rain, and nothing is more romantic or John Cusack than that."

"And... you're in a bra." He looks down at the sheer lace on my chest. "Is that part of the fairytale too?" I instantly cover my face with my hands. Embarrassed is the only word to explain the burning sensation in my cheeks. I was so caught up in the moment I forgot I am practically naked.

"I had to cover my cast! I didn't have anything else in my car!" I am mortified, and I know my flushed face is giving me away.

"I understand. You had to preserve my work of art."

I giggle. "Exactly."

"I'm really sorry for showing up here like this, but I can't just let you go." Jack's words play like the lyrics to the most beautiful love song I've ever heard.

Without thinking, I blurt out what I wanted so badly to tell him, the reason I went to his house tonight. "I'm coming with you." He stares at me, his expression unreadable, and I am so terrified of what he will say next, I just keep talking. "I love you, and I'm coming with you, and I'm really sorry it took me so long to figure it all out."

His eyebrows raise, forming deep wrinkles on his forehead. "To Syracuse? You're serious?"

"I'm serious. I'm all in. Syracuse better be ready for me."

Jack lifts me up and twirls me around in circles. I'm alive in his arms, more alive than I've ever been. But he sets me down after three go-arounds, a concerned expression on his face. "There's one problem."

A lump rises in my throat as I wait for what he will say next. What else could there possibly be? I can't handle another hurdle. I just want to be his. Finally his. Forever.

"I just..." He pauses. "Well, it's just that..." He stumbles over his words, unable to get them out. He finally manages to mutter, "I hope you don't have your heart set on Syracuse."

"Huh?" I'm confused and worried.

"I had an interview at The Ohio State University. I came straight here. I got the job! It's a tenure-track position and everything. One of their literature professors decided at the last minute he's going to retire and move to Barbados or something."

I grip his arms with my hands and squeeze. "No fucking way! *The* Ohio State University, as in a two-hour drive from Cincinnati? As in my dad's alma mater?"

"Yes, and yes. I thought you'd be more open to a long-distance relationship if I found something closer, so I've been working my ass off trying to find something. I didn't tell you because I didn't want you to get your hopes up if it didn't work. But just like that, a job opened up in Columbus. The universe told me not to quit on you, so I didn't." He clutches my wet hair in his hands and kisses me again. I don't want to stop, ever, but I force myself to pull away. There's one more thing I have to tell him.

"For the record, I went to your house tonight to tell you I'll follow you anywhere for the rest of our lives."

We slow dance on the porch soaking wet for a long time, a thunderstorm surrounding us, a boombox playing my favorite songs, and this is exactly how it's supposed to be.

Epilogue

"Congratulations," I say to Jack as we cheers our water glasses over a white tablecloth in an upscale downtown restaurant.

"I couldn't have done it without you." Jack lays his fingers gently over mine on the tabletop.

"So what happens next? I have no idea how all of this even works."

"Neither do I, but now that I have an agent, she's going to link me up with an editor to polish things up before we take it to publishers and see what happens." His eyes are beaming as he tips his glass to his lips.

"It's going to be amazing. I don't think there's even one thing I would change."

"Well, that's why you don't hire your wife as your editor," he says through laughter.

My hand graces my belly and pauses there, the way it naturally does so often these days. I can feel hiccups, a tapping just above my pubic bone, and I press into the sensation softly with the tips of my fingers as if to say, *Hello, I can't wait to meet you.*

Nothing is the same as it was last year when I was still afraid to leave, terrified to commit to the man I now call *Husband.* I had no idea the night we danced in the rain I was already eight weeks pregnant. And I realize no one probably believes that, and anyone who hears our love story must think the pregnancy made me decide to go with him, but I love that it isn't true. Jack, not our baby, is the one who made me change my mind. His love for me, his commitment to me, and the fact that there isn't another soul on this planet who can make me feel the way he does, that's why I wanted to go.

Jack proposed to me on our first night in our Columbus apartment. "There's no point in waiting. This is what I want," he said, down on one knee in the middle of our living room. There wasn't even a couch in there yet. I got out of the shower and had a towel wrapped around my wet hair and another around my body. Jack received my dad's approval earlier in the afternoon when he and Mom dropped off a car full of my things. He said he couldn't wait any longer to ask me. That night, we ate pizza for dinner and slept on a mattress on the floor. We spent the next day unpacking boxes and planning our wedding.

Jack and I got married two months later at the end of October, a couple of weeks after finding out I was pregnant. It was a small outdoor ceremony and reception. We had a taco bar from our favorite Mexican restaurant and donuts from the bakery we now frequent every Saturday morning in Columbus. I never dreamed of a big wedding the way a lot of girls do, but I did always dream of being a mom, and knowing our baby was there with us made it even more perfect.

Jack started working seriously on his first novel right after we moved. He said he needed a creative outlet separate from work and the classroom, and he already started a draft of something back in Cincinnati. So, he spent his mornings writing, most of the time on the patio while I worked in the kitchen. He said he wanted to finish the manuscript before the baby came, and now, eight and a half months pregnant, he just signed with a literary agent.

Sarah has flown to Columbus to visit us twice since she stood by me as the maid of honor at our wedding, and Jack and I were able to make it down to see her and the kids over his holiday break. We talk a few times a week, and she plans to visit again when the baby arrives. It's not easy to get away with two little ones.

She's managed to make a few friends at the hospital where she works in Florida. Sometimes they go out for margaritas after work, but they are always trying to set her up with their single friends or brothers. She tells me she never even considers it though.

"It's just going to take time," I tell her.

"No, I don't think it will," she says. "I know everyone says I'm young, and they think I'll eventually want to date again and maybe get married, but I don't think I want that. I'm okay with being alone for the rest of my life. Someday Mike and I will be together again, and that's all I want." And without any experience or advice, I understand.

"You live whatever life you want to live," I say.

"Thank you for getting it. You're the only one who does."

My parents are getting by too. Jack and I see them weekly,

whether I drive down to Cincinnati or they come up to Columbus. The two-hour drive is manageable and doesn't feel as long as I imagined it would. They recently toured some assisted living centers near their home for when Mom can't take care of Dad on her own anymore. He understands why it will need to happen, though Mom is hesitant and wants to wait for as long as she can to take that step.

I say prayers to the Man in the Moon every night for my parents and for Sarah and for Atlas and Ace and our little baby I feel so close to already. We found out it's a boy, and we're naming him Davis Everett after our dads.

Pregnancy insomnia has been a bitch, to say the least, and sometimes I lie awake at ungodly hours staring at the ceiling thinking about how much time I spent in the past worrying about the signs the universe was sending me, wondering how I would know whatever decision I made was the right one. What I didn't realize is that the universe isn't all-powerful. It can send you signs and try to push you in the right direction, but at the end of the day, everyone has a choice. If you aren't brave enough to see those signs and take action, you'll never get the life that was meant for you. It's a tough lesson to learn sometimes, and I'm grateful every day Jack was stubborn enough not to give up on me. Whatever time we have together, I'll never take it for granted. This I know for certain.

Author's Note

Dear Readers,

I've been an avid reader and writer for as long as I can remember. In the third grade, I recall writing long, passionate (and incredibly hilarious) short stories about King Arthur and Guinevere's fiery romance. I've never been an artist, so my mom was my illustrator. I've wanted to be a writer ever since.

I began writing this novel shortly after giving birth to my third son, and the majority of *Exactly How It's Supposed to Be* was written with a newborn on my lap. I quit my job and told myself it was now or never. So many people want to be so many things but let those dreams fade away for one reason or another. I wanted my boys to know I didn't give up.

When I sat down to write *Exactly How It's Supposed to Be,* I told myself I wanted to write a real love story. One where the characters deal with real life shit that feels impossible to get through at times. Love is messy. And so are all of the other parts of life. I wanted this book to reflect all of the bumps in the road. The older I get, the harder it is to read the storybook romances. I wrote the love story I wanted to read, and I hope you enjoyed it.

Thank you so much for reading. I hope this book will be the first of many.

Love,
Jodi

P.S. Keep supporting indie authors.

Jodi Niehaus lives in the big-little city of Cincinnati, Ohio with her husband, three sons, a dog, and a cat. She attended the University of Dayton and received her master's degree from Northern Kentucky University. Before writing *Exactly How It's Supposed To Be,* her first novel, she taught high school English for nine years.

Follow on Instagram @jodiniehauswrites

visit

www.jodiniehaus.com

Manufactured by Amazon.ca
Bolton, ON